MONSTERS WITHIN

TOOTH & CLAW
BOOK 4

AMELIA FAULKNER

Ravensword Press

Monsters Within © Amelia Faulkner 2014.
Cover design by AK Faulkner & Jen Fowler.

This book is a work of fiction. The names, characters, places, and incidents are products of the writer's imagination or have been used fictitiously and are not to be construed as real. Any resemblance to persons, living or dead, actual events, locale or organisations is entirely coincidental.

This book contains sexually explicit content which is suitable only for mature readers.

First electronic publication: December 2014.
First paperback publication: March 2025.
https://ravenswordpress.com

Monsters Within is set in the UK, and as such uses British English throughout.

CONTENTS

GLOSSARY

Areet: All right. E.g. *Y'areet there, petal?* or *It's areet, in't it?*

Aye: Yes. *Aye, it was me.*

Barmpot: Fool. This tends to be used as a term of mild frustration or exasperation. It isn't too derogatory, but it's not all that fond either. *The fella's a total barmpot!*

Cadge: Borrow. *Can I cadge a tenner? I'll pay it back…*

Daft apeth: Fool. This is a term of fondness or endearment while still expressing how silly you think someone's being. *You don't have to pay me back ten quid, you daft apeth.*

Earwig: Eavesdrop. This can either be in, on, or as-is: *I was earwigging in on Albert t'other day* or *Oi, stop earwigging, it's rude!*

Gradely: Good. Excellent, even, especially combined with reet: *Aye, it were reet gradely!*

Happen: Reckon. *I'll 'appen as it'll take a few days.*

In't: In the or isn't. *I'll be over in't morning* or *It in't time for dinner yet!*

Owt: Anything. *I didn't bring owt with me. Were I s'posed to?*

Reet: Right. Very. *I'll 'appen as it were reet gradely!*

Petal: Term of endearment. *Y'areet there petal?*

Tosser: Wanker. From 'tossing off', i.e. wanking. *Aye, 'e's a reet tosser, he is.*

Wazzock: Idiot. Mildly derogatory. *Then the wazzock dropped 'is trousers an' we all had a good laugh!*

PROLOGUE

Claws sliced into his gut like shards of glass, but there was no blood. There'd never be any blood. Only the living could bleed.

Randall's eyes were an amber colour and bright with rage, surrounded by fur too short to mask his expression. His bare fangs glistened white in the low light, and each one seemed as though it could be sharp enough to slice into metal. With lips curled back from his muzzle, he would have made lesser predators shit themselves before they ran off with their tails between their legs.

When Randall's claws pulled free, ash spewed through the air; it formed a light haze of dust which drizzled and fell across the desk.

Ellis kicked out at the creature which towered over him. The bulk of it alone was double his own, and it had more muscle than the strongest human had space for. Ellis' only hope was to break free, to find some shelter.

He heard laughter. Charles. No, it was Briar. Or Randall.

He rolled from the desk and burrowed beneath it.

The mahogany shook and splintered beneath the force of blows from unnatural fists. Then his shelter was gone, evaporated, and Randall was there.

Not the behemoth, not the huge beast with its dripping fangs and razor talons, no. Beautiful, sweet Randall, his dark eyes soft and caring, his hand outstretched.

"I won't ever hurt you," he said.

Ellis almost believed it. He wanted to believe it. So against his better judgement he reached for Randall's hand.

The monster erupted from Randall's flesh and surged in for the kill.

ELLIS' eyes snapped open, and in doing so robbed him of sight.

He lay in darkness and listened.

Randall's steady pulse thudded along at his side in the slow beats of deep sleep. His breathing was shallow. Faint burbles of digestion came from his stomach, too subtle for most people's ears. His lover's body heat permeated the right hand side of Ellis' body. The left was cooler, like it faced away from a fire.

Beyond, Tiberius slept out in the living room, making adorable little squeaks in his dreams.

Further still, he heard the water in the old house's pipework as the heating came on. Tiny bubbles of air percolated through valves. The pilot light for the boiler clicked as it reignited itself. The grandfather clock in the ground floor office ticked as the pendulum swung with soft monotony.

Did Ellis miss the press of neighbours in other flats surrounding his own? From here he could sometimes hear the Thames river traffic over the noise of buses and cars that crossed Vauxhall Bridge, but the house itself was so old that the walls between it and the next were solid, and he suspected that if anyone even lived there they were rarely at home.

It wasn't unusual for houses in this area to stand empty for months at a time. They were far too expensive for most Londoners to buy, so the majority were owned by the super-rich: Russian oligarchs; Middle Eastern sheiks; oil barons. Charles had purchased this one back when it was built, and while it'd been pricey it hadn't cost him the nineteenth century equivalent of fifteen million pounds.

The value of this house didn't even bear thinking about. Edison had cleared out hundreds of thousands of pounds' worth of antiques just to pay all the fees associated with transferring the ownership to Ellis. Charles had been an avid collector of nineteenth century Romantic landscapes, and auctioning them off had caused one hell of a stir. Even the gallery had picked up a few new clients, but Ellis was well aware they weren't interested in contemporary works. They'd lose interest once they realised he didn't have secret stashes of long-lost Turners up his sleeves.

Randall's breathing remained soft and even. He hadn't stirred.

Good.

On nights like this, Ellis' guilty wish was that he could forget he'd ever seen Randall's face. Charles' former office was a land mine to his touch. He'd watched Randall interrogated by the smug elder bastard, but other objects had revealed other visions. The desk offered up Randall's unwitting attack on Ellis, when ten feet of muscle and fur and teeth and claws and...

Ellis' fingers curled until he could dig his nails into his own palms.

Don't go there.

Randall was stunning. He had eyes like warm coals and skin of burnt umber. His hands were soft and nimble, and despite his shorter stature he was built like a brick privy. Without his visions, Ellis could only construct an idea of him in his mind, assembled through touch and description, but still nothing quite like the real thing.

That his bastard brain had chosen to convert those privileged glimpses into nightmare fuel pissed him off no end.

ONE

Randall chose not to wake Ellis. There was a strange peace to his stillness, and the way his soft, wavy hair splayed across his pillow gave him a dark halo around his pale, delicate features which was oddly cherubic. He wriggled free of the sheets and did what he could to get ready in silence.

There was no such thing as silence to Ellis, of course. His hearing was constantly amped up to a level Randall's wolf ears could only begin to match. How the vampire ever slept was a mystery to Randall. Still, he supposed Ellis could just lay there with his eyes shut and Randall would be none the wiser: he didn't breathe, his eyes didn't ever seem to twitch in REM sleep, and he didn't roll about or steal the sheets.

When asleep, Ellis was all but a corpse.

Randall eyed him while he stepped into his jeans. "Hey," he whispered. "Are you awake?"

Ellis didn't answer, and Randall's stomach released a tension he hadn't noticed it held. His lover *was* asleep.

He shook his head and tugged a T-shirt on, then leaned over to kiss Ellis' forehead. "Got to go to work. Love you."

Ellis' lips curled into a grin. "You're getting far better at that, petal."

Heat flushed through Randall's cheeks. "Oh, you arsehole!"

Ellis laughed. His eyes fluttered open, revealing their ice-blue irises and ever-so-faint preternatural glow. "You say it more when you think I'm asleep," he teased.

"Maybe I'll just stop altogether!"

"Misery guts." Ellis felt for Randall's arms and used his touch as guidance to Randall's face. He raised his head from the pillow and leaned in to kiss him. "I love you too. You've got clients this morning?"

Randall's chest tightened, and he caught his breath. "Yeah. Then lunch with Kieran. I'll be back around half-five, sixish at the latest. Depends on whether the tube's running properly."

Ellis nodded. "I've got a thing this evening. I'm getting hauled up in front of the Council again. No idea how long that'll take."

"Okay. I'll catch you when you get home, then." Randall brushed his fingers through Ellis' hair as he pulled away. "Go back to sleep."

Ellis' grumbling was short-lived, and by the time Randall reached the door the vampire was dead to the world again.

Or faking it.

VAPOUR SWIRLED around the rim of Randall's mug until it breached the lip and made its bid for freedom. As it rose higher, it fell apart and disappeared.

Randall cupped the plain white ceramic with both hands. They never served tea too hot here, so the best it could do was warm his palms through the thick wall of the mug while he nursed it. This wasn't one of your fancy coffee places. Tea was still fifty pence, and if you tried to walk out the door with it the dulcet tones of the cafe's owner would hound you until you either ran so deep into the market that you couldn't hear her anymore, or you were overcome with shame at trying to steal a cheap-arse cup and shuffled back inside.

Over in Westminster — and Mayfair before that — tea was something that cost you four quid and it was delivered in a snazzy take-away cup, double-walled cardboard with an additional cardboard sleeve to keep your hand from burning, and capped off with a plastic lid that had a tiny hole to let the steam out. People in Westminster didn't have time to sit and let their tea cool before they took a sip. They had places to go, people to see, and time was money — all the usual aphorisms.

He set the mug on the battered old chipboard table and plucked blond hairs from his jacket, then dropped them on the table as discreetly as he could. The morning had been two hours of puppy party in one of Westminster's more prestigious veterinary offices, and as such he'd been covered in fluff from young Labradors, Golden Retrievers, a tiny miniature Dachshund whose owner kept trying to pull it out of the fray, and a pair of Shiba Inu. The fad for designer puppies seemed to have largely passed his clientele by.

It was a far cry from Stepney, where just about everyone had a Staffie or a Boxer. People out east didn't do puppy parties to socialise their animals or get them used to the vet's office. That was what snobs did. Posh gits with too much money and funny ideas. Out this way you got your dog home, then you gave it a quick walk around the block once or twice a day. You daren't take it to any decent parks because everyone and their uncles would tell you your dog — your daft, soft dog — was a killer that should be muzzled or put down altogether. And because you knew your soppy animal wasn't a killer you told them to fuck off and mind their own business.

He snorted at the idea of any of his Westminster clients uttering the words *fuck off*.

"Oi oi saveloy!" A big hand landed heavily on his shoulder and squeezed. "Wakey wakey!"

Randall started and almost spilled his tea. "Kieran!"

His brother loomed over him with a wide grin splitting his face. "Thought you were enjoying the high life. What're you doing in my neck of the woods?"

Randall laughed briefly and rose to hug Kieran. It was like standing hadn't made any difference to their relative heights. Kieran had a good five inches on him, and he was just as broad. "Well, some arsehole suggested we meet up for tea, but he's running late. Because he's an arsehole."

"God, what a bastard." Kieran thumped him on the back before he sank down into a chair at the table. His bulk made it look like it was made for children. "Oi, Mandy! Can I get a tea?"

"Get some bloody manners," screeched the ruddy-cheeked woman at the counter while she grabbed a fresh mug from a pyramidal pile of them.

"All right, bruv?" Kieran leaned against the table and swept the pile of dog fluff onto the floor. "How's you?"

"Yeah, not bad." Randall gave a small smile. "What've you been doing with yourself?"

"Usual shit." Kieran's shoulders bunched, then relaxed when Mandy smacked his tea down on the table in front of him. "Cheers, Mands."

"Fifty p. This ain't a charity."

"Yeah, yeah, all right. Jesus." Kieran dug shrapnel out of his pocket and fished about in it until he found enough to cover the cost. The rest — and some lint — went back to where it had come from as Mandy stalked away. "You know," he continued as if there had been no interruption, "city's always going to need someone to keep the shit flowing."

"You make it sound so glamorous." Randall laughed louder.

Kieran grabbed his tea and snorted into it. "Yeah, well. I suppose now you're all hoity toity you aren't interested in the underground adventures of sewer maintenance man, eh?"

"Oi. That's not fair. And I didn't come down here to get lectured."

Kieran gulped tea, then grimaced and added some sugar.

"Anyway. I still don't see how you fit down those tiny little Victorian sewers," Randall prompted. The familiarity of a much-repeated conversation tended to get Kieran to relax.

He loved his brother. There wasn't any doubt about that. Through all the years they shared at the same schools Kieran was always there to defend Randall against bullies. Usually Kieran's version of defence was a good offence, but still, there was warmth to be had in the knowledge that Kieran would kick the living shit out of anyone who tried to put a bruise on Randall. When you were small and even kids in your own year were bigger, and they were all keen to pick on you because you were the latest in a long line of kids abandoned by their dads, it seemed right to pull together, to be there for each other on the playing field. Except it was usually Kieran doing the bigger part.

He'd missed that once Preeti found him. Kieran couldn't be there for him anymore. He couldn't protect his little brother against bullies, and Randall had no way of knowing how to defend against them himself. Even less when those bullies were his friends.

He blinked rapidly and buried himself in his tea as his last memory of Preeti rose to the surface like an oil spill.

"I'm smaller on the inside," Kieran said wistfully.

Randall inhaled warmth from his mug and held it in his lungs a second. "Missed you," he said when he released it.

"Oh, God." Kieran glanced out through smeared windows at the bustle of Spitalfields market. "Don't get all maudlin. You've bagged yourself a rich bloke. How's the stick insect doing?"

Heat suffused Randall's cheeks. "He's good, thanks. And he's not that rich."

"Pimlico, Rand." Kieran grinned to him. "Art gallery. We're talking the definition of rich bloke. Plus mum loves him, so he's rich *and* nice. She's a good judge of character. Usually." His gaze hardened and he looked out the window again.

"Yeah." Randall frowned.

Kieran's temper was a thing of legend. He'd never turn it on his family, but his moods fluctuated with each passing breeze, and he could switch from jovial to scowling at any stray thought whose end destination was their father. Randall had seen this look so many times it was as familiar to him as his own hands. His brother had delved down a well-trod path, but it was one Randall knew how to divert him from.

"Do you think I'm selling out?" He straightened in his chair and rested his elbows on the table.

Kieran blinked, and the wild look in his eyes fled, replaced by amusement. "It's funny, innit?" He looked to Randall and gulped a mouthful of tea. "Just 'cause someone catches a break and makes something of themselves they're a sell-out. You haven't compromised who you are, have you? In fact, I haven't seen you so happy in years. You haven't stopped going to work with your existing clients, and with the District Line being what it is it'd probably be easier on you to ditch 'em, right?"

"Yeah." Randall shifted in his chair. Neither the District

nor Circle lines were renowned for reliability. Sometimes it was better to just give in and grab the Piccadilly all the way up to King's Cross then switch to the Hammersmith and City. On the truly rubbish days it was actually faster to run all the way around town than to just sit on the line that should take him straight from Westminster to Stepney.

"But if you're asking, then you think you're a sell-out," Kieran surmised. "So what's eating you?"

Randall took a slow sip of tea while he tried to shuffle all his thoughts into order.

In Westminster, his clients were wealthy. There wasn't any quibbling about it. They bought pedigree puppies, and they had them neutered the moment the dogs were old enough. They attended puppy parties, they knew their local vet by name, and they fed their animals only the best — whether commercially available or raw diets. He knew a couple whose butler prepared the dog's food every day, which meant he knew people who in the twenty-first century still employed a butler. Westminster clients vaccinated their pets. They paid for a dog trainer as a matter of course, not because the dog had behavioural issues which had become too much to handle. In a month he'd picked up enough new business in west London to rival his east London income, and time wasted on the tube was time he wasn't with a customer.

The temptation to schedule more time for the west London half of his business wasn't a strong one, but he'd be lying if he told himself the thought hadn't occurred to him.

"More money in Westminster," he finally said.

"Well yeah." Kieran smirked. "But?"

"I've got clients in Stepney who need me."

"And you haven't walked out on them, right?"

Randall shook his head. "No, of course not."

"No," Kieran agreed. "Because only assholes walk out on their obligations."

There it was again. That hardness in Kieran's gaze. The glint of obsidian piercing the surface.

Randall fussed with his mug and watched shoppers outside. There weren't many of them today, but then it was so damn cold that the few who were there were bundled up like it was the Antarctic. Stallholders marched back and forth behind their wares to keep warm, and their breath followed them in little clouds. The few brave enough to shop in a market which offered little more protection from the elements than a 150-year-old roof were ensconced in scarves, hats and gloves, some of which looked new enough to have been Christmas presents.

"Ahhh." Kieran nodded to himself.

Randall blinked and pulled his attention back to his brother. "What?"

"You're worried you'll end up like Dad, right?"

"Uh—"

"Well, don't." Kieran's broad shoulders lifted. "You're better than he ever was, okay? You're nothing like him. I know you don't really remember him like I do, but that's better, I reckon. You haven't got all that bullshit."

Randall puffed his cheeks out until he felt the stretch in his skin. He couldn't rehash this. It wasn't fun to keep going over year after year, and Christmas hammered it home to Kieran more than it did Randall. His brother was older. When Dad never came home, Kieran had put on his big boy trousers and become the man of the house at the grand old age of twelve. Randall was still a child, and Kieran's response let him stay that way. But it haunted Kieran in a way it didn't cling to Randall. Even though his brother was a big guy with a soft spot for his mum, he preferred to work in the sewers rather than deal with people on a daily basis. It was quiet down there despite being below one of the biggest cities in the world, and it made him happy to get away from everything.

Television banged on about Christmas as a time for family, so every winter saw Kieran sink back into the doldrums, and Randall would do his best to pull his brother back out of them. He'd gladly accepted his mum's invitation to bring Ellis over for dinner, and the day had gone brilliantly, but still Kieran was floundering, and Randall wasn't sure what to do about it anymore.

"You wouldn't hurt a fly," Kieran said. "Let alone anyone you loved."

Randall put his mug down and laughed weakly. "No." He felt light-headed. "Of course not."

Not unless you count Preeti. Or Ellis.

He'd killed Preeti. Oh, not with his own hands, no. But with his actions. He should've walked away from Zev's pack. He should've convinced Ellis to let things go. Now her death, Zev's death, the deaths of everyone who lay rotting away in unmarked graves not three miles east of where he sat drinking tea were all on his conscience.

And Ellis? Randall had torn into his lover's flesh with his own claws. He'd shredded away at him even as Ellis' body struggled to heal itself.

He was a monster. How could Ellis bear to be near him? How could Ameera and Hasan put up with the presence of the man who killed their brother, let alone accept him as their Alpha?

All Dad had done was disappear without saying goodbye. Randall had blood on his hands.

"Oi." Kieran thumped the table.

Randall's throat clenched. His mouth dried up. "Eh?" he croaked.

"You wouldn't." Kieran stared at him. "You've moved in with a bloke, Randall. That's a big thing! You ain't done that before. You're bound to get the collywobbles."

A gulp of tea gave Randall the ability to speak again. "Yeah." He rubbed his eyes. "You reckon that's what it is?"

Kieran laughed. "Of course it is, you berk. It's a huge step. Especially since you only met the bloke a few months ago. I can only assume that as well as being minted, he's got a huge cock."

Randall coughed so hard that Kieran bounced up to slap him on the back.

"Yeah, yeah," Kieran cooed. "It's okay. I know the girls like a huge cock, so why shouldn't you?"

"Oh God." Randall groaned. His voice warbled with every impact of Kieran's hand against his back. "You're such an arsehole."

"Yeah. But I'm your arsehole! But not, like, your actual arsehole. That thing's gotta be like—"

"Kieran!"

TWO

Ellis sat on a hard wooden chair. It was smooth in the way that only wood which had seen the press of a few hundred years' of backsides could be, and as such it was probably more comfortable now than it had been when it was made.

He wasn't keen on all this pomp the Council adhered to. Even though he made sure to arrive on time, they liked to make him wait, as though their time was more important than his. He wasn't in a position to decide whether or not they were right, but the fact that they had such poor manners rankled him, so his small act of middle-finger retaliation was to spend his waiting time with his phone.

His pocket vibrated again, and he slid his fingers across the Braille reader in his lap.

Can we take £55,000 for the Koen?

Ellis sat forward sharply at Christy's message. The movement was so sudden that Tiberius' pulse quickened in readiness.

"It's okay," he murmured. "Not going anywhere."

No. The price is seventy.

Ok, she answered.

Ellis fidgeted with the reader. He didn't want to keep pestering Christy, not if she was with a customer, but asking to drop a whole fifteen thousand pounds off an original Koen was outrageous.

Bloody January. Almost everyone who came into the gallery this time of year was on the prowl for a "bargain", and the number who were outraged that there weren't any discounts to be had there had risen sharply since the year before. Everybody wanted something for nothing, which Ellis found irritating.

His phone buzzed, but this time the reader identified Randall as the source of the text.

I'm home.

Ellis' fidgeting stilled, and he tapped out his response.

Still sitting here. They haven't seen me yet. Be home quick as I can, petal.

He heard movement from the council chambers. Footsteps approached the door. Ellis didn't bother packing away yet.

Okay. Good luck.

The handle of the old doors ground faintly as it was turned. The hinges sighed in sympathy. Footsteps approached Ellis, brisk and officious.

His pocket buzzed.

No sale, said Christy.

"Time-wasters," Ellis muttered.

"Mr. O'Neill, the Council will see you now."

Ellis tilted his head and frowned at that boyish voice. "Is this a Constabulary matter?"

"Can't say," Aaron answered, his tone flat.

Ellis nodded. He packed away the Braille reader in its little pouch without any particular hurry, and nestled it into his pocket before he stood. Then he urged Tiberius to his feet, and took the dog's harness loosely in hand. It felt childish to waste a few extra seconds, but sod them. They'd kept him here for almost twenty minutes.

He gestured for Aaron to proceed, then murmured to Tiberius to follow. The sway of the dog's gait was a soothing sensation, a safety net in an otherwise unsafe environment.

Was it Aaron's presence that made this entrance feel as though he were walking into the jaws of a shark? Other meetings had been tedious interrogations over the circumstances of Charles' death, but there had been a variety of Constables on hand throughout those. Here Hughes was sent to fetch him like an errand boy, and Aaron was nobody's Vassal.

What the hell was this about?

Hughes touched his shoulder lightly. "Chair," he said. "About a foot in front of you."

Ellis inclined his head, then reached for it. He found wood at chest height, far more diligently carved than the seat he'd just come from. "Thanks," he said, and felt his way around it to sit.

Aaron's footsteps retreated. The doors closed. It wasn't until Aaron returned to Ellis' side that Ellis knew Aaron hadn't left the chamber.

"Who's here?" Ellis said.

"Councillor Asquith, Councillor Hillier, and Councillor Stanley," Aaron said quietly.

Ellis kept his face immobile.

"Mr. O'Neill." Asquith's voice was deep, with a rasp to it that suggested he'd endured some sort of bronchial infection before he was turned that hadn't cleared away. While he spoke with an accent every bit as moneyed as Devitt's had been, the slight rattle in his lungs turned his voice from silk to slurry. "We have questions for you."

Ellis pressed the tip of his tongue firmly against one canine to keep himself from resorting to sarcasm before things even began. Once he felt he could speak without loading his voice with contempt, he stated, "I've answered a lot of them lately."

"Well then, you won't mind answering a few more." Asquith was gruff. Irked at the lack of respect from a youngster, most likely. He'd ascended to the Council after the losses of the Second World War and had been there ever since, so dealing with the city's youngest official vampire was probably his least favourite duty. He'd have kittens if he knew about Han.

Ellis eased his glasses off, then tucked them away into his pocket. The chambers were lit well enough that he could make out a vague yellow glow to the room now, and the Councillors all melted into a single blob somewhere ahead of him, but he didn't do it to see. The Council — especially Asquith — were backwards enough that being able to look Ellis in the eye and know he couldn't return the favour caused them some serious discomfort. Ellis took a measure of joy in listening to them stumble over their words while he rolled his eyes back and forth like he was having a fit. Jay would've called it trolling. Ellis just considered it entertainment. His patience with the Council's staggering bigotry had worn thin after hours upon hours of them questioning everything from his homosexuality to being seen with a black man.

Satisfied with the creaks from their chairs and the rustle of their clothing, Ellis fixed a placid smile into place. "Fire away."

Stanley's voice was lighter, but also more working class. "What changes would you make to the way we run London?"

Ellis' expression froze. Alarm bells clanged somewhere deep within his head, and he fought the urge to fidget around in his chair himself. "I'm not reet sure I follow," he said cautiously. The moment the Yorkshire slipped past his lips he regretted not being more careful with his words. It was a clear signal that they'd rattled him despite his attempt at a calm demeanour.

"It's hardly a difficult question," Asquith snapped.

"I think it is." Ellis gave in to the urge and repositioned himself in the chair so that he could cross his legs and rest his left elbow on the arm. That way most of the work of remaining upright was being done by simple physics. "And not one that can be answered without some thought."

"You run a successful business." Hillier too had the ring of a formal education to his speech, from the sort of school which made sure everyone left with Received Pronunciation regardless of their academic prowess. "Surely you have some ideas?"

Ellis couldn't help but squint. It didn't do anything to separate the blobs out into individual entities. He had a horrible suspicion brewing, and it seemed absurd to even think of it, but if he was right this was the most ham-fisted meeting of its kind he'd ever heard of.

"Is this an interview?"

"We've got two empty seats on the Council," Stanley said.

"This is a waste of time." Asquith's ghastly rattle almost overwhelmed his words, and he paused. "There is an established path of succession in these cases," he added with far less energy. "Why are we even entertaining a mere Constable on this issue?"

"Because you know it's the right thing to do." Hughes spoke up from Ellis' side, and Ellis was surprised by the vehemence in his words. "The world's changed more in the past thirty years than it has in the last hundred, and more then than in the past thousand. Christ, we've gone from black-and-white telly to smartphones in your lifetimes. Twenty years ago you had to wait five minutes to get on the Internet and now everyone in the street is on it. The government records every little detail about every single person in the country. Orwell wrote about this and it was a *warning*; instead people are living in it and they've gone from objection to acceptance in ten years! O'Neill's the youngest vampire in London. He's *current*. He knows about modern life. He knows how to run a business despite the fact that half the devices in London can't even see us. Sticking to the old way of choosing Councillors was fine and dandy when the city didn't have hot and cold running water, but now?" Aaron huffed. "It's suicidal. You need him. London needs him."

Silence wrapped the room in a prickly embrace. The only breaths belonged to Tiberius.

Ellis sat still as stone. How often had Aaron made that argument to get this far? A month since Devitt's death and the Council hadn't yet filled the empty seats. Were there two vampires out there who thought those seats were rightfully theirs? Did Ellis want to make an enemy of those strangers if these dinosaurs decided to offer him the job? Did he want to make an enemy of the entire Council by declining it?

God, it was like navigating through a viper's nest. Toes would get stepped on no matter what decisions were made. Hell, they'd already been stepped on for a few weeks, unless those potential Councillors didn't yet know that Dickens and Clarke were dead.

It felt unnatural to think that there might be vampires unaware of the massive upheavals going on in their own city, but that was the parcelled-off nature of territories. Most probably wouldn't find out anything until they came to report to the Council once their year was over and they were faced with a new line-up. But then what of those Charles had controlled? Randall and Christy remembered everything he'd ever done to them now that he was dead. Charles had even had mortal Thralls who witnessed Randall's gigantic werewolf form. He'd had to fumble about and adjust their memories quickly before the Constabulary arrived, just as he had to with Victor's, but how many others littered the city and knew things they shouldn't? They had to know something had changed, even if they weren't sure what.

Asquith broke the silence first. "Mandelson's a rum cove."

"But he *is* next in line," argued Stanley.

"Yes, and so was Devitt." Hillier's words came softly. "Can you imagine having him back here right now? We'd be puppets."

"We'd be dead," Asquith countered. "He made that clear."

"And he might be a child, but O'Neill's got chutzpah." Hillier again. "He knows all this modern technology. He got rid of Devitt."

"He's a cripple and a whoopsie." Asquith's made no effort to mask his disdain. "God alone knows what else is wrong with him."

Ellis ran fingers over his stubble with his palm across his mouth to cover the snarl he couldn't hold back. The urge to force Asquith to eat his words was a powerful one, though he wasn't a hundred percent sure he could quite control Charles' power just yet. He'd managed through trial and error with Devitt's Thralls and his former Vassal, but it wasn't the kind of thing it was okay to just test on random people until he got to grips with it.

That and it'd be wrong to make Asquith grovel.

Was it more or less wrong than letting Asquith get away with being a total bastard, though?

"Tell you what." Ellis unfurled his legs and slowly stood. He approached the Council until their blobs spread apart somewhat, and he slid his glasses back on. "I'll answer your question now." He stuffed his hands into his trouser pockets and raised his chin. "I'd modernise this city. I'd give vampires the right to travel. I'd give them the right to meet with each other and to live halfway decent lives with others of their own kind who understand what it's like to be a corpse while they're sleeping and invisible to the modern world while they're awake. I'd let them start to form friendships now that might well last them a thousand years, so that when humanity totally evicts us from the cities they can still survive in the wilderness because they have each other. Because that's where the world's going, esteemed Councillors. You're already obsolete, and in ten or fifteen years I will be too. One day the humans will decide it's a good idea to use facial recognition for banking or to replace Oyster cards. You know what an Oyster card is, right? Little bit of plastic with a chip in it that lets you use the tube? Of course, they're already phasing them out so people can just use the smart chips on their bank cards to do the same thing. What are you going to do when you can't hail a self-drive taxi because your computer doesn't recognise you and the taxi itself can't see you?" He drew his lips back into a contemptuous snarl. "This cripple can see the future, and he'll survive it long after you've all fallen to dust."

"You little weasel!" Asquith all but exploded.

"Christ," said Stanley. "You've got a bloody nerve."

"No." Ellis jabbed a finger toward the Councillors. "You've all got a nerve dragging me across town then making me wait for you when all you've done is sit in here bickering like small children. I saved your lives. I own Westminster and Mayfair. I've taken away one of the most dangerous threats to the freedom of every vampire in London, most of whom don't even know who I am, and I did all this in under a year. What am I going to get up to if you *don't* give me the seat?"

He stuffed his hand back into his pocket in the uproar which followed.

"Hughes! Get him out of here!"

"No, he's right! I haven't used the tube in three years now!"

"Who needs the damned tube?"

"Everyone?"

Ellis tuned it out and turned his back on them, using the steady pump of Tiberius' heart to steer himself back toward his dog. When he was a foot away, he took his hands from his pockets and gestured to his side. "Tiberius, here."

Tiberius' claws clicked against the flooring as he walked around to Ellis' left side and stood patiently.

"Good boy!" Ellis took the handle of his harness, then turned back to the Councillors. It was impossible to make a dramatic exit, so a flounce-off was out of the question. Better to be dignified, then, so he waited.

"All right," wheezed Asquith. "Then we may as well try it out. But if it doesn't work, we go back to the proper way of doing things around here."

Ellis blinked.

"Five years," said Stanley. "After that, we'll re-evaluate."

"Agreed," said Hillier.

A chair scraped over the floor. "Welcome, Councillor O'Neill."

Ellis turned his face toward Asquith. "You're joking."

"No. Now, take a seat. You can worry about assigning a Vassal later."

Aaron's footsteps approached, then stopped at his side. "Here," he whispered.

"Thanks." Ellis took the Constable's arm and followed him to a wholly new chair, one carved from wood and with plush leather upholstery on the seat, back and arms. As he sank into it, it enveloped him.

It felt very much like a throne.

He released Tiberius' harness and murmured for the dog to lie down, then felt for the table he knew to be in front of him. There it was, only inches away, and smooth as glass.

Asquith sat again. "That leaves the last seat."

"Well," said Stanley. "We have the Constable's recommendation."

"No," snapped Asquith.

"A woman?" Hillier roared.

"I suppose you're all for it, O'Neill?" Asquith's voice came at him like a freight train.

Ellis gave a languid shrug. "If we're talking about Barbara Applegate, yes. I am."

"What sort of degenerate turns a woman to begin with?" The rattle of Asquith's lungs was even more disconcerting up close.

"Oh, yes. Because gender matters once you're a walking corpse." Ellis rubbed his stubble. "Give her a seat. See what she can do."

"Why?"

Ellis flashed his teeth. "Because if it wasn't for her help, Devitt would have had four of these chairs taken away by now."

The arguments died away. They'd questioned Ellis enough these past few weeks to know he was right.

All that remained was to see whether the sexist old bastards would find out the hard way what Barb was capable of.

THREE

RANDALL'S BUZZING phone roused him, and he grabbed it to silence it before it woke Ellis. "Sorry," he mumbled.

"It's fine." Ellis' voice was odd, and Randall's sleep-stained thoughts struggled to work out why.

He sat up and looked to his left, but Ellis wasn't there.

"El?"

He rubbed his eyes to clear them. He distinctly remembered getting Ellis' text at around half eight last night advising that he'd be home late and not to wait up, but Randall had tried it anyway. By midnight there was still no sign, and after another quick exchange of texts to make sure his lover was okay he'd given in and gone to bed.

"Right here, petal." Ellis wandered into the bedroom, wearing only trousers and a shirt. Everything else had been shed somewhere.

Randall blinked at him. Had Ellis come home so late he'd slept in another bedroom rather than disturb him?

Then his brain did a little skip backwards. He pushed the sheets aside and looked up to Ellis. "You're up early!"

"Well." Ellis came closer, walking around the room with the surety of intimate knowledge of its layout. "I missed you last night, so I didn't want to miss you this morning." He gave his little lop-sided smirk and added, "When do you have to go?"

"Um." Randall checked his phone again, as if somehow his alarm could have gone off half an hour before he'd set it to. But no, it was only a couple of minutes after seven o'clock. He hadn't miraculously summoned an extra thirty minutes out of his day. "Half past," he groaned.

Ellis' eyebrows rose, and the light from the phone glinted across his ice blue irises. "You don't leave yourself much time."

"Nah. I try to get out without waking you."

"I better not hold you up, then." Ellis' smile twisted into a sly thing. "Which means we'll be multitasking." He touched his free hand to Randall's wrist and stroked his fingertips up toward the crook of Randall's elbow. His touch was cool, almost ghostly, and Randall's stomach fluttered.

"How—" he croaked. He licked his lips and swallowed. "How many things do we need to do at once?"

"Just the two." His fingers reached Randall's shoulder, and Ellis leaned in until his cheek rested against Randall's and his hair fell against Randall's nose. The ghost of a touch flitted downward, crossing Randall's collarbone and sending a jolt of arousal straight to his groin. "You're going to shower," he whispered, "and I'm going to suck your cock."

Randall sucked in a breath, but all his air was lost to a moan of desire when Ellis' nimble fingers found a nipple and circled it.

Ellis tipped his head down and grazed Randall's shoulder with his teeth. His finger and thumb closed around Randall's nipple and gave it the gentlest of pinches.

Randall's head fell back. He dropped a hand behind himself to keep from falling over, and his knees parted almost of their own volition.

"God, the things I'd do to you if we had longer," Ellis breathed. "I'll have to save them for later."

He withdrew, and Randall whimpered in the back of his throat.

I could cancel the first appointment.

Randall toyed with the idea as he watched Ellis tug the shirt off over his head and toss it to the bed. When Ellis pushed his trousers down and took his boxers with them, the sight of his stiff cock almost made Randall willing to ditch a brand-new client.

Ellis crooked a finger at him, but didn't wait, and strode to the bathroom.

Randall scurried to follow.

He'd grown used to using the bathroom without turning on the lights, but he hadn't memorised it the way Ellis had after they'd moved in. Still, everything non-essential had been moved out of the room or outright sold off, so crossing to the shower in the dark wasn't difficult. It was an old thing, though, not like the power shower in Ellis' old flat, and it took a few seconds to really fetch up enough hot water to avoid freezing bodyparts off in the morning.

Ellis' hand found Randall's chest, then trailed down toward his stomach. "You first," he whispered.

"God, El, you're enough to drive a bloke mental." Randall reached into the cubicle to start the shower, and by the time he'd withdrawn his hand Ellis' closed around his shaft. "Oh, fuck," he whimpered.

"Later." Ellis tugged gently until his palm smoothed over Randall's eager head. "Get in."

Randall stumbled forward until the warm water trickled

over his hair and ran in rivulets down his back. Droplets broke free and trailed down his chest, and their warm touch stirred his nipples until they were hardened bolts of flesh.

The door closed behind them. Ellis' hands felt cold in contrast to the water, and they fell to Randall's hips in a possessive grip. His erection slipped in the wetness between Randall's cheeks and nudged demandingly at the small of his back.

"Fuck me," Randall pleaded. "Oh, God, El…"

"No time," Ellis said. His lips pressed against Randall's shoulder. His hips ground into Randall's arse. His hands slid forward and coiled around Randall's dick.

"I don't care!"

Ellis laughed and ran one hand along Randall's length while the other wrapped finger and thumb around the base and gripped tight.

Randall writhed, desperation taking hold over his body. His thighs quivered as he pushed his arse back against Ellis' erection like a cat in heat, and he splayed his hands across the cold tile wall to steady himself. "God, if you keep that up—"

"Turn around."

It didn't occur to Randall to disobey, and he turned in the confined space. Ellis' hands left him for only a moment, then pressed against his hips and forced him back against the tile.

"Ah!" Randall gasped with the cold. It made everything in him clench, from arse to toes, but before he'd adjusted to it Ellis had dropped to his knees. It was all Randall could do to grip Ellis' shoulders before the vampire's mouth found his cock.

Then nothing else mattered.

He was enveloped in the cool confines of Ellis' mouth, tiles at his back, warmth running down his chest like a thousand hands all touching, caressing, teasing every inch of his skin, and he shuddered with arousal.

"Oh, shit… Jesus fuck, Ellis…" Words spilled out of him, and none of them made any sense. It didn't matter. Ellis suckled on him like his life depended on it, and Randall's hips bucked. He shifted his hands to Ellis' hair, soaked through into thick, heavy strands, and he gripped at them as he began to thrust deeper.

He could feel the muscles in Ellis' throat as they swallowed around his head. Squeezing. Coaxing. Pushing him toward the edge. Fingers drifted between his legs and inscribed slow circles around his entrance, while a palm closed gently around his balls.

A growl rumbled from Randall's diaphragm up through his chest until it clawed free from his lips, and he fucked Ellis' mouth, going deep with every thrust.

"Fuck," he snarled. "Fuck, I'm gonna come in your mouth, El."

Ellis' responded with a nod, and he ran his thumb tenderly across Randall's sack.

"Fuck!" Randall's body shook as he came, and the force of it left him quivering against the wall as his cock twitched and spat with every heartbeat. "Ohhh God. Oh *God*."

Ellis eased free and placed a kiss to Randall's stomach, then chuckled. "You dirty bastard."

"Me?" Randall barely had the strength to squeak.

"All that swearing. I'll tell your mum what a potty-mouth you are if you keep that up." Ellis stood and felt behind himself for the shower door.

"You wouldn't dare!"

"Try me!" But he darted out of the cubicle before Randall could grab him, and laughed as he closed it behind himself. "You've failed at multitasking," he called out.

"Oh, shit!" Randall pushed away from the wall and grabbed the shower gel.

HE ASSUMED Ellis had gone to evacuate the contents of his stomach in one of the house's other bathrooms, rather than do so in the same room as Randall. He checked the time while he dressed in a hurry, and the relief that he still had five minutes flowed through him like a balm.

He dragged a jumper on over his head and hurried off downstairs. By the time he reached the ground floor, the place smelled of tea and hot buttered toast. He broke for the kitchen and found Ellis there, wearing only a pair of boxers, wet hair dripping over his shoulders as he poured a jug of tea into a travel mug. His fingertip hung over the lip of the mug so that he could judge when it was full without creating a mess, and his head tilted toward Randall with a smile.

"I'm guessing you only have a few minutes, so I thought you could take tea with you." He laughed, then added, "It wouldn't do for a Yorkshireman to let his fella out into the world without a cuppa inside him."

"What, would they revoke your Yorkshire card?" Randall stepped in and kissed Ellis lightly.

"Too bloody right they would." Ellis set the mug down and felt for the cup's lid, then screwed it into place. "Toast's yours," he added somewhat redundantly.

"Cheers!" Randall grabbed the top slice and chewed on it quickly. He let his gaze rove over Ellis' lean frame as he swallowed. "So what happened last night?"

"Oh, well." Ellis rubbed his stubble and turned to rest his bum against the worktop. "We ended up in a huge argument, then they made me and Barb Councillors, and we spent the rest of the night in tedious administration rubbish. I only got home about an hour ago."

Randall almost inhaled his toast. "Wait, *what*? You're on the Council now?"

Ellis' features crumpled into a grimace and he crossed his arms like a petulant toddler. "Schoolboy error," he groused. "They got me so riled I ended up arguing why they *should* give me the job instead of why they shouldn't. Talk about a failure of negotiation."

"But this is great..." He looked up to Ellis and frowned. "Isn't it?"

"I have a gallery to run." Ellis' shoulders hunched as he pulled his arms tighter to his chest. "I just want to do that in peace and quiet. It's Barb who wants to overthrow the Council, and that's great. Good for her. She's got a seat, maybe she can start to change things for the better. Or what she thinks will be better."

Randall stuffed another bite of toast into his mouth and quickly chewed on it. At least if he gave himself indigestion his physiology would fix it after a burp or two, but he usually preferred to eat in less of a hurry. "Can't hurt to give it a go though, right?" he finally offered. "I mean, with two of you, that's like forty percent of the Council. All you ever have to do is win over one vote and you guys get to make changes. You can really help people out here, can't you?"

Ellis fidgeted. His arms unfurled and he tugged on one earlobe, looking like he'd just bitten into a lemon. "I suppose, aye," he grumbled.

"Right. So why not give it a few months and see how you do?" Randall crammed in the rest of his toast and grabbed the travel mug.

Ellis' eyes flickered toward the ceiling, then he huffed. "They've made it probationary anyway."

"There you go then! How long for?"

"Five years."

Randall stared. "Wow. They really think long-term, eh?"

"Aye, seems that way."

Randall leaned up and kissed Ellis' lips. "You're cold," he said. "You going to be okay today?"

Ellis nodded. "Yeah, I'm okay. It's more the weather than hunger. Go on, I'll catch you this evening."

"Okay. Be back quick as I can."

He hurried out of the house and quickly found the world caked in frost.

FOUR

"ELLIS! Hey hey! How's my favourite ex-employer?"

Ellis laughed and took Jay's arm. "Don't you only have two ex-employers, one of whom you're working for again?"

"Oh, no! I temped my way through uni!" Jay's humour infected his voice and made it bubble with glee. "There's hundreds of you stowed away in my past. Well. Maybe ten. Hello, Tiberius! Oh my God, did you fatten him up over Christmas?"

Ellis followed Jay's lead through a lobby which smelled of plastic and cleaning fluids. "I think Randall's mum might have slipped him a few bits of turkey. She thinks everyone's skinny."

"In the woman's defence, though, you are."

"Oh, this from the poster child for the twink look?"

Jay feigned a gasp. "My God, no! I've gained a hundred pounds since you went blind!"

"I didn't realise it affected you so badly!" Ellis grinned.

Jay led him through what sounded like an open-plan office. There were too many keyboards and mice clicking, heartbeats thudding away, stomachs gurgling over their lunchtime contents, and people chattering to each other and using words like *function* and *variable*. It all turned into a background level of utter nonsense, and his fingers gripped Jay's elbow a little more firmly.

"You know me, sweetie," Jay answered dismissively. "If people aren't ogling my sexy bum all the time my self-worth plummets."

"It's always about you." Ellis faked a long-suffering sigh, and was rewarded with a laugh.

"That's right!"

A door squeaked and Jay led him through into a room which, once the door was closed behind them, cut out most of the office chatter and made it an indistinct murmur that was much easier to disregard.

"Ellis!" Han's voice, now. "Thank God for this lousy weather, eh? Keeps the clouds out in force." His footsteps came in, and then his arms wrapped tightly around Ellis.

Ellis grinned and released Jay's elbow so that he could return the hug. "Han. Glad you could fit me in."

"Always, mate. You want to take a pew?"

"Aye." Ellis made his way to a chair and settled into it, then let Tiberius relax and lie down. He waited until Han and Jay both sat, footsteps and creaks his only guide, then he ran his fingers over his watch to feel for the ball bearings. Ten to three.

"You're a bit early," Jay said. "But it's all good. Oooh, I feel all weird not offering tea. Would you like tea?"

"No," chimed Han and Ellis at the same time.

"Bliss!"

Han chuckled. His chair creaked faintly. "I've got some discoveries for you, so it's great you came over."

Ellis leaned back and dropped his hands into his lap. "Really? Have you figured it out?"

It was fast becoming the Holy Grail. Han searched and searched, but he couldn't find it, and it seemed to be stretching beyond his reach. While it had only been a few weeks, the idea that he might wake up one day and suddenly work out what his power was and how to use it had been slipping further away with each attempt. It had occurred to Ellis to try and order Han to use it, to see if that would force it to the surface, but that seemed weird at best, and downright rude at worst.

"The power thing? No. No, still don't have a clue. And it's getting a bit bonkers trying different things on the off-chance, you know? How do you even work out that you can fly, for instance? Do you just give up on everything else at last and leap off a tall building?" Han chuckled. "It'll come sooner or later. I've been working on other problems."

Ellis' brow furrowed into a frown. "Problems? Is everything all right?"

Jay huffed. It wasn't one of his fun huffs, either. There was nothing playful to it. It was an angry little sound, and was followed by the sucking of air through teeth.

Ellis leaned forward. "What is it?"

"Dipshit here has been experimenting," Jay snapped.

"We need to understand the parameters of this condition if we're to make it work." Han's tone came with the reason and calm of a man who'd made the same argument several times.

"Hang on." Ellis raised a hand to try and stop them before they cycled an old argument he was usually absent for. "Experimenting? Han?"

"There are hundreds of different myths and stories about vampires, right?" Han sounded sure of himself, and Ellis suspected his friend had already done more research on the subject than Ellis had in two years. "If I'm to work out what we can and can't do I need to test them."

"He burned his bloody hand off!"

Ellis blinked. "You did what?"

"I was testing the effects of exposure to sunlight. Ultimately to destruction. I wanted to know how long I could endure direct light if push came to shove. That's not the kind of thing you want to find out in an emergency, is it?"

Ellis grimaced. That was exactly how he'd discovered it after a visitor to his previous flat had opened the curtains mid-afternoon. "No," he had to agree.

"Oh my God!" Jay sounded appalled. "Don't encourage him!"

"I'm not! But you know what it was like for me when that bloody woman from the guide dogs came over. We went out for a walk after that to work out just how bad it was, and don't you try to tell me that you haven't filled Han in on what happened with that." Ellis turned to face Jay's pulse. "He's right. Maybe if I'd done a bit of experimentation instead of just listening to what I'd been told like a good little boy I would never have been in that position in the first place."

Jay didn't answer. His chair shifted, then his heartbeat rose higher, and his footfalls carried him across the room.

Ellis turned toward him, ready to ask him to stop, but he heard the run of water and then the click of a kettle, so he turned back to face Han.

"Logically," Han said softly, "this seemed the best time of year to begin testing. The sunlight is so weak that a significant percentage of the population suffers seasonal affective disorder. The cloud cover is often thick, and there's frequent rain, further reducing the potential strength of the light. I bagged a light meter and a stopwatch and started doing a variety of exposure tests. Just one hand," he added, "nothing more. I reckoned if it turned out to be a burn-on-sight thing then at least it'd just be a few fingers, and from what I understand they'd grow back, right?"

"Slowly," said Ellis.

"But they would grow back. So I ran tests under various conditions. Partial cloud cover. Full cloud cover. Low light temperature, medium light temperature. Morning, afternoon. Blah blah blah. The TLDR of it is that I think Randall's blood is helping you a lot."

Ellis eyebrows climbed. "You're sure?"

"Well, no. It's hardly scientific when our sample sizes are one vampire on werewolf blood and one vampire on human blood—"

Jay snorted.

"—but operating on the premise that all things would be equal if not for our diets, then yes. I can be awake all day and sleep all night with no problem, but the fact is that I don't think summer will be something I want to try going out in. As it currently stands sunrise is around half seven in the morning, and sunset's at half four. That lets me get to the office before sunrise and not leave until after sunset. I can get straight to and from the tube in the dark. That's nine hours of sunlight in this office with cloud cover, bad weather, and poor quality light. Add to that I keep the blinds in here closed and after those nine hours I'm itching like I've got fleas. I've got to find a better solution for when summer rolls around or my staff is going to wonder why there's a pile of ash on my desk."

"And your hand?"

"Took around two hours of poor quality light exposure to reach serious sunburn stage, another two for blisters, and at the five-hour mark fingers started to fall off."

"Bloody hell, Han! And you sat through that?" Ellis' eyes widened reflexively and his spine stiffened.

"You see what I have to put up with?" Jay stomped back across the room, the scent of tea accompanying him, and his chair protested as he sat heavily. "He just sits at the window for hours on end with one hand through the blinds taking notes. It's horrible. And I thought it wasn't going to grow back, it took so long!"

"A week. And it was only a few fingers. I didn't wait for the whole hand to go."

"Areet, stop." Ellis leaned in again and rested his elbows on his knees. "Han, you can't keep treating this like some kind of science project."

"I can."

"No, you can't! Have you thought about what this is doing to Jay?"

The room became uncomfortably quiet, punctuated only by Jay's soft sips and swallows.

"I had to do something," Han eventually said. "I can't just sit at home all day every day. I'm sorry, baby." The modulation of his voice altered slightly, like he'd turned away from Ellis. "I'm sorry. I must've put you through hell and you've put up with all of it."

"I'll forgive you," Jay said slowly, "if you start listening to me. I'm only trying to help."

"I'm sorry."

Ellis leaned down to fuss Tiberius between the ears while Han and Jay decided to kiss and make up. They'd never had any fear of public intimacy, and that hadn't changed now that Han was dead it seemed.

Good for them, Ellis thought. In a way it was another reassurance that being turned hadn't driven Han insane.

He sat up sharply. "You haven't tried crossing the Thames above water, have you?"

"Oh hell no." Jay snorted. "I might not be able to stop him

baking his hand all day, but I will put a table leg in him rather than let him do *that* to himself!"

"I'm willing to accept anecdotal evidence on that one," Han said. "Anyway, while I was waiting for my fingers to come back, I started experimenting with capacitive touch screens, camera lenses, photographic film and the like. I've only really just begun those lines of experimentation, but I'm already at a loss as to how any of that can possibly fail to work."

Ellis slouched back in his seat. "What've you found?"

"It's context-sensitive. The pickup on reflections and lenses and such," Han explained. "Whatever's at work gives the appearance of understanding the difference between things which are worn and things which are carried, and it differentiates between the two."

Ellis nodded slowly. Both Jay and Randall had explained to him how reflective surfaces showed Tiberius' harness, but not Ellis' clothes. It had been one of the clues the werewolf picked up on back when they'd first met, despite Ellis' care in selecting routes which minimised his exposure to mirrors and windows. "But you don't know what it is."

"No. And so far as I understand it it's impossible."

"Why?"

"Okay. Physics time. Light is actually invisible."

"Er—"

"Bear with me. Light is invisible until it bounces off something. You can only see light when it hits your eyes directly after it's boinged off another surface. Now, light bounces off different surfaces in different ways. Some objects absorb some of the light's wavelengths, and what you see is the section of the light that's left over. So technically red items aren't actually red, they're every colour *but* red. Red's just what managed to break free and—"

"Han, Han, Han!" Ellis waved his hands in surrender. "This is all going reet aboon my head!"

"Basically the law of reflection suggests that if I can see you, a mirror should also reflect you." Han sighed faintly, like a child robbed of the chance to show the class how clever he'd been. "The same with cameras. Likewise the vibration of air molecules—" He cut himself off this time. "If I can hear you, so should a microphone. That none of this works is inexplicable to any law of physics I know, but your mileage may vary. I am not a physicist, I'm just a nerd."

"I think there's a really obvious answer that you're both missing," said Jay.

Ellis turned to face him and lifted his eyebrows in a silent question.

"Magic!"

"Jay—"

"Baby—"

"Hey, don't be so quick to chuck it out with the bathwater." Jay snorted. "I am sitting in a room with two vampires. One of them can see the past by touching stuff. The other one has some potentially awesome superpower we just haven't figured out yet. I mean, come *on*. Even if you had reflections and could use the phone, you have powers and abilities people just don't have. Your hearing is like, I don't know, a bat's. Han can see a speck of dust on my lapel from across the room. Both of you have the kind of poise now it usually takes ballet or tai chi to learn. You can feel minute changes in temperature and air pressure. You're both like walking barometers. It's ridiculous." He huffed. "So maybe, just maybe, magic is a thing, and you two are it."

Ellis scratched the back of his hand.

Jay had a point. There was no way anyone could deny that there was anything supernatural in being a vampire.

Regardless of the troubles with technology, the simple facts were that his body could do things a living creature's couldn't. He'd regrown an entire arm. He'd seen Randall's face after touching a chair. Of all the things he could pick apart, Jay's theory wasn't one of them.

And so far it was the only one they had which made any sense at all.

FIVE

RANDALL SAT COILED in an armchair and flicked through channels on Ellis' dodgy little old telly.

Charles' house held little in the way of comfort for the average living, breathing individual. Most of the ground floor had been the blond bastard's office, and the rest was kitchen, a tiny loo under the stairs that probably never saw use, and this study with its armchairs and ancient wallpaper which now had clean spots that showed where paintings had once hung. They'd rescued Ellis' things from his flat and found impromptu homes for them, but this place was old and Charles hadn't really kept it up to date. The place needed to be rewired, because the fuses were in that downstairs loo and looked like they were made out of Bakelite. The heating was hit and miss, and it seemed the closer to the ground you were the worse the radiators got. Of all the bathrooms and bedrooms, Charles had clearly only ever stuck to the master suite on the top floor, and had had a bathroom installed as an afterthought once plumbing was a thing. It was a mishmash of different fixtures and decor with a claw-footed tub and a shower cubicle that had to be at least twenty years old. The toilet was a horrible lump of ceramic probably installed just to stop the plumber wondering what kind of man wanted a bath but no lavatory.

It was a step up from the other bathrooms, though. No showers in those. Nothing but sterile whiteness and cold water.

There hadn't been a single television in the entire house. The only kind of broadcast device Randall had found was an early wireless radio the size of a small suitcase, and Edison had sold it along with all the paintings. Randall had let his old landlord keep everything in his flat to cover the costs of the repairs — though he'd snuck in first to at least collect clothes and his laptop — so they were down to Ellis' single TV that was a remnant of the days before his eyesight deteriorated too far for it to be of use to him anymore. He'd work with it on as background noise, or tune it in to one of the radio stations up in the 700's on the Freeview box, but otherwise the vampire mostly ignored it now that it was tucked away on a sideboard in the study.

Randall really wanted to ask whether there was enough money left over from Edison's legal fees to get the wiring and plumbing sorted out.

'Course, if Preeti were still alive, she'd do it for peanuts.

His eyes stung, and he rubbed at them with the palms of his hands.

She'd been there for him right at the start. She'd saved Kieran's life, and his mum's, by making sure Randall's first ever change was away from home. She'd taught him everything she knew about what he was, and over the years she'd stood between him and Briar like a force field. She was a sister to him and he'd never see her again.

How could that happen? How could the world be so cruel as to snatch away *two* people he'd loved?

Would he forget what she looked like over time? Was that how things worked, or was that just because he'd only been a kid when he lost Dad? Was the world filled with people who couldn't remember what their loved ones looked like because they'd lost them too long ago? No wonder people were so fixated on taking pictures of everything from their pets to their children to their Gran in the retirement home.

Did anyone have pictures of Ellis from before he was turned? They had to, right? Those pictures had to be out there somewhere. He'd Google it later or, failing that, drop Edison a text.

The front door shut with a bang and shook Randall from his melancholy. "El?"

"It's me," Ellis called.

Randall heard the rip of Velcro, then Tiberius bounced into the room, free from his harness and tail thumping ten to the dozen. He slobbered all over Randall's hand and Randall fussed his shoulders. "Good boy! Who's a good boy? You? Yes, it's you!"

"Good? I'm stellar!" Ellis stepped into the room with one hand against the door. "You after a new house already? We only just stole this one!" He thumbed toward the television.

"Er." Randall glanced toward the TV and found he'd landed on one of hundreds of relocation programmes. "Oh, I was just hopping." He turned it off and put the remote aside. "How was Han? Has he learned to fly yet?"

"Nope." Ellis picked his way carefully around Tiberius, his hand flitting to the sideboard for guidance. "God, one month is not long enough to learn an entire building," he grumbled. "Especially with a great hairy backside in your way." He patted

Tiberius' rump fondly, then settled into Randall's lap. "Is this seat taken?"

"It is now." Randall slipped his arms around Ellis' waist and leaned up for a kiss.

"Perfect." Ellis' lips were cold as ice.

Randall shivered and grabbed Ellis' hand. "God, El, you're frozen!"

"Bloody minus two out there, isn't it? And I've had to get back here from Blackfriars." Ellis curled his fingers around Randall's. "Give it a few minutes."

"You walked the whole way?"

"The Thames Path is all gardens and absolutely no windows."

Randall eyed him. The vampire's lips were set in a faintly smug little line. "And you're a Councillor so you can go where you damn well please," he surmised.

"I may have decided to stretch my legs because I can, aye." The line twitched upward at the ends.

"So you're warming to this Council idea, yeah?" Randall grinned. "Aaahh! Bastard!" He writhed to try and escape the hand which had snuck into his shirt like a ninja and pressed its icy touch against his skin.

Ellis lips parted into a wolfish grin and he slid free of the shirt, then smoothed it over with affected innocence. "So no, no flying from Han," he said as though he hadn't just partially frozen Randall's nipple off. "He's been using himself as some sort of guinea pig, though. Got Jay properly wound up, he has."

"Is that at all sensible?" Randall leaned back and drew Ellis against his chest to try and warm him more rapidly. "Either the science experiments or winding Jay up," he added.

"I wouldn't go with either." Ellis tugged his glasses off so that he could rest his head to Randall's shoulder. "Bloody fool burned his own hand off. Decided to leave it baking in the sun to see how long it'd take. It's fine, he's regrown it since, but it took days."

Randall turned his head to rest his cheek against Ellis' hair. "So it's my blood," he surmised.

"Aye. That's Han's conclusion, though he did some hand-waving about needing more data." He ran his fingers lightly over Randall's collarbone while he spoke. "He's trying to work on the electronics problem, too, but it doesn't seem to be going anywhere."

"He's had a few weeks," Randall reasoned.

Ellis' lips quirked. "Jay thinks it's magic. I don't know. A curse, or something else maybe. But when you have eliminated the impossible…"

"For Sherlock Holmes to work on this you have to know that magic is possible." Randall glanced down to Ellis' hand.

"Oh, aye. But I'm a blood-sucking corpse and you're a shape-changing Wookiee. Except your claws aren't only for climbing."

"Geek." Randall sighed against Ellis' soft hair and ran his fingers through it.

It was so strange. Even this close to Ellis, even something as porous as hair held no scent. It was as though he sloughed off the city's odours. They'd find someone else to adhere to, while Ellis continued untouched by the bus fumes and cigarette smoke. They might find their way into his clothes, but they never gained traction on his body. Scents had to be applied far more directly to linger: soap, shampoo, toothpaste. Even then they were pale imitations of the scents clinging to a living body, the faintest traces of humanity desperately trying to hang on for as long as they could.

Randall grimaced. "I, uh." He scrambled to jump his brain onto different tracks. "Oh. I could ask Mrs. Uddin?"

"Hm." Ellis sat up slowly, peeling away from Randall's chest. "Do you think she'd know?"

"I think she's the only person I know who *might* know." He dug in his pocket for his phone and scrolled through the contacts with his thumb, then dialled and held it to his ear. There was no need for speakerphones with Ellis' hearing, that was for sure.

"Randall," came Mrs. Uddin's welcoming voice, rendered two-dimensional by the phone's speaker. "Is everything all right?"

"Yeah, yeah. Thanks. Everything's fine. Are you doing okay?"

"Of course." She chuckled. "What can I help you with?"

Ellis laughed softly. "Straight in there."

Randall almost answered him, then just smiled and nodded. "I didn't want to take up too much of your time, Mrs. Uddin, but I just wanted to ask a quick question." He licked his lips. "You, er. You haven't any idea of whether magic actually exists, have you?"

Ellis' head tilted slowly as he tipped one ear toward the phone, his smile drifting away. "She's worried," he murmured.

"It seems silly," Mrs. Uddin finally said, her speech slow and careful, "that people like ourselves would wonder such a thing."

Randall glanced to Ellis. "I suppose. But I mean we're pretty self-evident, right? We know we exist."

"Are you calling for a philosophical debate?"

"No, no. For your expertise." Randall blinked. "You know something, don't you?"

"Oh I know lots of things, young one. But magic?" She sighed. "I would imagine there must be. It's just difficult to know what's a story and what is true."

"Hm." Ellis slowly eased himself from Randall's lap to perch on the arm of the chair instead.

Randall rested his hand on Ellis' thigh. "Which logically suggests you have heard stories," he prompted.

Ellis nodded in agreement.

"All that I've heard is that those who have magic are dangerous to everyone around them. To us, to humans, to anyone they ever meet, but most of all to each other. Sorcerers are power-mad. Magic warps them. They kill each other for power then get killed and have it stolen from them. They will use anything and anyone they can get their hands on as weapons. They're not for getting their own hands dirty, which is why all you'll *ever* know about them is stories. The lucky never meet the sorcerer, and the unlucky don't survive it."

"That seems to be the answer to a totally different question," Ellis said quietly, echoing Randall's own thoughts.

"Stay away from sorcerers. Got it." Randall nodded to Ellis.

"You haven't heard of any in town, have you? I thought they all died off years ago." Even Randall could hear the fear in her voice now.

"No, nothing like that. It was just a thought. I wondered if maybe things like vampires or... or even us... might have come about because of magic or something like that..."

"Oh." Mrs. Uddin cleared her throat. "Oh, I see. Well, er. I suppose that's possible."

"Okay then." Randall fished for something else to say, but all he came up with was, "I'll see you later, yeah?"

"Any time."

"Thanks." He hung up, then stared at Ellis.

"Touched a nerve there," Ellis mused. "What do you reckon that was about?"

"I don't know. That was weird though, wasn't it?" He slid his phone away. "I mean, proper weird?"

"Aye. Maybe Ameera knows what it was about?"

"Maybe." Randall rubbed Ellis' thigh slowly. "Sorry. That didn't help at all, did it? Just muddied the waters."

"Wouldn't worry about it, petal."

He gazed at Ellis and reached for the vampire's hands. They were cool now, rather than the ice-like cold they'd been earlier. It might take longer for the warmth to reach Ellis' core, but at least his extremities were room temperature at last.

Those fingers couldn't elicit a response from modern touch-screens. They conducted heat and cold like living flesh, but they wouldn't provide the slightest current needed to operate a phone or a tablet. Maybe that wasn't so bad for Ellis — since he needed interfaces to communicate with him through his hands so the sleek glass of a screen would never be enough regardless — but he faced other problems. He couldn't use biometric security systems, and couldn't speak over the phone. The longer he lived, the more that was likely to become a problem. People were already testing self-driving cars. By the time Ellis saw the end of the century would he be able to use any transportation other than his feet at all? Would the entire world leave Ellis behind one day?

Randall sprung to his feet and took a deep breath. "Right. The way I see it we've only got one option."

"Give Han more time?" Ellis suggested.

"Okay, two options."

"Then what's your one?" Ellis faced him, his gaze missing him by mere inches.

"Well. We'll have to find a sorcerer, won't we?"

Ellis stood with deliberate care. "I'm sorry, Randall. I've got bad news for you."

"What?"

"You seem to have gone insane."

SIX

"Wow. You really can tell the difference once you've eaten, can't you? Is it eaten, or fed?" Christy gasped and her pulse raced. "That's not an offensive question is it?"

"I don't know." Ellis paused at his desk and raised his head. A satisfied smile wanted to break out, so he let it. "A little of both."

The eating had come first, but since he'd already had Randall down his throat in the morning he didn't stick with it too long this evening. Besides, he'd kept the werewolf waiting on a promise the entire day, and the little shivers from the hot body under him sang to him in a way that no words could, so after the eating had come the fucking.

And the feeding.

The winter left him alone now. He felt alive in a way that people never noticed while they possessed vital signs. The simple ability to remain above zero Celsius was one which was often overlooked by those who had it.

"Right, right." Christy's awe suggested she'd completely

missed his inference. "Well if you ever need to, you know. I mean, if you're ever—"

Ellis tugged his glasses off and tossed them onto his desk. "What?" It was difficult to keep the incredulity from raising his voice.

"Well, now that Jay's not here, and—"

This time Ellis failed. "Jay? I've never touched him!"

"Oh," she breathed. Her heart fluttered. "Sorry, I just… I thought, well… I mean…"

"He's married!"

"I'm not."

"W—" Ellis clamped his lips together. His eyes narrowed until he could make out her blob as it merged with the blob of her desk, both occupying a small spot in the centre of the slightly larger dot that was his entire field of vision. "What is it," he said once he had a tighter hold on his bemusement, "with humans wanting to coddle me?"

"People," Christy corrected.

Ellis fumbled for his glasses and slid them on to distract himself from the fact that she was right. "People," he repeated reluctantly.

"Because you're a decent bloke," she said. "Because your friends care about you. And it doesn't hurt that vampires are sexy. Anyway, it's not coddling. It's friendship."

He laid his hands against his keyboard and fumed in silence. Since Christy remembered what Charles had done to her, it seemed unfair to take that knowledge away again, especially since she'd been helpful in searching Charles' house for paperwork and art alike. She really did know her art history, despite her shaky interview, and finding out about Ellis and Randall seemed to have given her a new confidence. It hadn't solved her clammy hands, but nobody was perfect.

But like Jay before her she'd begun to fuss over his well-being. She worried over whether he was feeding enough, going out in the sun too much, getting to the gallery too early in the day. She asked questions almost nightly in her quest to better aid her employer, then constantly apologised if she'd caused offence. She pulled long hours, worked weekends, and tried to do her best to let Ellis turn up as late as he liked, which was pointless since if he wasn't in the office he was working from home more often than not. Either way it took two people to run the gallery regardless of whether they sat here at the same time as each other.

It all felt horribly like he was being pitied.

God, he wanted Jay back. At least Jay had moved on from the pity party fast. He still fussed like an old man, but that was Jay's nature. He fussed over everyone he cared about regardless of how alive they were or whether they could see.

"Look," he said with practised care, "I appreciate your concern." Like hell he did. "But I don't need all the worrying over, areet? I'm fine. Thank you."

"Okay." She paused. "Huh," she added.

His lips parted, then he heard the door downstairs close. Footsteps came toward the stairs without any hesitation.

"You in, Councillor?" Aaron's question was asked quietly.

"Aye." Ellis nodded toward Christy. "It's fine," he said to her.

"Oh, okay, because the door, like, moved on the CCTV but then there was nobody there and so..." She tailed off. "Oh, Constable!"

"Evening." Aaron entered the office. "Sorry to interrupt."

"It's fine," Ellis murmured. "Come in, have a seat."

"Do you want me to go?" Hope tinged Christy's voice, but Ellis doubted it was on the expectation that Aaron would agree.

"Nah, it's fine. You already know the properly secret stuff." Aaron sniffed and came closer. "Don't think it's really fair to shoo you out just for our nonsense."

Christy's faint sigh of happiness proved Ellis' guess correct. "Great, thanks!"

"Plus God knows how many other people know now that Devitt's carked it," Aaron grunted as a chair creaked under him. "Seems it's a good idea to have someone able to keep an ear out for loose lips, innit?"

Ellis withdrew his hands to his lap. "What can I help you with, Aaron?"

"Well, Councillor—"

Ellis scowled.

"—I need your help with a case. Don't give me that look. Now you know what it's like to have a shitty title you never wanted."

"Then why'd you put me forward for it?"

"Because the people who want power are usually the ones worst suited to it. Now, there's a couple of guys who have missed their annual check-ins. I've been 'round to their places and there's no sign."

Ellis felt like his brain's wheels were spinning trying to keep up. "Annual check-ins," he surmised, "with the Council?"

"Them's the ones," Aaron agreed. "One of 'em's our mutual friend Victor. He was due in last week, never showed. Have you seen him around?"

"No. Not since the clean-up." Ellis shook his head. "He turned up for all the questioning, didn't he?"

"Yeah. So we know he was okay three weeks ago. Whatever 'appened to him, it weren't Devitt. His house looks like a bomb hit it, an'all. Total mess. There was some ash, but nowhere enough to be all of him. I've taken samples and handed 'em to me other 'alf, and he's got access to some sort of science shit he can do to it. I just want to be sure it's not paper or something innocuous."

Christy sucked in a quick breath.

"Yeah, yeah, he knows too. Keep yer mouth shut about him, eh?"

"Not a word, I swear," said Christy.

"Good stuff."

Ellis leaned forward slowly. "Are you suggesting something was strong enough to take Victor in a fist fight?"

The thought alone was enough to make his balls crawl up into his stomach. Of all the seemingly random powers vampires took on after they were turned, Victor's was at once one of the simplest and most terrifying. He had the strength to tear through steel. He'd been Charles' Vassal back while Devitt still sat on the Council, and his bodyguard — willing or otherwise — ever since. Victor had picked Ellis up like he was a child's toy and slammed him into a stone floor so hard that it broke several of his bones, and he'd done it one-handed. The man was in every sense a juggernaut, and if anything had taken him down inside his own home it had to be even more monstrous.

"Yeah." Aaron sounded as grim as Ellis felt. "If he'd been destroyed there'd be more physical evidence on the scene. Cooper's wasn't so bad, but then he wasn't a thug. He probably didn't put up anywhere near as much of a fight."

Ellis shook his head slightly. "Name doesn't ring a bell."

"Turned in the late Fifties," Aaron said. "Decent enough bloke, though he's all post-war spirit, you know? Moans about the kids of today a lot. His thing's ghosts."

"Like, dead people ghosts?" Christy sounded excited.

"Yeah. Can see 'em. Can't hear 'em or anything, so maybe he just went crazy when he was turned and he's seeing stuff?" Aaron's clothes made a brief *shh* sound. "Either way, not gonna protect him from something capable of going toe-to-toe with Victor, is it?"

"I'm guessing not," Ellis muttered. "But he's missing, aye? And there's some ash?"

"Far less, but yeah, I found a bit."

Ellis ran a hand through his hair and tugged it back from his forehead. "Doesn't make any sense."

"Yeah. So I wondered if you minded lending me a hand on this one."

"Me?" He drummed his fingers on the arm of his seat a moment, then shook his head. "How?"

"I was hoping if you had a spare evening you might come with me to look it all over."

Ellis ran the tip of his tongue along his upper teeth. For a moment he had the baffling idea that Aaron had forgotten he was blind, then he had a sinking feeling. His shoulders slumped. "Oh."

Aaron wanted Ellis to use his power. The one Aaron knew he had, anyway. But if something awful had happened to Victor and Cooper, Ellis would have to watch it in glorious Technicolour. He'd seen far too many things for his own good lately, and as much as he might have hated losing his sight, it was only the things he'd *seen* which gave him nightmares.

Not true.

He grimaced as he sank further down in his chair. No, not true at all. If it wasn't Randall's attack it was the sound of flesh torn from towering bodies, snarling and screaming and dying, and the scent of blood threatening to take him over. He knew that extreme hunger led to a loss of control, but now it seemed that being near so much blood was a threat to everyone around him too. That wasn't a normal human thing to do. He didn't remember ever going into any kind of feeding frenzy over the sight of a buffet; not even in his student days when he'd made a tenner stretch an entire week at a time. One night he'd dreamed of nothing but that scent and woken up ready to eat the first living thing he could get his hands on. Thank Christ it had been Randall.

"Ohhh!" Christy's epiphany dragged him back to the here and now. "You mean with his hands!"

"No, with his eyes," Aaron deadpanned.

Christy's heart did that little *whump* people did when they were uncomfortable. She squeaked like a cornered animal.

"Oh, God." Aaron's chair slid back across the carpet and his clothes swished. "Kiddo, if there's one thing you've gotta learn, it's that if someone wants your pity they'll ask for it." The chair bumped back toward Ellis after Aaron's voice came from high enough to suggest he'd stood. Aaron was one of those people who returned Ellis' chairs to their starting point.

"And I don't need a white knight, Constable." Ellis sighed and pried himself from his seat. "C'mon, Tiberius." He took the dog's harness and walked around his desk, all the while imagining that he could feel Christy's embarrassment from across the room. "It's fine," he said to her. "He's old and cranky. He probably yells at kids to get off his lawn."

"If kids were on your lawn in the middle of the night, you would too," Aaron muttered.

"It's okay," Christy said. "Just remember I'm new to all this, okay?"

"Fair," Aaron said.

"Okay." Ellis drew himself up and squared his shoulders. "I want to take Tiberius home and drop him off first. Grab a cane instead. Then you can loan me your elbow, Constable." He was damned if he was going to take his dog anywhere that might be even remotely dangerous.

"Yeah." Aaron stepped to the door and it opened with a

soft sweep of wood against carpet. "Sorry, kiddo. He's right. I'm an arsehole."

"That's not exactly what I said…"

"Close enough."

Ellis snorted. "Close up whenever you feel like, Christy." Then he headed out after Aaron. "Let's go put my hands all over your crime scene."

SEVEN

AARON WALKED Ellis up to Victoria station so they could get the tube out to Parsons Green, then led him through a myriad of turns that rendered him completely unable to find his way back to the station if anything happened to the Constable. The District Line train sounded like one of the newer ones, at least, so the journey hadn't hammered at his ears like nails on a chalkboard for ten minutes.

The area sounded suburban. Not with blocks of flats, but with rows of houses instead. He could hear televisions and snatches of conversation, or snoring from those who had gone to bed already. None of the sounds of life came from higher than a couple of storeys, and the wind hadn't picked up the more extreme speed that might indicate tower blocks. Still, it was bitter, and felt like it had tiny shards of ice in it. It made boughs groan overhead, but the only leaf rustles were at hip height. Bald trees and short hedgerows, then.

Something cold and wet fell against his cheek.

"Where are we?"

"Fulham."

Ellis grimaced. Fulham was virtually outside London as far as he was concerned. "Is it snowing?"

"Just started, yeah."

Every flake that hit his coat was a tiny little *pat*. Those which fell against his face melted in a second or two thanks to the warmth Randall's blood provided. A couple snuck down the back of his collar and he gave a sniff of disapproval.

"Doorstep coming up," Aaron advised.

Ellis felt for the height of the step with his cane and waited while Aaron scratched at the lock. Then the bolts chunked back and they were inside. A quick sweep of the cane was enough to tell him that they were in a tight hallway. People in houses either side. To his right, two adults and three children, along with some tiny pulse which could be a cat. To the left, further away, one adult and two children. He couldn't make out any pets in that direction. That they were further away suggested that the front door didn't sit centrally, but that wasn't unusual for terraced houses, which were usually built as reflections of their neighbours.

"Mind your step." Aaron moved slowly. "Once we get into the living room it's a bomb site."

Ellis nodded and bounced his cane off every surface he could find, measuring and assessing. He heard Aaron kick or sweep detritus aside, but there was still the occasional piece of something underfoot, and he hesitated to lift his feet more than a few millimetres.

"So, what do you need?" Aaron asked.

"Eh." Ellis stopped and tightened his grip on his cane. "It's hard to say. Whatever has the most emotional resonance on it. If there's a discarded weapon he used to defend himself that would be ideal."

"Don't remember seeing one." Aaron paused, then Ellis heard a series of clattering sounds from all around the room, all running together into almost one single noise, and all done within mere seconds. "No. No weapon, but Victor was one for his fists rather than anything clever."

"Then something directly involved in the struggle. Ah." Ellis put his hand through his hair, only for it to come away damp with melted snow. "I don't know. Something he might have grabbed to defend himself with, or any marks his attacker made, anything like that."

Aaron snorted. "Marks. Yeah. There's marks. Come this way."

Ellis took his elbow, and they picked their way through the debris, then Aaron said, "Right in front of you."

He released Aaron and reached forward until his fingers felt solid wall. The paper was sleek, slightly bumpy.

"Left about three inches. Uh. What's that? About six centimetres?"

"Closer to seven and a half. It's fine, I'm old enough I can go with either." Ellis smiled tightly as his palm slid across the wall until he found a rough edge.

He felt along it, and then into it. Plaster had powdered away and left edges like the scales of a fish which jutted out from the wound, trapped there by the wallpaper they were stuck to. Beyond the long, almost-straight ridge of scales was a trench which cut through paper and plaster alike until it gouged into the brickwork beneath.

"That's not the only one," Aaron muttered.

Ellis shook his head, numb. "Are they parallel?"

"Yeah. Kinda reminds me of Charles' desk. Well, your desk now. But—"

The room flashed into view. Ten feet by twelve feet at most, a poky little living room for a family but for one man living alone it was probably plenty. How ironic that Charles had relied on Victor for over fifty years, yet Victor's home was so humble.

There was a cheap three-piece suite to match the cheap wallpaper. Everything had an aura of the Sixties about it, with vinyl upholstery and brown wallpaper, both dulled with age. Table lamps were round, organic shapes. Tables and sideboards were simple G-Plan affairs. Even the carpet was orange, well-worn to the point of threadbare in the areas nearest the doors and armchair. The brown curtains were closed, and had enough cobwebs at the edges to suggest they hadn't been opened in several months.

Victor backed into Ellis' field of view, a mask of determination on his face. He didn't look afraid. He was too alert for that, too focused to have time for fear or panic.

Claws sliced through the air and gouged into the wall where Victor had stood only a second before. For a big man he was light on his feet. He moved like a boxer, his eyes evaluating his opponent even as he danced away from the massive, furred forearm that lunged past Ellis' face.

Ellis didn't want to see any more. He didn't want to turn away from the wall again.

But there was a werewolf in Victor's house, and Aaron needed to know what happened here.

He forced himself to turn. To watch.

The monster was bent over to fit into the little room, which made it near impossible to judge its height. With a man Victor's size in here as well it made the place positively claustrophobic.

Victor landed solid, heavy blows. His aim was damn good. His fists would ram into the creature's stomach or sides. Sometimes he got behind it and slammed a flurry of blows into its back. Sometimes he picked up a table or a sideboard with single-handed ease and smashed it across the monster's brown-furred form.

It was all for nothing.

A broken bone here and there. The snap of ribs. But it wouldn't ever be enough to stop a werewolf. Victor would need silver, and no vampire was stupid enough to leave the stuff lying around his home.

Claws caught Victor's chest, and he healed.

They raked across his back, and he healed.

His expression became grim as the futility of his situation sank home.

Ellis shook. His hand trembled.

Victor couldn't win this, and he knew it. He couldn't inflict enough damage to make the werewolf stop, not even for a moment, and every wound it inflicted on him took its toll on his reserves of energy.

Every chunk it tore from him fell into dust before it hit the floor. Every opening it tore in him took more and more time to close.

You have to bite him, *Ellis urged in silence. It was the only way to stop this horrendous engine of destruction from destroying him.* Bite him. For God's sake, Victor!

Victor's fangs had descended now. He launched himself at the werewolf, an uncoordinated assault which brought him another gash to his flesh.

It didn't heal.

The werewolf grabbed him by the waist and dragged him across the tiny room to the remains of a shattered table. Victor snarled and writhed and pulled fistfuls of fur from it, but it ignored him and reached into the mess.

Victor's realisation hit at the same time Ellis' did.

"No. No! Stop!"

The werewolf hefted the table leg in one hand. His gigantic grasp made it seem like little more than a twig.

"What do you want?" Victor's features contorted in fear at last.

The werewolf snarled and drove the wood through his heart.

"Oh God." Ellis shook his head, but the vision had ended abruptly the second the stake did its work. Had the werewolf experienced no emotion at all during the entire fight? Surely if he'd been angry, if he'd lost himself to the full moon, his fury would have been more than enough to continue the vision past Victor's loss of consciousness, but instead it cut out.

"O'Neill?" Aaron's voice was so close it startled him.

"Werewolf." Ellis snatched his hand from the wall. "Oh God, it was a werewolf. They fought, but Victor didn't stand a chance. It staked him."

"Right." Aaron stepped away from him again. "How many of these buggers have we got hanging about in this city, eh?"

"I... I don't know. I'd have to ask Randall—" His throat closed around his words.

Could it have been Briar?

Oh, God no. It couldn't, could it? Randall said Briar was something like fifteen feet tall when he was in what they called their war shape. The creature would have been bent double to fit in here if it was Briar. No, it had to be someone else. Someone who could still move around in this cramped space.

Someone shorter.

Claws raked across the desk, ruining in an instant an antique which had stood immaculate for three hundred years. The brown-furred arm shot past Ellis' shoulders as the vampire threw himself at Charles Devitt in one final, frantic attempt at killing the Elder before Randall could destroy him.

Ellis crushed the cane's handle in his grip and began to fumble his way toward the exit.

"Ellis?"

"Out," he whimpered. "Got to get out."

He stumbled down the narrow hallway and out into the street. His thigh smacked into a solid iron gatepost, and he reached out to grab hold of something but all he found was wet, prickly hedge.

The door behind him slammed, and Aaron was at his side before he could fall, hand on his elbow to keep him steady. "O'Neill," he said quietly. "Stop."

Ellis did as he was told.

"What's the panic?" Aaron kept his voice to a whisper. "Wait. Did you recognise it?"

"I can't see," Ellis snapped. "How can I recognise it?"

Aaron released him gently. "We should get back before the tube shuts down for the night."

Ellis rocked his jaw. He wiped the damp off his hand and onto his shirt, but the snow came thick and fast now. It was a wasted effort, so he took Aaron's elbow and held it like a drowning man.

He had to be wrong. It couldn't have been Randall. It *couldn't*.

No matter how much it looked like him.

EIGHT

Parsons Green tube station was far enough out of Central London that its platforms were above ground, exposed to the elements.

Ellis sat huddled on a wooden bench. The snow which had been on it subsequently soaked through his trousers to chill his thighs, so he hunched forward rather than have the same thing happen to his back. He didn't know that huddling really achieved much, but any reduction in the surface area he made available to the weather had to be a good thing so far as he was concerned. At least he was immune to shivering or goosebumps.

"Where's the bloody train?"

"Five minutes," Aaron said. The Constable had decided to stand instead. "I need details. What kind of stake?"

Ellis shook his head. He didn't want to revisit that vision.

"If Victor's been taken I need to know everything you saw."

He ground his teeth slowly then sighed, and haltingly relayed the entire fight.

"Right. So it stopped 'cause he got staked, right?"

Ellis nodded, then unfolded his cane at the sound of distant rattling on the rails.

"Is that unusual?"

"In a way." Ellis leaned forward to stand without touching the arms of the seat. He rested the cane against the platform's slick surface. "It suggests the only emotions strong enough to imprint on the room were Victor's."

"That's bad, then."

Ellis turned toward him slightly. "Why do you say that?"

"'Cause generally in a fight people feel something. But this werewolf just goes in and whittles Victor down, then sticks him with a table leg calm as you like. Suggests he had a plan. Also suggests he's a fucking psychopath."

The train screeched and rattled closer, setting Ellis' teeth on edge. An older train, then. He spared a silent curse for the continued existence of antiquated rolling stock. "Reet, so." He pushed his hair back, and the amount of wet in it kept it in place for once. "He can't have walked into the house like that. He must've arrived in some other shape. He probably didn't even shift until he got into the living room."

"You didn't see that part?"

Ellis shook his head. "No. Victor's emotional state wasn't enough to imprint at that stage."

"So he invited whoever it was in, maybe." Aaron's voice drifted closer. "Train's pulling in."

"And you tend not to invite stray wolves in after they've knocked on your door." Ellis found Aaron's elbow and followed him onto the train, which was so elderly it still had the slightly bumpy plastic-coated floor which made his cane skip every time he hit one of the bubble-filled humps. At least the carriage didn't smell of bodily excretions.

"No, not that one," Aaron said before Ellis could sit. "'S got chewing gum on it. This one."

He almost fell into his seat as the train jerked to life. There were three other people in the carriage, but over twenty feet away and chattering together, so odds were they wouldn't overhear. Still, he kept his voice low. "Thanks. Areet, so you reckon Victor either knew the fella or was expecting him somehow, aye?"

"Or the werewolf has some funky powers of persuasion, yeah."

Ellis folded his cane and rested it across his lap. "Or a weapon."

"Yeah. Victor wasn't the smartest, but he wouldn't have done a fight on his own doorstep. Take 'em indoors, beat the snot out of 'em, toss 'em out on their ear, whatever. Still, he's been taken, so at least I've got places I can go now. I'll canvass the street, see if anyone saw anything. Big fight like that, maybe the neighbours heard it. See if we can't pin down when exactly it happened. Don't suppose you know, do you?"

"No. Unless a vision conveniently includes a calendar somewhere I'm pretty limited on guessing when something happened. And the curtains were shut, so I don't even know if it was night or day."

"Logically it's gotta be night," Aaron reasoned, "'Cause he let someone in."

"Right." Ellis fixed a smile into place. If Han's experimentation should've drummed one thing home it was that most of the vampires in London didn't have the daylight freedom he did.

"And if our werewolf wanted to nick 'imself a vampire intact, he wouldn't then take the damn thing out in the middle of the day."

"You'd make a good detective."

"Oho, so funny." Aaron tutted. "You know what I gotta ask though, right?"

The train's sounds *whumped* into dullness, and the air pressure dropped enough to make Ellis' ears pop. "No."

"Victor knocked you about a bit, didn't he?"

Ellis pressed his lips together and turned toward the cold air radiating inward from the side of the train. Of all the memories he didn't want to relive, he had to admit that having Victor toss him around like a small toy and introduce his face to a stone floor at high speed wasn't at the top of the list, but it was still on there somewhere. For all Victor's readily-used violence and strength, though, there was a simple truth on the man's side. "He didn't have a choice."

"Does Randall understand that?"

"I might be wrong," Ellis said with care, "but I think you're implicating Randall somehow."

"I'm covering all possible lines of enquiry. C'mon, O'Neill, you know it's my job."

The cold began to seep into Ellis' cheeks, so he turned away from it and faced Aaron. "Right," he sighed. "You're right. Feelings aside… I honestly don't think Randall would do this. He's got no reason to. Victor left us alone after Devitt died. There wasn't any kind of vendetta we were aware of. That and we had no idea where he lived, and I don't know how Randall could have found out."

"Barb, maybe?" Aaron sounded thoughtful. "She probably doesn't respect borders, she might know where quite a lot of us live."

"Or there's the Council, their Vassals, and the entire Constabulary," Ellis said.

Aaron seemed to take his sarcasm seriously. "Right, yeah."

Ellis shook his head. "Okay, so where's Randall hidden

Victor? And this Cooper fella? What's he got to do with anything?"

"Yeah. Doesn't sound all that likely, does it? Odds are that it's got to be some other werewolf. And I don't know that anybody but you, me, and Barb knows werewolves even exist, let alone who might be one or how to get in touch with 'em."

Ellis flinched as a brief memory of a vision flickered across his thoughts.

You smell like a werewolf. It's quite distinctive.

"Devitt knew," he said softly. "So we can't assume others don't."

The train clattered its way through two stations as they sat without talking. Aaron didn't respond, and Ellis had no desire to push further.

From his knowledge of Devitt's personality the chances were that the Elder had knowledge which was of limited availability to others in the city; Devitt preferred to accumulate rather than to share. His drive was personal survival and power, and damn everyone else if they got in his way. He'd pulled on the strings of countless puppets throughout the years. The evil old bastard had forced Aaron to kill his own lover, and almost done the same to Ellis and Randall. Ellis couldn't envision the devious little shit sharing information he might have use for one day, such as knowledge of werewolves or how to tell them apart from human beings.

He'd known, though. He'd smelled it on Randall without hesitation. That distinctive scent, woodsy, earthy. Many colognes emulated it, but to the sensitive nose and taste buds of a vampire nothing could come close to the real thing.

To know that they existed wasn't enough, though. To know where Victor lived, to have a werewolf agree to go there, for the werewolf to know how to wear down and then stake a vampire...

"We're missing something," Ellis grumbled at last.

"Yeah. Even if somehow everything comes into play and makes sense for Victor, how does it make any sense for Cooper too?" Aaron sighed. "If it's not Randall, though, if it's some other werewolf, we've got a big problem."

Ellis lifted his chin. "Why wouldn't it be a problem if it was Randall?"

"'Cause he's got reason for Victor, he might have reason we don't know about for Cooper an'all. But some third party? We ain't got a clue about motive. Don't even know where to start." He paused while they screeched through another station and a couple more people got onto their carriage.

Ellis ran his thumbnails along the surface of the cane in his hands. Sleek, clean, a layer of paint over hollow aluminium. It wasn't his preferred mode of transportation, and every time he used it he returned to Tiberius like long-separated friends. Still, the cane couldn't get hurt.

He didn't want to go home. Not right now. Not to Tiberius and not to Randall. Aaron hadn't said it, but he knew what the Constable wanted: he was coming with Ellis to question Randall, and Ellis wasn't a hundred percent sure he could be there for it. Aaron would let him stay, of course, but what if Randall was guilty? What if he described what he'd done? Suppose he wasn't guilty, but he showed Aaron what he was capable of so that Aaron better understood what he faced in the course of his investigation?

The nightmares would be back when he finally slept, he knew it. He'd found new fuel for them, a new monster to ruin his dreams and prey on his thoughts.

And if they found this creature, what then? Ellis knew what happened when werewolves fought one-another. Oh, God, he knew, and it made him sick to his core. Nothing could stop them once they went at it. They would tear into each other until one of them stopped moving, and he wasn't willing to lose Randall. Not like that, and not any other way.

"We should take this to the rest of the Council," he said once the train was in motion again. He hoped it sounded as light as he wanted it to, as though it didn't eat away at him to let someone like Asquith find out about werewolves.

"I don't think we should," said Aaron.

Ellis turned toward him. "Why not?"

"You want them to know about Randall? 'Cause that's where it'll end up, mate, if we get them involved. Trust me, I've been doing this shit for donkey's years. Better to solve a problem and just tell 'em it's dealt with than let them start turning over all the rocks to see what's underneath."

Ellis grimaced and shook his head in frustration. "You want to talk to him, though, don't you?"

"Gotta be done."

He was right. But that didn't make it any easier to swallow.

NINE

RANDALL SNOOZED off and on throughout the evening. Ellis had left him a pleasing combination of stuffed and drained, and Randall fully intended to bask in it for as long as he could. He did well, too, until Tiberius' cold, wet nose dug under the duvet and smeared snot all over his arm.

"Gah!" He wriggled away from the intruder, then sat up. "Why? Why do you do this?"

Tiberius' tail thudded against the bedside table, and his tongue drooled onto the sheets.

"Yeah. I take it all back about you being a good boy, you know." Randall scratched between Tiberius' shoulders as he picked up his phone and squinted at the time. "God, it's only half eleven. What'd I do to you, eh?"

Tiberius licked his lips and belched, then trotted off out of the bedroom. His paws thudded off downstairs.

Randall grabbed some clothes and dressed quickly in case the dog needed the loo, but then he heard familiar voices from below. Ellis was easy to pick out, even from three floors up, so no wonder Tiberius had woken him then run off. The other he had to listen to a little as he hopped about pulling on his socks, until he figured out it was Constable Hughes. And the only way to work out whether it was a social call or Constabulary problem was to get his butt down there. Neither voice was raised, at least. He hoped that was a good sign.

He walked down the stairs unhurried, but there was no chance of him eavesdropping on them on his way down. Bloody radar ears meant they stopped talking well before he was within sight, so when he reached the office which occupied the majority of the ground floor, he found Hughes with a thin smile plastered on his youthful face, and Ellis seated at the desk he seemed to hate.

"Okay," he said slowly. "You two look like something's up. What is it?"

Hughes' smile slid away, which only confirmed Randall's suspicion, so he sat himself down in a chair which predated the Boer War and waited.

"Aaron has some questions," Ellis said quietly. He had one hand on Tiberius' shoulders, and the dog's head rested on his thigh. It was a gesture which sought comfort, and the dog was empathetic enough to offer his support accordingly.

Randall frowned slightly. Ellis was ill at ease, that much was obvious. He hadn't sought any form of comfort from Randall, either — hadn't reached out to him or beckoned him to the desk. Whatever was eating away at him was enough to make him retreat into himself.

He'd been doing that a lot lately.

"Okay." Randall faced Hughes. "What can I help you with, Constable?"

"Hopefully it's something you *can* help with." Hughes perched on the arm of the bulky wooden chair Devitt had once made his men zip-tie Randall to. He planted a foot on the seat of it with as much disdain for the piece of furniture as Randall himself felt. "You remember Victor, right?"

"Big fella?" Randall nodded. "Used to run around after Charles? Yeah. Hard to forget him. Why?"

"Got any beef with the bloke?"

Randall shrugged. "Who hasn't? But he's left us alone since then, so no."

"Do you know where he lives?"

"Haven't got a clue, sorry." He watched Hughes, but the Constable was either skilled at faking his body language or he really was as relaxed as he seemed. "What's this about?"

"He's gone missing." Hughes slid off the arm and into the chair. His boot was still on the edge of the seat, so he ended up with one long leg sprawled out and the other folded up against his chest. "Better than that, he was taken."

"Well, I didn't take him." Randall chuckled. "Good luck to whoever did. The bloke's pretty ballsy from what I gather."

"It was a werewolf." Ellis spoke so softly that it was barely above a whisper.

Randall looked to him and something unpleasant twisted within his gut. Ellis looked tired. His shoulders had slumped and his body was still. His face was slack, wet hair hanging around it in lank waves, and he faced the table rather than the room.

It could be hard to read a vampire. They didn't have all the autonomic clues which would tip the hand of a living, breathing human being. Their pupils only ever dilated to adjust focal length or adapt to light conditions, not as an emotional response. Their flesh never turned to goosebumps, at least not that he'd observed. Their skin didn't flush unless they'd fed, and never from embarrassment, and likewise they didn't turn pale with fear or shock. It all came down to their movements, their posture, and whether they were habitual fidgeters.

Ellis was a fidgeter. He wasn't one to stay still. He'd put his hands all over the place while he worked things through in his head: he'd mess with his hair or scratch his stubble, sometimes he fiddled with his glasses or hid his hands away altogether. It humanised him, but Randall wasn't sure Ellis was aware he did these things. He suspected they were habits from Ellis' living days.

Randall didn't know Hughes well enough to recognise all of his fidgets, but the Constable certainly liked to pace while he was thinking. Some of Hughes' cues, like Ellis', were verbal too. Hughes' Cockney accent became more pronounced when he was relaxed, and dwindled away when he was being professional, whereas Ellis' Yorkshire accent and slang would rear their heads when Ellis was excited or afraid but generally settled to a background rhythm when he was going about his daily life.

Now, though, Ellis sat stock still, and Hughes was all business. These two facts collided with Ellis' statement, and Randall felt ill.

"And you think it was me," he said. "Right?"

"No," Ellis said.

"Nah, I don't think so," Hughes agreed. "But gotta be thorough."

Randall puffed out his cheeks. "Then why the long faces?"

Hughes jerked his thumb toward Ellis. "Councillor managed to bag himself a vision of what went down. Yer big walkin' rug came in, started a ruckus, then put a table-leg in Victor's heart."

Randall stared at Ellis, who hadn't moved at all. "Can you describe it?"

Ellis' fingers twitched and he withdrew his hand from Tiberius. He seemed to curl in on himself a little.

"Brown. Like…" Ellis trailed off. "But taller. He had to stoop in the room, so… maybe eleven or twelve feet? Hard to really tell." He wrung his slender fingers together in his lap. "I don't know, Randall. It was all so fast…"

Randall exhaled slowly. "It's okay. It wasn't Briar, or Nazim." That didn't seem to be the reassurance Ellis sought, though, since it did nothing to alleviate his hunched posture. "I doubt it was any of my pack. Where did this happen?"

"Fulham," Hughes said.

"No, not my pack then."

"How can you be sure?"

"Because Fulham's nowhere near our territory." Randall looked to the Constable. "We'll travel for work, or for… other things… but mostly we like to stay at home."

"Okay. I think theorising further at this point's not going to get us far," Hughes said. "I'm gonna go check Cooper's place. I'd appreciate it if you could come with and check it out for me, Councillor."

Ellis shrank further and turned to face the wall. "It's lousy weather out," he grumbled.

Randall blinked.

"Yeah but if Cooper's been taken an'all, the quicker we can work this out the quicker we can find 'em."

"And if he hasn't?"

Randall stared at Ellis. Deliberately hanging back when someone was in danger wasn't the man he knew and loved.

Then it all clicked into place. Ellis' posture, his reticence, his vision…

He was *terrified*.

"I'll come with you," Randall offered.

Ellis turned to face him slowly. "What?"

"Why?" said Hughes.

"If there was a werewolf there," Randall reasoned, "I'll be able to pick up his scent. I can tell roughly how old it is, if the place is relatively undisturbed. And if it's anyone I know, the scent will be a dead giveaway. Either we can pick out exactly who to look for, or we can eliminate like thirty potential suspects with a single sniff. Seems like it might be valuable knowledge either way, yeah?"

"Nice!" Hughes dropped his booted foot to the floor at last. "Then I'd appreciate it. Cheers!" He glanced down at himself as a buzzing sound came from his jeans, then added, "'ang on."

"'Course."

Hughes wriggled his phone from his pocket and dug out a sleek black stylus to go with it, then poked at the screen swiftly. His gaze flitted over the message, and within a second he was tapping out his response in a way that Ellis never could.

"It's Jude," he said as he jabbed with the stylus. "Says he's run spectroscopy on his ash sample and it's coming up blank. I assume he means the machine can't even read it or whatever, but he says it means it's not any known substance."

"Which we already know," Ellis muttered, "because it's Victor."

"Yeah. But every little bit of evidence counts." Hughes put his phone away. "And anything I can get which corroborates your vision's a good thing as far as I'm concerned. I much prefer multiple sources for any given fact. Makes it more likely I'll reach the truth."

"Okay. I'll grab my coat." Randall stood and moved to Ellis, and placed a hand on his shoulder. It was freezing cold, and soaked through, but he didn't let go. "El, why don't you go change into something dry?"

Ellis tipped his head back to face Randall. "Seems pointless," he said weakly. "If we're going out in it again."

"Yeah," Randall breathed. "But I'm going with you this time." He frowned with worry and leaned down to kiss Ellis' forehead, which was damp, but not as cold as he'd been earlier on, before he'd given Randall a damn hard fucking and driven his fangs into Randall's shoulder. "It'll be okay," he whispered against his lover's skin.

Ellis sagged against him slowly. The damp from his clothes soaked through Randall's T-shirt. "All right," he said. "Fine. We'll go. But this is the last one, Constable."

"Sure," Hughes said.

Randall fussed with Ellis' hair, but there was no use in asking him what was wrong. Not with Hughes here. He'd have to ask later, once they had privacy. Once Ellis felt comfortable enough to talk.

It didn't take a genius to have some idea, though. If Ellis had a vision of some werewolf attacking a vampire and winning, well... Randall's gaze fell to the claw marks which were etched through the surface of the antique desk, its perfect mirror-shine surface forever marred by the evidence of Ellis' narrow escape.

Randall stepped away with sluggish reluctance and went to fetch his boots. "He means it, Constable," he said as he tugged them on. "This is it. Where are we all going?"

Hughes stood. "Chiswick."

Ellis straightened in his chair. "You are joking, right?" His hand darted to his left wrist and felt for his watch. "The tube will have shut down by now!"

"Yeah." Hughes drew his phone and poked at it. "But there's an Uber five minutes away. Let's see if they're up for the job."

"Have you lost your mind?" Ellis stood, and Tiberius

padded out of the way. "We can't go bagging some random fella off the Internet!"

"Yeah, we can, 'cause we've got a breather with us." Hughes nodded to Randall. "You two go in the back so at least Randall reflects, and I'll go up front to keep him talking and his eyes off the rear-view. Easy peasy." He tapped with his stylus. "There we go. Piece of piss."

Ellis stood and waved for Randall, so Randall hurried to his side and offered his arm.

"We'll go, then we'll come straight back," Randall said. "Job done."

"Yeah," Hughes crowed. "Come play detective with me. You get to like it after a while!"

Ellis' expression suggested that he felt otherwise.

TEN

THE CAR DROPPED them outside a semi-detached house just a couple of minutes beyond a golf course. Randall had covered for the vampires leaving the car, then he followed.

It was almost a half-hour drive out to Chiswick, and Hughes had refused to accept any money for the ride. Randall wondered whether the Constabulary had expense accounts, or whether they had to pay for these things out of their own pockets, but before he could ask Hughes was at work on the front door's lock.

Randall looked around quickly. The street was quiet, and far enough out from Central London that every house had off-road parking for at least one car. A tall hedge shielded them from view of casual observers at street level, so he kept an eye out for any curtain-twitchers up in their bedrooms.

"Bingo," Hughes said.

The lock clunked, and Randall looked back in time to see Hughes easing slender picks away into a pouch, which he then dropped into a pocket.

Hughes shouldered the door and led the way, and Randall waited for Ellis to retake his elbow before he followed.

"Wow," Hughes muttered. "Nowhere near as bad, but yeah. There's been a fight in here."

"Doorway," Randall said softly as he led Ellis into the living room.

The place was a mess. If this wasn't as bad as Victor's home, then Randall dreaded to think what that must've been like.

Cooper's house was some sort of cosy suburban middle-class dream in which a bomb had been detonated. Furniture was scattered and torn, and one set of bookshelves had come down, scattering its books all over the floor. The others were intact, and the room must have been floor to ceiling with books until the fight broke out.

Randall parted his lips to inhale fully. "Yeah. There's been a werewolf in here."

"You can tell that?" Hughes looked impressed.

"It's really faint, but yeah." Randall looked around, but there were no claw marks in here, no convenient and obvious signs of supernatural violence. "I dunno if they had a piss while they were here or if it was only yesterday or something, though. I'd have to switch noses for that."

Ellis released him. "Let's get this over with. Find me something."

"Right," said Hughes. "Something defensive, or a weapon, or..." The pages of upturned books fluttered in a sudden gust of wind, and Hughes stood in front of Ellis with an iron poker. "Try this?"

Ellis reached forward and Hughes placed the poker in his hands.

"It wasn't by the fireplace," Hughes said. "It was under a couple of books. Stands to reason he might've..."

Ellis' features contorted. He clutched the poker tightly, and his head moved like he was watching something Randall couldn't see, but his expression quickly ran toward horror. He let out a strangled cry, and his arm trembled with strain.

Randall grabbed the poker and wrenched it from his grasp. He threw it to the floor and pulled Ellis against his chest, holding the taller man against himself while Ellis' fingers dug into his sides. "It's all right, baby," he whispered against Ellis' neck. "It's all right."

"Same werewolf," Ellis breathed. "I think. I don't know."

"Staked Cooper?" Hughes asked bluntly.

"I don't know," Ellis repeated.

"I probably broke it off before he could see." Randall glanced to Hughes.

The Constable's expression was not unsympathetic, but he didn't look best pleased either.

"He had a stake." Ellis spoke more loudly now, and gently unfurled himself from Randall's hold. His fingers fussed with smoothing out Randall's T-shirt where they'd been clinging for dear life moments before. His back straightened as he pulled himself together. "Wood. Very nicely turned. Could have been a fid that was sharpened for the job, or it could be completely custom."

"Fid?" Randall squeezed Ellis' hand.

"It's a tool for working with rope and canvas at sea. Like a marlinspike, but made of wood."

"Didn't realise you were a yachting man," Hughes smirked.

Ellis gave a light shrug. "They're not uncommon as *objects d'art* in auctions."

"Right." Hughes' gaze flit to the poker, then settled on Randall. "Wanna do your thing?"

"Yeah," he said. But he watched Ellis as he said it. "You gonna be okay, El?"

"I'm fine."

It didn't take an expert in Britishness to know he didn't mean it, but Randall leaned forward and kissed his cheek to show that he understood. "We'll talk later," he promised.

Ellis' head bobbed just a couple of millimetres.

Randall released his hand and stepped away. There wasn't any need to undress, but it'd make putting his clothes back on after a lot easier if he unfastened everything now rather than fighting with his bootlaces while his bits were dangling for all to see. He crouched to unlace them and nudge them off, then removed coat and T-shirt before he unfastened his jeans and slid them down.

Hughes was politely pretending that something on the ceiling had captured his interest, which for a guy who'd already seen him butt naked was a nice gesture, but not one Randall found necessary. Werewolves saw each other in the buff plenty of times; he was over any shyness he once felt about it long ago. Still, maybe it was Hughes who was uncomfortable seeing a guy naked when that bloke's lover was right there beside him, so Randall got rid of his boxers and didn't wait around after that.

He dropped to all fours while his body snapped and twisted itself into a new shape, and shook himself out once it was done so that his fur felt comfortable.

"God, that sounds grim," Hughes muttered.

Ellis said nothing. His face was rigid.

Randall gave himself a couple of seconds to adjust to his wolf senses. The room had lost almost all colour saturation right away, leaving almost everything at the slow end of the spectrum tinged mostly greyscale with a faint yellowish overtone to it. Even blues were muted, though, to let him pay more attention to all the detail laid out around him. Much more of his field of vision was in focus, which was what was the majority of his disconnect between the two shapes was, especially when he went from wolf back to human.

Scents were almost entirely absent. It was as though he'd somehow forgotten to change his nose, though that wasn't possible. Two vampires in a room owned by a third would do that, he supposed, when the owner never had living guests. No food in the kitchen, no items which came into contact with the living, no skin to create dust from...

It made the werewolf pheromones in the room stand out like a splash of bright paint across a monochrome canvas.

Randall backed out of the room and trotted to the front door. The scent entered here, though it was dimmer.

The werewolf had been human when he entered, then. Not a wolf, or the scent glands in his paw pads would have imprinted the scent into the carpet.

He followed his nose. It was difficult. The scent was around two weeks old, and only blossomed once over the threshold into the living room. This was where the werewolf had taken on his war form, then. His feet had left blots of bright scent across the room, and Randall picked through scattered books to follow them.

Slow movement at first. He tried to corner his prey. Then he lunged and it ducked aside.

That was the fate of the bookshelf, then. The scent was heavy across some of the scatted books and splintered shelves.

The prints grew further apart, but not as far as a werewolf in his war form could have stretched. Confined by the room, he'd decided not to pussyfoot around anymore and gone straight for the attack. The prints slowed and danced about.

Here. Here's where he began to wear Cooper down.

His nose found little scattered dots of ashes that smelled of nothing, and he licked them off to get them out of the way and moisten his nose to enhance his sense of smell further.

He took on human form after the attack. The weaker scent returned to the front door.

The werewolf's scent was oddly familiar, like a well-loved recipe someone had made some small alterations to. It wasn't Briar or Nazim, but nor was it anyone from either his or Mrs. Uddin's pack.

Maybe there was a pack this side of the city who resented having vampires on their territory? Fulham was only three or four miles from Chiswick, so easily well within a single pack's range, and Chiswick was close to plenty of green spaces, especially if the pack straddled the Thames.

"Reckon you can track it?" Hughes said.

Randall flicked his ears back while he thought about it. With a trail two weeks old from a werewolf in human form, who may or may not also be carrying a scentless vampire with him, the odds were negligible. But he couldn't rule it out without trying it, so he looked up at Hughes and raised his shoulders in a shrug while he vocalised his answer.

"He says maybe," Ellis murmured.

"Well, we got naff all else. Councillor, you better stay here in case we find trouble."

"Fine." And this time Ellis wasn't lying.

Randall glanced back to him and rumbled softly.

"Just come back," Ellis said quietly.

Hughes opened the door and they headed out.

RANDALL FOLLOWED his nose as best he could, but as he'd expected the human shape was a bugger to try and track, even in a suburban area with lighter foot traffic than somewhere like Westminster. The snow was falling more heavily, but even if it wasn't, two whole weeks of rain and people soon turned his trail into nothing more than a wild goose chase.

Hughes kept pace with him easily, loping along with his long legs and saying nothing while Randall backtracked time and time again. He didn't question Randall, didn't interfere with his concentration, and it was almost though he wasn't there for most of the time.

Randall sighed and looked up at the Constable, then shook his head.

"Nuffin'?" Hughes nodded. "Yeah, not to worry. Gotta try these things, eh? Come on, let's go get your fella."

Randall turned back toward the house. Ellis opened the door for them, and Randall nuzzled his hand before running a cheek along his thigh. At least his own scent would stick to Ellis for as long as the man kept those trousers on, just in case someone came and tried to take him away.

Not that Ellis would allow it. He was far more adept at defending himself than he looked.

With the door closed, Randall shifted back. His skin pricked and itched as it drew his fur back inside itself, and his sight was flooded with colour.

"Don't know who it is," he said as he dressed quickly. "Maybe it's someone who crossed Briar's territory once? It's like I should recognise the scent, but it's just sitting there on the tip of my tongue. I don't think it's anyone I ever *met*, you know?"

"And it's well gone now?" Hughes was looking away again.

"Yeah. It happened a couple of weeks ago, give or take maybe a day or two. He was human when he came and went. Didn't change until he was inside."

"But if he's carried Cooper off, maybe someone saw it. I'll canvass 'round 'ere an'all." Hughes shook his head. "Why them? They got nothing in common—"

"They're both vampires," Ellis interjected.

"Right. But why take them? Why stake them? If you've got a beef with vampires and don't care which ones you're bagging, why keep 'em alive and drag 'em off somewhere instead of just kill 'em if you can get access to their homes? If you know where they live…"

Ellis nodded grimly. "Which brings us back to *how* he knows where they live."

"Yeah." Hughes sucked his teeth. "How the hell do we find 'em? We leave no trace, no footage, no smell, and the werewolf's scent's bloody disappeared by now." His cold blue eyes fixed on Randall, every bit as eerie as Ellis' were. "You reckon your pack can help out, maybe? If they can come here and pick up this guy's scent, maybe some huge search pattern can get underway? It's a long shot, but I'm reckoning at this point it might be all we've got."

Randall tucked his T-shirt in, then fastened his coat. "Can but ask," he agreed.

But first, he'd speak to Mrs. Uddin. If anyone knew whether there was a pack out this way, she would.

ELEVEN

THEY TOOK a taxi back into town and walked home from
Vauxhall Bridge rather than have the cab go straight to the
house. Ellis would have vastly preferred to be dropped on his
doorstep, but Aaron's logic was it was better to all leave the
taxi at once. It made a certain sense.

It was unusual for snow to fall in more central areas, no
matter how close it got in the suburbs. The city was several
degrees warmer than the outskirts, even in the middle of the
night, so even when it settled it didn't last anywhere near as
long. While this meant that the stuff falling on him from the
sky wasn't snow anymore, it was still drizzling miserably and
settling on him, so it made very little overall difference.

Randall was a step ahead. He'd got much better at leading
since his first few attempts, and Ellis was content to say
nothing until they were safe and sound at home.

He was delaying the inevitable, and he knew it.

"What's up?" Randall said it the moment the front door
closed.

Ellis grimaced and peeled his coat off. "Can we at least dry off first?"

"'Course."

There was no avoiding it. Ellis fussed Tiberius and told him to go back to bed, then checked the dog's food and water. He headed up the stairs to the master bedroom. Undressed. Took a towel from the bathroom to pat himself dry.

And always, Randall at his heel.

That isn't fair, he told himself.

He slipped into bed and folded sheets around himself while Randall settled by his side. The werewolf's pulse was strong, unhurried.

"I saw him," he breathed. "Randall, I don't know what to say. You probably think I'm being a reet Jessie, but he was…" He failed to find the courage to describe the powerful creature which moved so easily for something that huge.

"Let me tell you something." Randall curled a muscular arm around Ellis' shoulders and drew him into a warm embrace. "People in cities, civilised places, they don't know what it's like to meet a predatory animal in the wild. We've domesticated cats and dogs, and the closest we get to a tiger or a pack of wolves is in the safety of a zoo. We can stand there, just a few feet from animals which could kill us with ease, and admire their beauty and their form. Even if they show us their teeth there's no threat there because we know they just can't reach us, but most often they don't. They're well-fed, they're relaxed, they know we can't reach them either." His fingers slid through Ellis' hair and gently warmed his scalp. "Plus humans are usually top of their food chain. They don't have to worry much about predation from above. So you aren't a Jessie, El. You're just a bloke who's seen something which might sit further up the chain, and your instincts tell you to save yourself."

Ellis wasn't sure whether Randall had meant to imply that werewolves could eat people if push came to shove, but he preferred to believe that wasn't his intention. "Have there been man-eaters?"

"Ew. No." Randall's muscles tensed at the suggestion. "No, that's gross!"

Ellis wriggled closer and pressed against Randall's heat. "Sorry. God, I'm a reet mess lately. It'll settle down, it will."

"Is that all that's bothering you?" Randall kissed him tenderly. "Just the visions?"

"Yeah." The lie came with ease. "He's just huge, and those claws—" He shook his head. "I thought Victor was bad, but Cooper didn't stand a chance. He tore chunks out of Victor, but at least Victor fought back, you know? He knew what he was doing. Cooper…"

Cooper snatched up the iron poker while the beast wrecked one of his bookshelves. It was the first thing his hands managed to find after his panicked but surprisingly successful dodge, and he snapped it toward the creature.

The thing had dropped the stake, but paused to pick it out of the mess on the floor before it flung itself at Cooper with more speed than he'd expected of an animal that size. He barely had time to swing the poker at its outstretched arm before it had him in its grip. Its claws dug in, and little trickles of ash fell free of the wounds.

"Who are you?" Cooper struggled, but he didn't have Victor's strength.

His eyes widened in fear as the beast settled the tip of the stake over his chest.

"For God's sake—"

The stake drove in, ripping through his shirt and penetrating flesh.

Ellis drew a breath. "He wasn't a fighter, petal. He wasn't at all able to protect himself. And this thing, it just stuck the stake right in, and—"

"Shh." Randall ran a hand down Ellis' arm. "It's not coming in here, okay? It's not going to get you."

"What if it does?"

"I'll rip its fucking nipples off is what," Randall growled.

Ellis sighed against his skin. The potential which lay below the surface of Randall's body was phenomenal. Not only the sheer brawn of his human body, but the puissance he could muster within seconds offered a level of reassurance which Ellis had initially found intoxicating.

Until it had been turned against him.

It wasn't Randall's fault, and Ellis knew that Randall wouldn't ever hurt him under his own volition. But that it had happened at all gave his doubts a little scrap of material to cling to.

He didn't want to sleep tonight.

"I thought I'd give Mrs. Uddin a bell," Randall said softly. "Or at least drop her a text, see if she's awake."

Ellis closed his eyes, relieved by the change in subject. "Reckon she might be?"

"Worth a shot."

Ellis nodded and pulled back so that Randall could fetch his phone. He listened to the soft *bloop bloop bloop* as he typed out his message and sent it.

The phone rang moments after.

"She's awake, then," Ellis said, offering as much of a smile as he could.

"Apparently so." Randall sat up and answered it. "Hi Mrs. Uddin! I didn't wake you did I?"

"Only a little." Her voice stopped off for a yawn, then she continued. "What's up, dear?"

"Hopefully just a quick question. You wouldn't know if there are any packs out Chiswick way, would you? Fulham, maybe?"

"Uh." Someone snored in the background. "Well, it's possible. Why do you ask?"

Randall laid his hand on Ellis', and Ellis nodded. "Might as well tell her," he said in answer to the unasked question.

He listened as Randall explained that a rogue werewolf had attacked and staked two vampires in their own homes, then became vague about how he knew the details. The man was an adorably poor liar.

"I don't know," Mrs. Uddin finally declared. "It's not proper behaviour, is it? And most of the youngsters don't even know the vampires exist, I don't think. Not really something you think about. We destroyed one a long, long time ago, but it was before Zev was even born."

Ellis leaned back and frowned.

"Oh?" Randall clicked his tongue. "Mind if I ask what that was about?"

"Damn thing went for me. Bit off more than he could chew, that's all. First and only time we ran into one. They don't seem to like hanging around in parks, so I think we just don't meet. Funny thing is, though, they don't smell of anything."

"Huh."

"But since you're sleeping with one, you already know that."

"Uh—"

She chuckled. "Ameera talks. But she says he's a good sort, so what you two do together is none of my business. Just, you know, think it through."

Ellis frowned and sat up. "What the hell is that supposed to mean?"

Randall's touch brushed over his thigh and he fumed impotently.

"Well, back to your question," Mrs. Uddin breezed. "There might be a pack out around Kingston upon Thames. I went there shopping once and I thought I picked up a scent or two, so I left and haven't gone back. If there is a pack, it'd be rude to trespass, so we stayed away after that. Honest mistakes happen."

"How long ago was this?" Randall asked.

"Oh, years. Hasan was still in his nappies." She chuckled. "They might have moved on by now, who knows?"

"Okay. Thank you, Mrs. Uddin. I'm sorry to wake you."

"Try just a little earlier in the day next time, would you? There's a good lad."

Randall snorted. "I will. Thanks again."

The line went dead and Ellis waited.

"She means," Randall said with a sigh, "that whether you and I are having sex is between me and Allah."

"Oh." Ellis felt tension slowly ease from his shoulders. He hadn't realised he'd bunched up until the relaxation came. "Nothing to do with what I am, then?"

"Not in any way other than gender, nah. She gave me this small sermon about how acting on homosexual desire in a sexual way was a sin that even Allah might not forgive, and about how she was just looking out for my next life, but she doesn't go on about it." Randall sounded more amused than anything else.

"Right, yeah." Ellis smiled tightly. "Nothing like centuries-old dogma to replace good old personal judgement."

"People always find some reason, El. You know morals change over time."

"Aye." Ellis had to admit Randall was right. Hell, just a few hundred years ago European aristocrats found tossing animals into the air until they were dead to be tremendous sport. Homosexuality had gone from okay to illegal to a hanging offence and all the way back to legal, and even socially acceptable again in the space of a couple of centuries. In that context, it was hard to be too offended by one middle-aged lady's slight concern for Randall's eternal soul.

"C'mon. Let's get some sleep, then I'll pop out to Kingston after work and have a sniff around."

He let Randall draw him back down to the mattress, and wrap arms around him. "And if there is a pack?"

"I'll apologise and leave. But if the scents match we'll have that information and we can take it to Hughes."

Ellis pursed his lips. "I don't want you to go alone."

"Eh, I can't go in there mob-handed. They might be okay with one werewolf on their turf, but half a pack will look like an invasion."

"Then I'm going with you."

He heard Randall's breath catch, and his heart thump a little faster for a moment. "Are you sure?"

"No." Ellis laughed weakly. "I don't ever want to be in the vicinity of any werewolf who isn't on your side, petal. But you're not going alone, and that's the end of it."

Randall settled around him like a protective blanket. "We'll be in and out in a jiff. I love you."

"I love you, too."

He meant it. He absolutely meant it.

But that didn't make it any easier to sleep.

TWELVE

It seemed to Randall that if they were going together and his job would be to smell everything he could before they were discovered and challenged, it made sense for him to take the right nose for the job. Ellis had needed persuading, but Randall understood his reticence better now. Not only about possibly encountering new werewolves, but also Randall's previous and awful attempts at guiding him around while wearing Tiberius' harness.

They didn't use boot polish this time, though. Randall stopped into a chemists' on his way home from his last client and picked up some spray hair colour that was supposed to be black. Ellis had sprayed the floor, but most of it had hit Randall, and it looked passable once the fluorescent coat covered most of his fur.

He led Ellis through the tube down to Vauxhall station to get them past the river, then they had to switch to overground services. The train took over forty minutes from there, during which time several people asked Ellis whether they could pet his "dog," and Ellis answered with the patience of a saint that, alas, his dog was working at the moment so he would appreciate it if they wouldn't. It saved strangers walking away with spray-dye on their hands.

We're here, he rumbled as the train rocked to a halt at a station. Norbiton was as far as they could go on this line.

Ellis reached for the harness and took it as he stood. "Right," he murmured. "Let me know if there's a gap, aye?"

Yes.

Randall padded to the train doors and peeked down. The carriage was almost flush against the platform edge. *It's okay,* he rumbled, and stepped off.

Ellis' hold on his harness was loose and easy. He seemed comfortable with Randall's lead, so Randall continued toward the exit barriers.

They walked out into snow-dusted suburbia. The train station was rife with scents from pastries to coffee, but once they were past that and into the car park they were immediately in a residential area. The only businesses present were a small supermarket and a funeral home.

"Over to you," Ellis murmured.

Randall had studied maps before they left the house. There were two main areas of open parkland near Kingston, but Hampton Wick was across the river. If he were forced to check it he'd have to find somewhere safe to leave Ellis, and since Ellis probably wouldn't be pleased if he tried, Randall made his mind up long ahead of time that they'd try Richmond Park first. That meant he'd have to lead with the train station's car park to his left.

He chose the side of the road without lampposts dotted down it right in the centre of the narrow pavements. With Ellis on his left, Randall was perilously close to the kerb, and the situation worsened when he peeled off down a smaller street which had low-hanging tree branches. He grumbled in frustration and wove around the trees to save Ellis from frequent smacks to the face.

"Trees?" Ellis sounded sympathetic, at least.

Yes.

"Aye. Pain in the arse. You're doing grand, petal."

Randall had to watch out for overhanging branches, uneven pavement, randomly-placed lampposts, other people, parking meters, traffic, pedestrian crossings, and just about everything else with a view to not only whether both he and Ellis could navigate it safely, but also how to communicate to Ellis what he needed to do to avoid bumping into anything or tripping over. It was hard work, and people trained dogs to do it. No wonder the training programme was so meticulous about which dogs it took on.

Richmond Park was vast. With over two thousand acres of gently rolling hills intersected with small roads with hefty speed limits, the size of it still took Randall by surprise despite his map scrutiny. He stuck to the paths rather than risk Ellis on bumpy ground, and stopped to sniff.

It was a riot of scents. Everything from small rodents all the way up to wild deer lived and — more importantly — defecated around here. The particularly pungent whiff of fox poo wasn't hard to miss, either.

But he found what he was looking for.

Wolf urine.

It was fresh. Certainly placed within the last day. There were twelve distinct scents mingled together to form the pack's marker, and Randall followed the trail to better pick those scents apart and work out whether any matched their unknown werewolf.

Seven females. Five males. They seemed healthy, if their wee was anything to go by, but he couldn't tell much more than that other than none of them were the one he was hunting for.

"How's it going, petal?" Ellis asked after a while.

Randall wasn't sure he could convey everything without some body language, so he just answered *yes*.

"Have we found our man?"

No.

"Ah. But others, aye?"

Yes.

"Best get off their territory and go home then, aye?"

Randall huffed, but Ellis was right. The one they wanted wasn't here, and the longer he hung around the higher the risk of encountering the locals. He couldn't know whether they were a pack of shifters who knew where they came from, or whether they'd pieced it together the way Briar had been forced to, but either way they might be aggressive. He couldn't take any more of a chance than they already had, so he turned and led Ellis the way they'd come.

They almost made it out of the park undiscovered.

Her scent gave her away, despite her human shape. She approached curiously, her eyes on Randall and not Ellis.

Randall supposed that her hair was probably brown. It was dark, and her skin was some mid-tone he couldn't identify. She wore jeans and a puffy coat which bore trace scents from the rest of her pack as well as her own, and he could make out the stray hairs that were stuck to her clothing like a pet's fluff. They were a deeply social pack, then, if they liked to mark each other this much.

She came in so close that Randall swerved to walk Ellis around her, but she sidestepped in front of him, so he had to stop.

Ellis ground to a halt. "Hello?"

"All right?" she said.

She leaned in to sniff Ellis, then looked confused and tried again.

"Well at least let me buy you a drink first," Ellis said, his tone flippant.

She stared down at Randall, then said, "Are you lost?"

Randall swept his ears back and tucked his tail between his legs.

"You two may as well talk." Ellis was a picture of calm and self-control. Compared to last night, he was back on form.

He was damn good at faking it when he had time to prepare, and Randall felt a glow of pride for his resilience.

"Right," she said slowly. She looked Ellis over again, then down at Randall. "What's this all about then, eh?"

Sorry, Randall rumbled. *No offence meant.*

"We're trying to find someone," Ellis added. "But we don't know what he looks like. Only his scent."

"Found it?"

No. Randall took the opportunity to sniff her jeans, though, just in case. *No,* he said again. There hadn't been an obscure thirteenth scent hidden in there.

"We're sorry if we've caused any disturbance," Ellis said softly. "We'll get out of your hair, if that's all right with you?"

She nodded slowly. "Yeah, okay. Where are you guys from?"

"Central London." Ellis stuffed his free hand into his pocket.

"That's a long way to come for a sniff."

"Aye."

She stared up at Ellis, but she didn't seem aggressive in the slightest. Eventually she merely shrugged and said, "You came in through Norbiton?"

"We did, aye."

"Mind if I walk you back there, then?"

Ellis laughed softly. "Making sure we leave?"

"Yes." She didn't blink or smile, but there was still no aggression in her.

"Sounds fair. Then no, we don't mind at all. Just so long as you don't mind a very slow walk."

She stepped out of Randall's way. "Why slow?"

Randall wagged his tail in brief thanks and began to lead again.

"Lot of obstacles, and I don't know the area, so we're having to be careful to avoid banging into stuff, that's all."

Her own hands disappeared into the pockets of her coat. "Oh. So you're actually blind?"

Randall's ears pricked forward, but Ellis just laughed.

"Aye."

"Oh." She paused. "I thought it might just be a ruse to get a wolf out and about in public."

"There's that, too. But no. Blind as a bat."

Randall knew it wasn't strictly true, but he also knew Ellis wasn't going to volunteer that sort of information to a total stranger.

"So this is your pack's territory?" Ellis asked it glibly, as though he were asking about the weather.

"Yeah," she answered. She blinked.

"You've all scent-marked it, right?" he murmured.

"Uh huh..."

"Nobody's been left out?"

She stared at him. "No."

"So if the scent we're looking for isn't here, that means he isn't one of your pack?"

"Right..."

"I suppose the entire park is your territory, aye?"

"Yeah..."

"You've been really helpful," Ellis said smoothly. "And

thank you for steering us back to the train station, too. We're not from around here, don't know the place at all, and I think we maybe could have taken a shortcut if we'd known any."

She looked a little bit confused, and frowned down at Randall. "Uh. Just... past the hospital, really. It's the quickest way."

Yes, Randall agreed.

"Oh, that must be the way we came, then. I thought I heard—" Ellis' hand emerged from his pocket to wave vaguely through the air "—hospital noises."

"What kind of noises does a hospital make?" she asked, looking up to the vampire.

"Eh. Gurneys coming out of ambulances, lots of people coming and going. And people loiter around and smoke a lot outside hospitals, too. So I suppose that's noises *and* smells. You learn to combine everything together for the bigger picture when you can't see anything."

Ellis continued with his disarming chit-chat the rest of the way to the train station, and Randall was left wondering whether any of his own pack would have told a total stranger exactly how many of them there were or where their turf was. Especially a stranger who wasn't a shifter and very clearly wasn't human either.

Maybe she was just the trusting sort.

Or maybe this had been too easy.

THIRTEEN

It was a strange sensation, like something had coiled around his breath as it left his lungs and shaped his words when he spoke.

Ellis maintained what he prayed was the best damn poker face he'd ever pulled while he fast-talked like a pro on the way to the train station, hoping to distract this new werewolf from what he'd just done. He heard suspicion in her voice to begin with, but it abated as they walked.

Maybe he'd get away with it.

They passed the hospital. It was too densely-occupied and with too many faint beeps to be anything but. Ellis kept talking, careful to neither mention any names nor ask for any.

Just keep swimming.

"Station," she grunted when they reached it.

"Wonderful. Thank you. And again, we're sorry for the intrusion. We won't be back."

"It's fine."

She didn't leave.

Ellis lifted his eyebrows and smiled slightly. "You don't

have to see us off. We've got nothing more to do here. We just have to wait for the train. Cross my heart and swear to die we'll be getting on it." Then that odd *thing* slipped around his words as he said, "You can go now."

"Right. Okay." Her boots scraped, then she was walking away.

Shit. Shit. Shit.

He took out his Oyster card and felt for the edge of the barrier, then pressed the card to the circular pad on top of it, and the barrier beeped, but he didn't hear the gates open.

Randall led him forward regardless, and he pocketed the card. The barriers must have been already open, then. It wasn't unusual, especially at night.

He didn't like trains. Everything about them was horrible, from the noise and tunnels and sometimes the crowds through to the CCTV, and the fact that Oyster cards were tracked as they moved around the city. If anyone ever noticed the fella who just beeped his Oyster didn't show up on CCTV it wouldn't be too hard to work out whose card it was. On the rare occasions he used the tube he wasn't so worried, since the tube was almost always busy and he could slip through among the crowds, but out here he was one of only a handful of people on the platform, and as he sat to wait for the next train he tried not to worry about it.

Randall sat by the bench and panted a little, but otherwise made no sound.

Had Randall noticed what Ellis had done?

He *had* to, surely? The woman didn't know what Ellis could do, but Randall did, and he'd be displeased at best.

Ellis rested his elbows on his knees and listened for the train.

What could he say? That he was sorry?

Was he sorry?

He didn't know. He hadn't meant to push her into answering his questions. The power had leaked out unbidden, but at least it had been relatively subtle, and they now had the information they needed. Nobody was harmed. Nobody was even lightly threatened. The whole thing was civilised and — most importantly, as far as he was concerned — hadn't led to anyone transforming into a massive killing machine right in the middle of a public park.

Nobody had fought and nobody had died.

They were in and out in maybe an hour, possibly a bit less, and the job was done. All it took was a tiny sprinkle of mind control.

So why did he feel so uncomfortable about it?

Because you know it's wrong, you idiot.

He pressed his lips together and closed his eyes. When had he begun to even think that Devitt's power could be a useful thing? Had it been around the time he first used the word *human* to describe living, breathing people, or had it come later?

He'd eaten two vampires and stolen their abilities. He drained Jonas and Devitt both. Oh, sure, in self-defence, but he'd *done* it. Every last drop he could get out of those bastards, he'd taken. That wasn't a thing people did. They didn't eat each other to protect themselves.

He'd put a knife in someone and left them to bleed out in the gutter. Oh, another excuse though. More self-defence! Jasiński would have killed him with that damn silver knife of his. The one Devitt had paid for and placed in his hands. Jasiński had already taken his arm. He would have come back to attack again if Ellis hadn't put an end to it, and perhaps if he'd had Devitt's power back then he could've fixed the situation peacefully.

You can't think like that.

He'd drained his best friend dry and turned him into the very thing Ellis himself hated being. He'd endangered Han's existence by turning him without permission, too. In front of Jay, Ellis had sucked Han's neck, and in such close quarters it was impossible to pretend Han wasn't aroused by it. The poor bastard hadn't stood a chance. That's what the bite *did* to people. They had no choice, no ability to say no, no power at all once the fangs were in. Jonas had done it to Ellis, and now he'd done it to Han. It was like some sick ripple effect.

He fed from Randall. God alive, Ellis lived off the blood of the man he loved. There wasn't any way he could pretend that was a normal human thing to do. People didn't do that. They didn't fall in love, move in together, then start eating their soulmates. Not without some serious mental illness, anyway. No, that's what parasites did. Oh, Randall enjoyed it, but that didn't change a damn thing, did it? He was convenient and willing, but if Ellis didn't have him he'd be necking strangers in pubs still. Briar had been right to call him a flea. His only saving grace was that he was immune to disease. He never caught anything, so couldn't transmit anything.

So if he had the power to find peaceful solutions to their problems, how was that any worse than all the heinous things he'd already done?

Maybe this was how Devitt started out. He was human once. Young, handsome, with a beautiful bride by his side and plans for a bright future raising children in his newly-built home. That's all the man had wanted back then, before his wife found that she was barren. Before she'd died. Before Charles had been turned and gained the power to make others do his bidding.

Had it seemed like a godsend at the start? Had Charles been in such pain from the loss of his wife that he'd used his power to find some peace? Had he withdrawn from his family, from hers, and woven a web of control around himself so that no one else could hurt him again?

Devitt had been young once. Even before the First World War, when there were still Elders in London who had been there since before the Regency, maybe before even the Reformation, had Devitt felt the way Ellis did when he discovered that his new existence was ruled over by some untouchable Council who told him where he could and could not go within his own city?

Was it Charles' power that had turned him from naive young man to conniving bastard?

It wasn't something Ellis wanted to dwell on, but without the damn train to distract him he had little else to think about. He'd taken Charles' power. He'd used it. He was wrestling with whether or not it was somehow acceptable for him to use it. But it wasn't the only power Ellis had in his arsenal. And it wasn't just his own, or Jonas'. It wasn't that he held the combination Charles had wanted to possess — the ability to control people in any language. No, Ellis had all of that, and a seat on the Council to boot. He hadn't even been a vampire for two years and he was one fifth of the ruling body.

Then there was the financial freedom. Thanks to Devitt's century or so of collecting art and artefacts, Edison had transferred the house to Ellis, paid off the debt to their father with interest, covered his own legal fees, *and* left Ellis with a significant slush fund. If he ever chose to sell the house in Pimlico and downsize he'd net himself a very tidy profit indeed.

On every level he could think of, it was a dangerous amount of power.

He'd never asked for it, no. And it wasn't like he could have turned most of it down. Hell, without being a vampire he wouldn't have the sensitivity required to read Braille. He would have been utterly dependent on Jay to run a business, and probably would have been forced to sell up and go home with his tail between his legs. Han would have died, too, without some miracle intervention.

Ellis would never have met Randall. If Jonas hadn't turned him, if Ellis hadn't had his gallery in Mayfair, if Devitt hadn't sent Jasiński to kill him, Tiberius wouldn't have acted out and Ellis wouldn't have hired a trainer rather than risk Guide Dogs for the Blind taking the German Shepherd away from him.

He sighed and placed a hand against Randall's shoulders. It didn't feel right to pet him like a dog, but he needed contact. "God," he whispered. "It's like the Farmer's Son."

Randall's muscles shifted, and he made a gruff, questioning sound.

"Oh. It's one of Han's mother's many favourite stories. She's full of these things, and Han likes to pop them out whenever he wants to fake some wisdom." Ellis smiled tightly. "There's an elderly farmer. He has a horse, but one day the horse runs away and so all his neighbours try to console him. 'Such misfortune,' they say. And this old farmer, he just says, 'Maybe'."

Randall sniffed slightly. Ellis couldn't blame him. All this must've just come out of nowhere as far as the werewolf was concerned.

"So the next day the horse returns, and has brought a dozen wild horses with it, and the neighbours rally around. 'Such good fortune!' The old farmer says, 'Maybe'. The day after, the farmer's son is out in the field trying to train the wild horses and he's thrown and breaks his leg. 'Such misfortune,' cry the neighbours. 'Maybe,' says our farmer. But the day after that soldiers arrive in the village to conscript all the young men, and the farmer's son is left behind because his leg is broken. 'Such good fortune!' say the neighbours. 'Maybe,' says the farmer."

Randall huffed, and it sounded a little like a chuckle.

Ellis nodded to himself. "I'm sorry."

Randall's body moved until his head was against Ellis' knee.

"It was an accident. I didn't mean to make her tell us the things she did. I need to get on top of controlling it before someone notices." He shook his head. "But there at the gate, that was deliberate. I wanted her to leave. I just needed the space. I couldn't bear the thought of her waiting her with us. I made her walk away, and I'm sorry. I had no right."

Randall's tongue was hot and wet against the back of his hand. It was weirdly comforting, so long as Ellis didn't think too hard about the fact that his lover was sitting on the floor with his tongue on Ellis' skin in a public place.

For weeks Ellis had endured nightmares, visions of grotesques and horrors which plagued his sleep. He'd been frightening himself over the idea that he shared his bed with a savage beast, a wild creature who could destroy him in an instant, a terrifying demon which had almost turned him to ash with its claws. But with his apology to Randall, and with Randall's gentle comfort and acceptance, Ellis had to admit that he was lying to himself.

It wasn't Randall who was the monster.

FOURTEEN

THE TRAIN BACK into town was as slow as the one out in the first place, but time dragged while Ellis stewed in his own thoughts, and in some way he was grateful that Randall wasn't in a position to talk to him at any great length. He didn't want his lover to offer any platitudes or assurances, because that would mean Ellis had to hear them.

Alas, without conversation, all he was left with was more time to think. And he didn't like where his thoughts led, because it meant that it was time to assemble the Council, which meant that being on the Council held some level of responsibility. It wasn't all long walks along the Thames.

He poked at his portable keyboard and sent out a few text messages. Barb. Aaron. Stanley. They could do the rest.

By the time they arrived home, Ellis was tightly wound. He didn't want to talk. But it would happen.

Best to just tear the plaster away in one go.

He removed the harness from Randall while Tiberius pranced around them both, and stood as Randall's body made those wet, grinding, tearing noises.

"God, that was a hell of a trip," Randall muttered. "Are you okay?"

Ellis leaned back, startled. "Me?"

"Yeah, you. You seemed to be taking things pretty hard."

"I don't know how to get to grips with the mind-control thing without actually attempting to use it," Ellis muttered. "And it doesn't seem like the sort of thing decent people do, does it?"

Randall chuckled and leaned against him. His naked warmth permeated Ellis' clothes almost immediately. "I don't know." His hands curled around Ellis' hips. "What's worse? Practising it so you can stop having accidents with it, or not practising it and having it pop out in front of people?"

Ellis pursed his lips. "You've changed the subject."

"I haven't." Randall's voice lifted with amusement.

"You're totally talking about my penis."

"You wouldn't want it to pop out in front of people, would you?" Randall chuckled.

Ellis sagged against him and laughed a little. "Thank you."

"Any time, El." His palms rubbed Ellis' back through his shirt. "What was all the texting about?"

"Eh. I need to go see the Council."

"Now?"

"Aye." Ellis kissed Randall's shoulder softly. "I won't mention werewolves, I promise you. But I do need to talk to them about this, so I'll have to go." He began to peel himself back. "And you're naked," he added.

"Yeah. I do that a lot. You haven't noticed yet?"

Ellis' laugh returned, easier this time. "I've had my suspicions."

Randall pressed a tender kiss to his lips. "Okay. Go. I'll do dinner while you're out."

Ellis' lips twitched gratefully. He didn't object to Randall eating. That would be ridiculous. But he did make the house smell fantastic while he did so, and Ellis couldn't indulge without, well... without it being a waste. So Randall preferred to eat around Ellis' absences where possible. Another small consideration from the most wonderful man in the city.

How could Ellis even have entertained the idea that Randall could hurt him?

"Where the hell would I be without you, eh?" Ellis mused.

"Somewhere with more clothes."

"Aye." Ellis reached out to find and squeeze his rear. "Somewhere terrible."

ELLIS HAD MEMORISED the route to the Council's chambers in Aldwych back when he first learned that he'd have to take himself off there all by himself to report in every year, but now that he'd moved house Aaron had helped him come up with a new route. It was a couple of miles on foot and took advantage of Westminster's maze of residential streets to avoid both the Houses of Parliament and Whitehall, where CCTV was at its most rife. It met up with the Thames Path after that, which he followed to Temple station, and then up the hill on Arundel Street. Aaron had assured him Arundel Street was all parking garages or Seventies concrete at ground level, so either side of the road was fine, and then it led straight to a pedestrian crossing on Strand. Overall it was a safe route. It just took damn near an hour to walk.

By the time he arrived the Council were all present, and he could hear Asquith's wheezy complaints from beyond the heavily soundproofed doors, so the old get had to be in full swing.

"Why are we here when the damn fledgling can't be bothered to turn up himself?"

Ellis didn't bother to interrupt as the door was opened for him. He walked through to his seat with care in case some arsehole had decided to move things around, but thankfully everything was as he last remembered it. He sank into his chair and softly urged Tiberius to lie down.

"Good to see you at last!" Asquith bellowed in his ear.

"And you, Councillor Asquith," Ellis replied blithely.

Asquith hesitated, and Barb laughed from across the table.

"Who's here?" Ellis asked.

It was Aaron who answered. His voice came from near the entrance, where presumably he'd been patiently waiting. "Councillors Asquith, Hillier, Stanley, and Applegate. Vassals Walters, Hodges and Williamson. Myself, as requested."

Ellis nodded. "Thank you, Constable." Still only three Vassals? Barb hadn't chosen yet either, then. Or she was deliberately refusing to choose, since she didn't intend for this Council to exist for much longer.

"Right." Stanley's tone was tired, like he'd borne the brunt of Asquith's temper for the past half hour. "What's this about, O'Neill?"

Ellis ran his hands slowly across the table in front of him, then rested them near the edge of it. "Victor and Cooper are missing from their homes. Constable Hughes is working on it, though I'm sorry for dragging you away from that, Hughes. I hope you'll see why in a minute."

"We know they're missing," Asquith barked. "That's Hughes' concern. Why are you involved?"

"The Constable requested my aid." Ellis flicked his fingers as though that were immaterial. "But in the course of doing so he mentioned something critical."

"Which was?" Hillier asked.

"That we knew they were missing because they had failed to report in."

"Obviously," Asquith snapped.

"Oh," said Barb. "Oh, *shit.*"

Hughes hissed softly.

"What?" Hillier remained patient.

Ellis tapped his nails against the table surface a moment, then laid his fingers flat to stop himself. "A year goes by between Council presentations. The year begins shortly after someone's turned, so everyone's year begins at different times, scattered through the entire year."

"We all know this."

Asquith's rasp grated on Ellis' nerves, but he kept his features still rather than let the Elder know how unsettling it was.

"Which means that absolutely anyone not in this room could be missing," Ellis stated quietly, "and we wouldn't know until they failed to show. This could have started anywhere up to eleven months ago and we haven't noticed it yet, or it may only just have begun. We've been working under the assumption that Victor and Cooper are the only missing persons, but we don't know that. Half the population could have vanished and we will not find out until each one fails to arrive, because nobody is allowed to talk to anyone else, visit anyone else, or check in on anyone else." He raised his head slowly. "Our system of managing this city might have killed half of us off already. Ironically, every one of us in this room is blind now."

The only sound was Tiberius' pulse, his stomach rumbling, and his light snoring as he dozed at Ellis' feet.

"We're all here because there's work to be done." Ellis turned slightly toward Asquith. "We need to assemble all our records and identify every single vampire in this city. And then we have to visit every last one of them to check whether or not they're still alive." He clicked his tongue faintly. "We have to audit the entire population, because until we know the scale of this, until we have more information, Hughes' investigation is missing a few wheels."

"I'd damn well say so," Hughes growled. "Jesus, if this is widespread…"

"We could be looking at some kind of extinction-level event," Barb supplied.

"This is a friggin' nightmare!" Hughes' boots stamped toward the table and stopped abruptly a few feet from it. "Council, excuse me a bit and I'll get the rest of the Constabulary here as soon as possible."

Ellis nodded slightly. "The more the merrier."

"If by 'merry' you mean 'sheer bloody panic'," Hughes answered.

"Close enough. Go."

Hughes left without listening to the uproar from the rest of the table. Ellis was sure he heard Barb spit some choice names at Asquith under her breath while the raspy Elder barked orders at the remaining Vassals.

Bodies came and went in a flurry of activity, and papers rustled as they were spread across the desk. Someone even placed a heavy ledger in front of Ellis, who ran his hands across it only to snort at whoever had placed it there.

"Maybe start keeping records in Braille," he said.

"You total dipshit," Barb snapped. "Give me that!"

The ledger was whisked away and Ellis leaned back in his seat. Without any ability to help search through records himself, this was going to be a damn long night.

FIFTEEN

BY THE TIME Randall left to meet his first client of the morning, Ellis hadn't come home, but he was responding to his text messages so he didn't worry too much. Hughes was there with him, which meant at least he had protection. Randall fired off a text to remind Ellis of the time, though. Whatever they were up to over in Aldwych, most of them had to be gone by sunrise, regardless of Ellis' own luxury.

Snow fell during the day. February had come at last, and it was determined to make a go of it, even in the warmest parts of the city. It melted within seconds of landing on the pavements, but it was able to last a few seconds longer on lampposts and parking meters. A couple of his clients' dogs hadn't ever seen snow before, and one of them found it wildly exciting.

When he got home late in the afternoon, Ellis was already up and dressed. He had the gentle scent of soap about him still, and his hair was a touch damp.

"You're up early for someone who was out all night." Randall moved around the scarred desk to kiss him gently.

Ellis tipped his head back and cupped Randall's cheek. "Aye. I was hoping to ask for your help."

"Anything." Randall smiled and sat on the edge of the desk.

He listened as Ellis detailed his night, including the potential for far more missing vampires than the two they knew about, and the hours on hours of bickering and reading that had carried them through to the morning.

"We're parcelling out the audit," Ellis explained. "The Constabulary are covering the Greater London area. Barb's going to speak to her people herself. Most of the Council are basically only going to look in on those they give a damn about. I've volunteered to cover our doorstep."

"But you need an elbow?" Randall nodded. "Of course, I'll help out."

Ellis smiled slightly. "Not quite that simple."

"Never is."

"Aye. Well, so far as anyone but Barb and Aaron are concerned, you're a living breathing human being and you can't know what we are, which means I can't go around knocking on doors with you at my side."

Randall watched him, then groaned softly. "I'm gonna put Tiberius out of work at this rate."

Ellis grinned crookedly. "I'm sorry. Do you mind?"

"Baby, if you're going places trying to find a werewolf, I'd feel better if you weren't doing it on yer own, eh?" Randall ran a hand over his own hair briefly, rubbing at it. "Where are we going?"

Ellis tugged a folded piece of paper from his inside pocket and handed it over. "There's the other catch," he admitted. "They haven't got a Braille printer, so they wrote it all down. I don't think they really get it."

Randall unfolded it and skimmed the list. There were only four addresses. "What about when they suss it out?"

"Eh." Ellis shrugged. "I'll tell 'em I got Aaron to text 'em to me. They don't like to think too hard."

"Right." He checked his phone to look up the addresses. "Covent Garden's the nearest." He paused. "Reckon it's that prick who got mouthy at us last year?"

Ellis flashed his teeth. "Be funny if it is, won't it?"

Randall thought back to the way the vampire had threatened them and smirked. "Yeah. Okay, I'm up for that. Let's go wipe the smile off his face."

"Assuming his face is still there."

⁂

RANDALL SAT on the doorstep while Ellis rapped on the door.

He hadn't picked up any trace of the werewolf here, but this area was a busy one. No weaker scents would survive more than a day or two.

Footsteps approached from within. The door unbolted, then pulled inward.

Randall looked up at the vampire who had opened it, and wagged his tail. It *was* the arsehole who'd given them the less-than-subtle threats back after the whole shit-storm with Briar during the Blood Moon. Ellis' slip of paper had listed the name *Mason*. Vampires weren't too bothered by people's given names, apparently.

Mason looked alarmed, but covered it in a jiffy. He ignored Randall altogether. "What are you doing here, O'Neill?"

"Councillor O'Neill, if you don't mind," Ellis said lightly.

Mason's eyes widened. "I, er. You..." His head shook, then he finally looked down at Randall. He didn't seem to see anything there worth worrying about, so he stared back up at Ellis. "Is this a joke?"

"Present yourself to us in five months and you'll find out, won't you?"

Randall resisted the urge to stare up at Ellis, but it was difficult. He was so fucking sexy when he did the whole quiet authority thing.

Mason gawped, and for a moment Randall saw fear openly cross his features. Then his whole posture shifted, turning inward. Submissive. It was a wasted effort. Ellis couldn't see it, and Randall didn't believe it.

"I know Devitt's dead," Mason blurted, as though he were relieving himself of a tremendous weight. "I'm sorry, O'Neill. He had me running around, testing your territory, spying on you, and I didn't have any choice. I don't even remember half of it—"

Randall stopped wagging.

"—but I couldn't stop myself. I was a total arse to you when all you were doing was passing through and I threatened your mortal and I shouldn't have. I hope you can find your way to forgiveness for everything I've done."

Ellis idly pocketed his other hand. "Of course, Mr. Mason. I think we all know what Devitt was like. You have a pleasant night, won't you?" He nudged Randall's harness faintly. "Come on, boy," he added.

Randall stood and began to turn, and Ellis turned with him.

Mason sucked in air. "But—"

"Wait."

Randall paused.

"But what, Mr. Mason?" Ellis turned his head back toward Mason idly.

"Uh, I mean..." Mason glanced around quickly, then stared at Ellis. "Was that all, Councillor?"

"Oh, yes. Just a social call."

"It… didn't seem very social…"

"Indeed." Ellis grinned, then urged Randall on again.

Randall glimpsed confusion in Mason's eyes, then his expression turned to a scowl as he shut the door on them.

Bullshit, he rumbled.

Ellis just laughed.

THEY HAD two addresses in Knightsbridge to visit, but both of those turned out to be populated, so they walked on toward Kensington. Randall did his best to avoid everything reflective, but he didn't know the area especially well and ultimately decided to cut a corner through Hyde Park to save himself the trouble.

"What if someone's just not in?" Ellis mused as they walked. "Can you pick locks?"

Randall chuckled. *No.*

"No, me either. I suppose if they've got a letterbox you can have a sniff through it, aye?"

Yes. Randall hoped that'd be enough. If a place had been abandoned for months, undisturbed, it might be possible that the scent had been trapped within if none of the windows were left open. And from what he'd seen, vampires didn't like leaving windows open.

"And if that tells us nothing, we can tell Aaron." Ellis nodded. "Should have thought all this through before I volunteered, I suppose."

Randall wagged his tail and thumped Ellis' thigh with it.

"Aye, well. I'm not a detective, am I?" Ellis chuckled. "Is this Hyde Park?"

Yes.

"Fair enough." He nodded. "Just think, if it weren't for all this we could be tucked up snug in bed right now." He laughed softly. "I'll have to make it up to you."

Randall rumbled in his chest and thumped his tail harder.

"Dirty bastard."

Me?! Randall laughed as he steered Ellis around some low-hanging branches.

"Oh, aye. Pure as the driven snow, me."

Randall snorted and shook his head.

They emerged from the park close by the ancient church Hughes had locked Ellis away in, and Randall fell silent. The place held an unpleasant set of memories for him, but at the very least if they ever needed it he knew where it was, and Ellis had the clout to get them in through the door.

He padded on in silence, checking the street signs high up on building walls as he found his way through the wide streets of beautiful old houses. Some even had blue plaques embedded in their walls, circular markers from English Heritage to note the past presence of events or people of historical interest. Kensington was littered with the things, it seemed. They stood out against the yellow-grey of the walls like lurid blobs to Randall's wolf eyes.

Campden Street. He turned down it when he found it. It felt more claustrophobic than the streets they'd walked through to get here, but it was just as quiet. The street was lined with flats one side and a terrace of old houses on the other, and the on-street parking either side left the road itself only wide enough for one car to pass through at a time. These roads hadn't been built for cars, or for anything to stop for any length of time. They were built for hansom cabs to drop off and collect their patrons directly at their homes.

The harness pulled slightly, and Randall glanced back up at Ellis.

His face was taut.

Randall's ears flickered as he went from relaxed to alert at that look, and soon he heard whatever had caused Ellis' hesitation.

Crash.

Snarl.

"It can't be," Ellis whispered.

Randall led forward as fast as he dared, and licked his nose to improve the sensitivity. He sniffed along the pavement all the way to the house, and picked up the fresh touch of the werewolf they sought right on the doorstep of the house they'd been heading toward.

The door was ajar.

Yes, Randall said reluctantly.

Something inside the house smashed. Something heavy.

He's here, Randall growled.

"Shit," was all Ellis said.

SIXTEEN

Randall had no desire to charge into a fight, but what other choice did he have? There was a vampire in there fighting for his survival, and Randall knew damn well he would lose.

Let go, he growled to Ellis.

Ellis released the harness and reached for something else. His fingers found cast-iron railings and closed around them instead.

Stay here!

Ellis nodded faintly. "For God's sake be careful."

Yes.

Randall slunk in through the door and kicked it behind him. It didn't close, but he didn't waste time with it. He ran toward the sounds of heavy collateral damage and took on his war shape as he ran.

The harness twisted and shredded around him, then the useless pieces fell discarded to the floor as he pushed himself through the tiny-seeming doorway into a tiny-seeming living room.

There he was. Oh, *God*, there he was! Bigger than Randall, though only by a foot at most, and raking his claws across a vampire who had lost his shirt and looked very much on the verge of giving up all hope. There was a look of surrender in his dark eyes that only worsened at the sight of Randall.

"You have *got* to be joking," he whispered.

Randall couldn't explain anything to the poor bastard. He didn't have Ellis' gift; he wouldn't understand half of what Randall meant by his vocalisations. Instead he launched himself at the other werewolf in the room. Surely nothing sent a clear signal of *I'm not here to hurt you* more than flinging yourself at someone's assailant.

The werewolf snarled in surprise and turned his attention to Randall. The vampire squirrelled himself away into a corner and stared at them both, but probably only because the bulk of them both blocked his exit.

Randall left him to his own business. Whether he stayed or ran didn't matter.

The werewolf's claws gouged across Randall's shoulder, and he yelped.

Like that, is it?

Yeah, this guy wasn't going to stop just because Randall had turned up. And Randall couldn't afford to pansy around with him. Their claws were almost as dangerous as silver. They slowed a shifter's regeneration right down, which meant that in close combat, shifters could readily kill one another.

And this one was damn well trying to.

Randall ducked and struck out, but the room was too small for two fully-shifted beasts to be going at it. It hampered his opponent, but it stymied Randall just as much, and his sparring partner was the better fighter.

He snarled with alarm the moment he realised it.

This shifter, whoever it was, had honed his fighting skills.

He was used to fighting in this shape, and he wasn't someone who pulled his punches.

He meant to win.

"Get out, both of you!"

They both snarled at the vampire to shut the hell up, and he curled into a ball.

The other werewolf leaped at Randall, and Randall managed to swipe his side as he ducked below the outstretched arms. Dark blood sprayed from the contact, and tufts of fur tore free. They clung to the black-looking liquid which coated his claws.

There was no red to his sight. Not like this. Blood was like ink. Wolves weren't creatures who gave much of a damn about the warning colours in the plant world. They needed to track movement; they didn't need to be told not to eat a particular berry.

He felt his own blood as it oozed from the gashes in his shoulder and seeped into his fur, weighing it down to try and clot the wound.

They smashed into one-another, jaws snapping, claws reaching for anything they could ensnare.

The stench of blood grew stronger.

Randall heaved the other away from himself and kicked debris off the floor at him to try and distract him.

There, on the floor, he saw a shaft of wood. Neatly-turned, almost two feet long, sharpened to a point that'd be enough to push through almost any vampire's ribcage, especially if the wielder was, say, five hundred pounds of muscle. He lashed out at it to toss it toward the vampire, and was rewarded with searing pain across his back.

Randall howled in anguish.

The vampire stared at him, need plain in his eyes. His lips parted, and the very tips of his fangs were visible.

Oh, Christ.

The person they'd come here to check up on had been so badly injured that the scent of blood was about to push him over the edge, and leaping into this fight would get him killed.

This was, all things considered, going really tits up.

The werewolf stared past Randall's shoulder and snarled a threat.

Randall didn't want to turn, didn't want to look. Because the only thing he could think of that might be behind him at this point was the man he loved. The man he'd left standing out on the doorstep.

Ellis took a breath, then let it out in a single word.

"Stop."

And they did.

ELLIS STOOD STILL as the world obeyed his command.

He could hear families in houses on either side of this one. They were watching television, eating dinner, laughing and chatting.

He heard the thunderous heartbeats of two werewolves in their war forms.

There was a persistent *drip, drip, drip* of blood as it hit the carpet. The smell of it was potent, but not enough to distract Ellis. He was well-fed, and it'd take more than that to get him started, but he had no way to know the state Baxter was in.

If Baxter was still alive.

"Baxter?" he said, as calmly as he could.

"What?" It was an unfamiliar voice, almost a squeak, and it came from a space where there was no pulse.

Ellis' fingers flexed.

He'd heard Randall's pain and stepped in to stop things,

but now there was a witness, and Ellis would have to handle this incredibly carefully or he'd be well and truly up shit creek.

He turned to face the unknown werewolf. "You're outnumbered," he said. He kept his tone conversational. Reasonable. He was going to pass this off as an element of surprise if he could. And if not? Eh. He didn't have time to think that far ahead. "You can't win this now. I know you're not unintelligent. Think about this carefully."

The beast's breathing was hard, heavy. A whine caught in his throat for a second, before he eliminated it.

God, Ellis wanted to know more. Who the hell was this bloke? Why was he staking vampires? Where the hell did he take them? How did he get into chaotic brawls in people's homes without the neighbours hearing a thing?

He could arrest the creature. Right here, right now, he could force it to surrender and to take his human shape. He could question the man, not the beast, and find out everything they needed from him.

All he had to do was use Devitt's power again.

And then explain how he'd obtained it. To Aaron, to the Council, to the Constabulary. And then the knowledge would be out there. People would understand why the law against cannibalism was in place, and all it would take would be a few angry fledglings or some greedy individuals and the city would sink into chaos as they all fought to eat each other while they scrambled for power. The Council and Constabulary had the edge there: they knew what everyone's power was, and where to find them. The Constabulary even had the opportunity, as they were undertaking a mass audit right now and could write off anyone they killed as absent when they checked on them. With a werewolf on the loose, who would care?

Devitt wanted power so that he could rule. Christ alone knew what anyone else would use it for.

His jaw rocked slowly. Blood fell still. The werewolves weren't healing, or if they were it was much slower than it should be.

He couldn't do it. He didn't *dare* do it. He bared his teeth in frustration and stepped back out of the room, his hand to the wall for guidance. "Go," he snarled. "Save yourself. Before I change my mind."

Randall growled in protest, but both shifters changed their shapes, and one sprinted past Ellis and out into the night.

The other came to nose at his leg, and Ellis dropped to his knees to explore the extent of his lover's injuries. "I'm sorry." He was saying that a lot lately. "You're hurt."

Randall gave a soft whimper and leaned against his hands.

The reek of blood was strong, and soon the warmth of it was sticking to Ellis' hands.

"Right," said Baxter. He sounded dazed. "What the actual fuck just happened here?"

"Shit happened, Mr. Baxter." Ellis sighed. "Absolute shit."

He had the sneaking suspicion he'd just let a killer go to protect his own interests.

SEVENTEEN

RANDALL'S BODY ACHED. His wounds throbbed in time with his heartbeat, and the blood trickled slowly down his sides, his legs. He wanted to close his eyes, to rest here in Ellis' hands, but the other vampire was asking questions.

"Who are you?" This Baxter bloke had a pretty middle-class accent, but then this wasn't one of Kensington's more expensive streets from the look of it.

"Councillor O'Neill," Ellis said softly. His head bowed toward Randall. His attention was clearly on the wolf bleeding under his touch. "How bad is it?" he murmured.

Randall twisted to look himself over. Dark lines ran over one shoulder and down his flank. *Not lethal,* he growled.

"Councillor?" Baxter paused. "I've never heard of you."

"Charles Devitt murdered Councillors Dickens and Clarke last year." Ellis stood slowly. "Where is your bathroom?"

"Oh, hell!" Baxter looked down at Randall. "It's, uh. It's upstairs. First door on the left."

Ellis nodded.

Randall moved past him to the stairs and waited. Once

Ellis used his hearing to figure out which way Randall had gone, Randall climbed the stairs slowly, checking over his shoulder.

Ellis followed him, his features grim-set as he left smudges of Randall's blood over the handrail and tested every step before he committed his weight to it.

Here. Randall nosed the bathroom door open.

"All right," Ellis murmured. "Let's get ourselves cleaned up enough to walk through town without making people scream, aye?"

Yes. Randall kicked the door shut and took human form, which pulled on his injuries and made him wince. But now that he had hands he could lock the door and use the shower.

Ellis fumbled to the sink and washed his hands thoroughly. He didn't say a word, and shook his head faintly when Randall took a breath to say something.

Randall shut his mouth again, then realised what Ellis meant.

Baxter can hear you.

He washed the blood from himself as thoroughly as he could without making the injuries bleed more, then he stepped out and helped Ellis clean himself off. The vampire's sense of smell was deeply acute where blood was concerned, but it didn't hurt to put a pair of eyes to the job too.

Ellis leaned in to kiss him lightly on the cheek, and nodded his gratitude.

Randall patted himself dry and dropped back to all fours. The bleeding would begin again, he had no doubt, but at least his fur was free of it now, and his undercoat would absorb most of it.

They looked presentable, and that'd have to do.

Ellis felt for the lock and they headed back downstairs.

"Mr. Baxter," Ellis said. "Do you have plans for the evening?"

"Er." Baxter stared around the wrecked living room. "Figuring out how to tidy this mess up?"

"Aye, well." Ellis grimaced a little. "If you'd like the help, I might be able to do something there. In the meantime, I'm going to have to ask your assistance."

Baxter laughed nervously. "I'm not chasing down whatever the hell that was—" He broke off and pointed to Randall. "Or whatever *that* is."

Randall sniffed.

"No. That's my job." Ellis shook his head. "It's much more simple." He waved his hand a little in Randall's direction. "He's broken his harness. I'm going to need some assistance to get home."

Baxter stared at Randall, then slowly up at Ellis. "I... what?"

Randall padded to the shredded harness and nosed at it, glaring up at the vampire.

"You're *blind*?" Baxter's voice rose with disbelief.

"Correct."

Randall watched as Baxter waved his hand an inch from Ellis' nose.

"But not insensate, Mr. Baxter," Ellis added dryly. "Come on. I'll give you a crash course in guiding someone. And if you're very lucky, you might also get an introduction to not flapping your hand around like a fool, after which we can move on to more advanced subjects like not telling people they don't look blind and how to avoid using the word *cripple* in casual conversation."

Baxter's gaze slid away in embarrassment, and Ellis brushed his fingers across the wallpaper to steer himself toward the front door. Randall eased out into the street at his side.

"Today, Mr. Baxter. I need to get this information to the Council quickly."

"Right. Right..." Baxter hurried out and shut the door.

———

RANDALL SNIFFED the fresh trail once they were out on the pavement while he kept an eye on Baxter's fumbling.

The other werewolf had fled the house on all fours, which meant that the glands on his paw pads had left a clear trace, but the fact that he was bleeding made it even clearer.

If the trail went too far, he'd have to come back to it later. He couldn't leave Ellis in Baxter's hands all the way back to Pimlico, let alone onward to Aldwych if Ellis did intend to go to the Council chambers. Who knew what kind of mistakes the man might make.

Randall wove back and forth along the width of the pavement as he tracked the scent. It moved at a running pace for a few feet and then veered toward the kerb and drove between two parked cars.

And disappeared.

Randall grumbled to himself. The bugger had got into a car, and that meant someone had been waiting here for him. But the car would have blocked the street. Randall would have seen it if it had been here when they arrived at Baxter's house. Had he heard one go by after the werewolf ran? He didn't think so, not even the soft tire noise from an electric car.

No werewolf would risk a very public shift to get into a car, would they? Not even one which broke into vampires' homes to stake and kidnap them? Randall hoped for everyone's sake that he hadn't done that.

He ran to catch up with Ellis and listened with half an ear

while Baxter tried to ask questions about whatever the hell had happened in his house this evening and Ellis deflected with instructions.

ELLIS HAD Baxter walk them as far as the gallery, then shooed him off and used memory and his hands to get the rest of the way home.

Randall did his best to help. He rumbled a warning whenever there was a kerb or some other obstacle. He kept an eye out for people who might mistake Ellis for a drunk and try to mug him. By the time they made it home and in through the front door it was well past midnight.

He shifted the moment the door was closed, and groaned as it reignited the fire in his muscles.

"Jesus," Ellis sagged against the wall a moment. "Are you all right?"

"Yeah." Randall grimaced down at the gouges in his abdomen. "God, that'll leave a scar, I reckon."

"Call an ambulance." Ellis bit his lip and pushed away from the wall. "We'll get you to a hospital, they can—"

"It's okay, El." Randall took his hand and squeezed slowly. "It just takes longer to heal, that's all."

"How long?" Ellis turned to face him. He looked so afraid that Randall wanted to hold him, to promise everything would be all right, but that'd just get blood everywhere again.

"Couple of days. I just need to lay off the massive parties for a little while." Randall smiled slightly and kissed him.

Ellis groaned and pressed his lips tight against Randall's. "You promise?"

"I promise."

"I'm so sorry. I had to let him go. The only way to make him stay was to *make* him stay, and Baxter—"

"I understand." Randall sighed and pressed his palm to Ellis' chest, then his forehead to Ellis' own.

Ellis leaned against him.

"It's not ideal," Randall whispered, "is it? But it's what we've got. We can't have Baxter running off at the mouth about what you can do."

"It'd start a shitstorm," Ellis agreed.

"Well if everyone behaves the way Charles did with that kind of information, I reckon it'd be over fast, Highlander-style." Randall grimaced.

"Oh, so you've seen Highlander?" Ellis' lips twitched. "Out of all the films I tell you to watch, you picked that one?"

"Gotta at least try to get into that geeky brain of yours, ain't I?" Randall laughed with exhaustion. "You're not really going to the Council right now, are you?"

"Bollocks, no." Ellis pulled back and drew Randall through to the office. "I'll let Aaron know. I assume all your running around back there was trying to pick up a scent?"

"Yeah." Randall shook his head and sat on the desk. It was cold against his bare arse, and he shivered. "He's not working alone. Got out of the house, jumped straight into a car. Not a parked one," he clarified. "One in the middle of the road. Someone came and got him."

"I didn't hear a car." Ellis sank into the leather chair behind the desk.

"Me either."

Ellis bit the tip of his tongue a moment, then pulled out his little Braille keyboard and set it on the desk. "Did you notice any CCTV in the street?"

"Can't say I did, but that doesn't mean there isn't any."

"Aye. Aaron'll have to do his best." Ellis' fingers pressed

the keys in random-seeming combinations that always reminded Randall of a stenographer's work. "You got a good look at the bastard, I take it?"

"Yeah. I'd recognise him again." Randall nodded. "At least, in two out of three shapes, which is a start."

"And you've got his scent."

"Yeah." Randall watched as Ellis sent and received messages, his fingers darting from keys to the pinboard and back again. "Aaron okay?"

"Aye. Just telling Han to watch out, too," Ellis muttered. "Until he works out what it is he can do he's a sitting duck. Hell, even if he's figured it out by now it might not be of any use to him."

"Hopefully this thing's just confined to the west." Randall leaned over to squeeze Ellis' forearm a moment.

Ellis laughed humourlessly. "Hopefully. Right, Aaron's going to talk to Baxter, take a statement." He grimaced a little. "At least that means Aaron's the only Constable who'll hear Baxter's werewolf stories for now. Then he'll work on pulling any footage from the area. Not a whole lot more we can do."

"Then let's go to bed, and tomorrow I'll call Guide Dogs for the Blind for you to arrange a replacement harness, yeah?"

Ellis nodded. "Thanks, petal."

"You're welcome." Randall wriggled off the desk. "And it's bloody nippy down here. We need to talk about modernising this place if we're gonna stay in it."

EIGHTEEN

So much blood.

Angry snarls and the crunch of bone. Flashes of huge, twisted forms, their fur matted with blood and their claws steeped in it.

Screams.

His screams.

He had to remember to breathe if he wanted to scream, otherwise it was some ghastly parody of fear, a mockery of helplessness. His mouth would open and no sound came out.

For a man who was blind, the loss of his voice too filled him with a nameless dread.

The blood.

It permeated his skin, his hair, his nostrils. He could almost taste it on his tongue.

He needed it.

Hearts faltered and stopped. Saliva accumulated in throats and made gruesome and unmistakable rattling sounds before they too failed.

Sometimes it was Tower Hamlets. Sometimes it was Baxter's house, or Cooper's, or Victor's.

Sometimes it was Victor slamming his face against the stone floor of the cell.

Sometimes it was Devitt's laughter and Randall's claws.

It all blended together as though leaping from one place to the next with nothing in between were a natural thing.

He lapped blood from cold stone, and it had all the taste but none of the power he needed to survive, and that drove him toward the living bodies as they collided against one another.

They collided with him. Tore into him. Roared with triumph as they devoured his flesh.

After they punctured his lungs, he couldn't scream any more.

ELLIS SCREAMED as he fought to free himself, but the moment he did, he was falling.

Dark. It was dark. He fell against carpeted floor and kicked out at whatever still held onto his ankle as he sucked in another lungful and let it out so loudly it rattled his own eardrums.

Pitch black.

He scrabbled across the floor until his head cracked against something solid, so he curled up and kept his head down.

Don't see me. Don't...

"Ellis?" Randall's voice croaked with fear. "Baby? What's wrong?"

Ellis clawed at the carpet. His fingernails found gaps in the pile, but it wasn't deep enough to grip. "Ra—" It came without sound.

Breathe.

"Randall?"

"Christ." A warm body coiled around him. It smelled of

sweat and blood and Randall. "What happened? El? Talk to me!"

His body shook with sobs that had no sound. He let Randall manhandle him into sitting up against his solid chest and he leaned into the body without any resistance.

"Just..." He faltered as he tasted the blood on the air. "Are you bleeding?"

"A couple of spots, nothing serious. Do you need me to wash?"

Ellis laughed weakly. "You're amazing. I don't tell you that enough."

"You tell me it plenty," Randall rumbled. His concern was vibrant, thrumming through him. It touched his voice and his heartbeat, it made his muscles tense and his breath short. But he didn't push. He waited with all the patience of a man who held a frightened animal in his arms.

He felt for the familiarity of Randall's collarbone. The skin was hotter there than it usually felt.

It had to be the injuries. There had been wounds on Randall's shoulder last night, on the wolf's body. He stilled his hand.

"I might have to take up boxing or something." Randall's tone was soft, and gently reassuring.

"You're a lover, not a fighter." Ellis mustered a faint smile.

"Maybe, but if I can't fight, I might have nothing left to love."

They fell silent then.

Randall had spoken a little too closely to the truth for comfort, and Ellis had no idea what to do about it. Did he dare try to assure Randall that everything would be fine?

No. No, they were past that. He was on the floor curled into a ball, for crying out loud. That would be absolutely nobody's definition of *fine*.

"It were just a stupid nightmare," he sighed.

"Obviously not all that stupid," Randall said. He pressed his lips to Ellis' forehead and held them there.

"I get them." It came out of him like a confession, and Ellis withdrew his hand. He curled it against his own chest. "Almost every night, I get them, and they *are* stupid because I know you'd never hurt me, and most nights it isn't even you, but sometimes it is and I'm so scared that you'd hate me if I ever told you or that you'll hate me when you work out what a monster I am. I'm terrified of losing you." He laughed weakly. "Isn't that ridiculous? I don't deserve you. How *could* you stay with me? I have to be so horrible to wake up next to. I'm *dead*, for God's sake. I'm dead, and without you I'm *nothing*. Sometimes I dream that you've worked it out, that you've realised you have to be rid of me. Sometimes it's Charles, laughing while you kill me. And when I think it's getting better, when I think I might go a night without one, something happens and they're back and they're getting worse and I don't know what to do."

"Oh, baby. No." Randall's fingers combed through his hair, and he began to rock Ellis' limp body in his arms. "Shhh, no. It's just dreams, baby. That's all it is. I'd never hurt you."

The wonder of it was that Randall didn't sound offended. *Upset*, but not angry or affronted. He wasn't accusing Ellis of being crazy, he didn't yell *How dare you think I could do that to you!* He was just… Randall. Kind, sweet, beautiful Randall.

Ellis groaned against his chest. "I should have told you."

"You weren't ready to."

"How do you know?"

Randall chuckled. "Because if you were, you would've. But you've told me now, El. That's what counts. We're right here, together, and you've trusted me with all this."

Ellis shook his head. "That's it?"

"No. I don't think so." Randall's fingers were so soothing, so gentle. They traced light strokes along Ellis' hairline and swept locks away from his forehead, and left electric tingles in their wake. "If something's bothering you enough to give you nightmares, I don't think it goes away just like that. But we can talk, try to work it out, and if comes to it I'll just tell Hughes you aren't getting involved anymore. You need time, El. You've been through so much—"

"And you haven't?" Ellis sighed and slipped his hand back to Randall's chest.

"People deal differently. That's all."

"How are you coping?" Ellis grimaced and turned to run his lips along Randall's skin, but caught another flare of dried blood and froze.

"Working all hours I possibly can?" Randall said it like it was an apology.

"Is it working for you?"

"Eh. I'm doing okay." There was a soft smile in the shifter's tone. "I can sleep at night. And if you aren't sleeping, stop pretending like you think I can't tell, right?"

Ellis bit his lip. How the hell had Randall figured *that* out? Ellis was lifeless as a wooden plank when he was asleep. All he had to do to fake it was not open his eyes. How hard could that be?

Too bloody difficult, apparently.

"Can't pull the wool over your eyes, eh?" he murmured.

"Not for long, anyway," Randall agreed. "We'll work through it, El. Together. I promise you." He brushed a thumb along Ellis' eyebrows, then back into his hair. "How about we get off the floor and have a bath, yeah? Not a shower, but a nice long soak together."

"Do you have clients?"

"Eh." Randall's broad shoulders rose in an easy shrug. "It's probably still the middle of the night. All this noise and Tiberius hasn't even stuck his nose in to see what we're up to."

"Maybe we should go back to bed."

"Oh, you reckon you can sleep, do you?"

Ellis groaned. "Areet. Bath then. Best we don't make a habit of this, though."

"Agreed."

NINETEEN

Randall worried that handling Ellis like he might treat a frightened dog was somehow diminishing his lover's fears, but he had to admit that over the next couple of days the gentle treatment seemed to help Ellis out far better than anything else Randall might have chosen to do.

It wasn't hard to empathise. Randall was used to a life in which anyone around him might undergo rapid transformation, whether physical or metaphorical. He'd spent thirteen years in the company of shapeshifters, let alone the fact that he was one himself. That was an extreme example, sure, but he'd lived through more subtle change. He'd gone from a life as a child in which racism was a common playground bully's friend to something nobody on the street would tolerate, and now it had come full circle and open racism in the streets was somehow acceptable again.

Except this time it wasn't aimed at him other than suggestive comments about the size of his cock back when he'd still been hitting up clubs on the scene. Now it was aimed at his friends. His family.

His pack.

How they endured random insults in the street along with the constant media bleating about "Islamists" he didn't know. They'd needed him more over Christmas than usual, and New Year's had brought out all the truths that drunk people pretended to hide when they were sober. They needed their Alpha to keep them level even once the full moons had passed.

Yes. Randall was used to change. But the biggest changes Ellis had ever been forced to endure were both sprung on him in short order. He'd lost his sight, then he'd been turned. The irony that Ellis had to live with was that if he'd been turned just a year or two earlier his sight would be as good now as any living person's.

But he'd adjusted. He'd been quietly continuing his existence, doing no harm to anyone. Subtle, withdrawn, and content to sell art in a small Mews in Mayfair for as long as he could.

Instead he'd been attacked by a madman, lived through a lethal battle between opposing werewolf packs, endured a near-fatal attack from the claws of his own lover, and witnessed with sight his eyes couldn't provide him the sheer viciousness of a wolf shifter's true power.

It wasn't any wonder the poor bloke was having nightmares.

Randall had suggested Ellis just leave the gallery in Christy's hands for a while, and he'd agreed. Randall had clients he couldn't cancel, but he spent as much time as he could at home, and they talked over simple, mundane things. They looked into the cost of rewiring the house, of having it re-plastered after the electricians had been in the walls, and of getting in a plumber to update all the Victorian pipework. They weighed up whether those renovations were worth the cost and whether they could afford to do any of them. They took Tiberius for nice long walks and talked about films and music.

For two days, life was almost normal, and for one night Ellis made it through without a single nightmare.

So when there was a knock at the door at seven in the evening, and Ellis couldn't hear a living person the other side of it, Randall felt a stab of resentment at whoever it might be for the intrusion.

"ALL RIGHT, RANDALL?" Hughes was on the doorstep. "His nibs home?"

Randall gave serious consideration to saying no, but Tiberius was here, and Hughes would've heard him by now. "Yeah. Come on in."

He led Hughes through to the study, where Ellis sat on the floor playing with Tiberius, and grinned at the sight of the vampire covered in dog fluff.

"All right, Councillor?" Hughes eyeballed the dog as he sat. "That dog's not giving you any trouble is it? I could arrest it for you if you want."

Ellis smiled softly and gave Tiberius the rope toy they'd been tugging on. "Maybe if he refuses to give the toy back." He stayed where he was, cross-legged and comfortable-looking, while he idly brushed strands of fur off his shirt and trousers. "What brings you here?"

Randall took a seat and gestured Tiberius over so that they could keep playing.

"Got a list of the missing at last." Hughes tugged a notepad out of his coat and flipped it open, then searched for a late page. "Here we go. Five missing in all, not including Baxter, since you saved his arse."

Randall glanced up to the Constable. "How did the canvassing go?"

Hughes turned up his nose like he'd just bitten into a turd. "Unbelievably badly. Doesn't make any sense. No neighbours saw or heard a bloody thing during any of the attacks, including Baxter's. Doesn't match the Councillor's visions or your own version of events in any way. I mean, I know people like to stick their head in the sand when the neighbours are arguing, but this is beyond that level of toss. They weren't lying, they weren't trying to be polite, they just didn't notice a damn thing."

Ellis frowned and stopped fussing with his clothes. He rested his hands in his lap and straightened. "That's unlikely, in't it?"

Hughes shrugged. "I mean, don't get me wrong. People are, by and large, lousy witnesses to everything. Even if it's a stabbing they saw with their own eyes, you'd be amazed just how much your regular bloke in the street just doesn't notice. Ten people watching the same stabbin'll give you ten totally different accounts. Some of 'em want to inflate their own sense of importance. Some of them really want to help, but they make up extra detail that they never actually witnessed. They're just extrapolating from what they *do* know. Some of 'em just weren't paying attention and couldn't even tell you whether there was a knife involved. Then there's people's prejudices, which overlay what bits of information they feel are important. They'll focus on the attacker's race, or what they think the victim did to deserve it. That's why the more sources I can get the happier I am." Hughes shook his head, and his spiked hair wilted a little with the force of it. "So when I don't get a single hit off any of six crime scenes? Yeah. Beyond unlikely. We're well into damn near impossible territory now."

Randall rolled Tiberius onto his back and rubbed the dog's belly. "What about camera footage? Did you manage to get any?"

"Yeah. I ain't got access to police stuff, but I managed to grab some private footage and council-owned recordings, and I've spent the past couple of nights going through it all." He grimaced again. "Fucking months' worth of the stuff, 'cause other than Baxter we ain't got a precise time or anything else to go on."

Randall opened his mouth, then shut it again. Hughes' power was his physics-defying speed. He probably could have fast-forwarded through ten years' worth of footage and it still would have been too slow for his abilities.

"Yeah, it wasn't exciting," Hughes grunted. "But there was some weird shit going on. Like, cameras which normally shot pretty clear would have patches of grainy footage, or they'd hit a power glitch and drop out for an hour, or there was lousy weather which reduced visibility to pretty much nil. Snow on the lens, rain on the lens, one had a fucking massive spider on the lens for half a damn night. 'E was impressive, I'll tell you that for nothin'."

"Convenient," Ellis mused.

"Ain't it just?" Hughes thumped his notepad against his thigh as he turned those eerie blue eyes on Randall. "Not some wazzy werewolf ability, is it? Stealth ninja stuff?"

Randall shook his head. "No. We don't get the variety you guys do. Three shapes, that's what we've got."

"Then maybe some vampires are working in concert?" Ellis tilted his head toward Hughes.

"I'd agree if it wasn't for the totally random footage blackouts. Even if we had someone who could affect electronics in any way, it'd be consistent, I reckon. But the fact is that just like we can't be seen, ain't nobody yet got an ability to actually mess with that sort of thing. I reckon it's them who develops that kind of stuff what goes mental when they turn, but that's just total unproven and untestable theory."

"How about just extremely competent people working together?" Randall shrugged. "I don't know. Is it possible someone just hacked all this CCTV stuff and did some Photoshop stuff or something? Maybe they've bribed the neighbours to keep quiet if anyone ever comes asking?"

Hughes waggled his notepad. "Jude reckons it'd be easier to just blat the footage completely rather than mess with it, but there's also a bunch of totally different systems involved, and some of the private ones weren't attached to the Internet. If it was hacking, those wouldn't be affected, but they are." He pursed his lips. "I thought about bribery, but it's a tricky thing. The more total strangers you pay off, the more likely it is one of 'em'll blab the moment they're asked. Most people just ain't skilled liars."

"Then maybe it's magic," Ellis said.

Hughes sucked air through his teeth. "Nah."

Randall's eyes narrowed and he stopped fussing Tiberius' chest. The dog stretched and yawned, then rolled onto his side. "Why not?"

"Well, er." Hughes blinked, then looked between them. "Wait, you're seriously suggesting magic?"

Ellis spread his hands briefly. "You've eliminated everything else, Aaron. Either there's some vast conspiracy, or there's magic involved."

"Right. Right." Hughes didn't sound convinced. "And you know all about magic, yeah?"

"Well, no."

Randall snorted. "No," he agreed. "We know bugger all about it. But we do know it exists."

Hughes eyeballed him. But he didn't argue.

"What connects the missing with Baxter?" Ellis said.

"Ha." Hughes picked up his notepad again. "You're gonna like this. Not a lot—"

Ellis groaned.

"—but you will! They're all Elders."

Randall sat back in his seat. "Is there a definition of that word that isn't just 'old'?"

"Nah, not really." Hughes tapped the paper in his hand. "We tend to use it to mean they were turned pre-Sixties. Before the war, though, it could've meant pre-newspapers. There's quite a few sprinkled across town, but most are in the West End or the suburbs. None of our missing were further east than the attempt on Baxter in Kingston. Whoever's doing it probably don't want to come too far into town, but they're skipping people further out who are way younger."

Should that information have pleased Randall as much as it did? He wasn't sure. All he knew was that it meant Ellis was off the menu of whoever was doing this, and so was Han, even if they did stump up the courage to come as far in as Westminster.

"How do they know?" Ellis tilted his head. "How can they tell who is an Elder and who isn't?"

"No way I know of," Hughes said.

"Magic?" Randall grinned at him.

Hughes poked his tongue out. "Maybe. Anyway, I've shortlisted potential targets. I'm trying to assign Constabulary who might stand a chance in a fight against this big bugger, but considering I thought Victor couldn't be taken down, I think my pool's a lot more limited than I might've hoped for."

Ellis' features twisted into a frown. He shook his head slightly. "No."

"Hear me out. Just—" Hughes raised his hand, "listen a minute."

"He's barely healed after the last time, Aaron!"

Randall huffed. "I'm right here, guys."

It wasn't hard to work out what Hughes wanted. Nothing else would have Ellis so adamant in such a short space of time.

He wanted to borrow Randall.

Hughes looked straight at him. "Yeah. So what do *you* say?"

"I say the bloke's a better fighter than me," Randall stated bluntly. "And if he gets the chance he will kill me."

Hughes looked surprised. "Seriously?"

Randall hooked a thumb into the collar of his T-shirt and tugged it aside. The scars on his shoulder were still pink across otherwise dark skin, and stood out like a straight bloke in a gay bar. They weren't sore anymore, but it'd still be a day or two before they were fully healed, and he'd probably bear the marks for the rest of his life. He tried not to get attacked by shifters often enough to find out.

"Shit!" Hughes' gaze flickered. "Sorry, mate. I had no idea."

"I'm not the biggest," Randall said as he pulled the material back into place. "And I'm not the most aggro. I'm pretty much the opposite of both those things, in fact."

Hughes gave a slow nod. "Right. But between you, me, and Barb, what do you reckon our chances might be like?"

Randall licked his lips and ran over the idea. Hughes had easily bested him on speed. Barb had agility, but better still she could run vertically up walls. He couldn't see how that'd help her in a fight in confined quarters, so it really boiled down to what he and Hughes could muster between them.

"Got something silver?" Randall said.

Hughes narrowed his eyes. "I might have," he said.

"Well. You're faster than me. You're faster than any shifter. If you can get silver into him before he can touch anyone, we stand a good chance, I reckon." Randall didn't like the idea. No shifter used silver against another — none other than Briar, anyway, which showed just what a staggering level of arsehole it took to do such a thing. And since silver was every bit as nasty to vampires, odds were that they considered it too much of a risk to take into a conflict. "It's a big ask," he added. "I know it is. But if you've got something you can stick into a living body, even if it's just silver plated, it's better than nothing."

Ellis' jaw tightened.

"I've got something," Hughes stated. "In case of emergency."

"Right. Then how do we go about doing this?"

TWENTY

GOING mob-handed out to babysit an Elder wasn't Ellis' idea of fun. Granted it wasn't anyone else's either, but he wasn't sure he could take any more violence.

But he was damned if he'd let Randall go off alone.

The shifter was in Tiberius' harness again. Brand new, and Randall huffed like it wasn't quite comfortable on him, but Ellis would take it off once they got there in case anything happened. He doubted the ladies back at the Guide Dogs office would be pleased at replacing it twice in one week.

There was no reason they should expect trouble though. That's what he'd tried to tell himself. It hadn't worked.

"I dunno," Aaron had argued on the way. "If they failed to grab Baxter they might try to move fast now."

"Or just go to another city," Barb had pointed out.

Ellis didn't like it. Baxter had been moved to a safe house in Brixton just in case, which meant that the next-oldest vampire on Hughes' list was a man named Mandelson.

"Here we go." Aaron banged on a door. "Open up, Mandelson," he added. "It's the Constabulary."

Aaron had no need to yell. Any vampire would hear him speak so long as they were within fifty feet or so.

Ellis turned an ear toward the door. Hughes' summons had borne fruit.

Three bolts drew back, and a lock turned. Hinges creaked.

"The *entire* Constabulary?" The stranger's tone held deep sarcasm.

Randall snorted. *Arsehole.*

Ellis pursed his lips.

"Peter Mandelson?" was all Aaron said in response.

"Obviously."

"Constable Hughes. These are Councillors O'Neill and Applegate. We'd like to come in."

There was a long pause, which Ellis couldn't read in the slightest. After it, Randall led him forward.

They settled into a room which sounded large enough to host a good ten more people if necessary. Maybe the house was old enough that the ceilings were higher, too. The way that sound echoed was more like the house in Pimlico than a smaller, terraced home.

Ellis sat and idly removed the harness from Randall while Aaron explained the situation to Mandelson. The Constable left out details like werewolves and magic, and left it at the barest of skeletal outlines.

He doesn't trust Mandelson, he mused, folding the harness into his lap and resting a hand on it. The other came to rest on Randall's head, since he didn't wish to place pressure on his shoulder.

"Is this what Constable Harris was 'round here for the night before last?" Mandelson snapped.

"Yeah."

"And, what? You lot just intend to sit here like lemons on the off chance whoever's doing this will try it on with me?"

"Yep."

"And these two are Councillors, you say?"

"Uh-huh."

Mandelson snorted. "Never heard of either of you."

"Wouldn't expect you to," Barb said.

"Nobody female in this city older than me. And you—" Ellis presumed Mandelson was addressing him now, "I've never heard of either."

Ellis smiled indolently. "I'm not all that surprised, Mr. Mandelson. I was only turned a couple of years ago."

Randall coughed, then pretended to hack up a furball.

"Stop your dog yakking on my carpet! This is real Axminster, this is! What do you mean you're only two?!"

Ellis tutted and shook his head softly. "There, there, Tiberius. Did you sniff up some dust?" He leaned back in his chair. It felt comfortably padded, and didn't creak at all. Good, sturdy furniture with well-fitted cloth upholstery, then. "I'm thirty-five."

"For fuck's sake. Only children count their living years. Who made these two Councillors?"

"Asquith, Hillier, and Stanley," Aaron said. "Devitt killed Dickens and Clarke, and was himself killed in turn."

"Then I should be on the Council," Mandelson snapped. "After Stanley."

"Thought they'd give democracy a go, didn't they?" Barb chuckled. "Not very good at it. They didn't open it to a city wide vote, but it's a start."

Mandelson snorted. "Democracy? I'll give those idiots a piece of my mind!"

"I'm sure you will." Ellis sighed. "Until then, we're here to try and protect you."

He almost wished the werewolf hadn't come as far into town as Kensington. Then they wouldn't have considered

Mandelson a viable target. But if Kensington was acceptable, then maybe Bayswater was too, and Mandelson had apparently been here all the way back to the late Fifties.

The thought that they might all have to sit here night after night just waiting on the hope that something might happen suddenly seemed even less appealing than it had back home.

As if reading his thoughts, Mandelson said, "How long are you lot intending to be here?"

"Hopefully no more than a few nights," Ellis answered. "We've had two kidnappings and one attempted, all within the space of under a month. We can't confirm the times of the other three kidnappings, but it doesn't make much sense that they were months ago and then nothing happened for most of a year. I'm thinking if anyone's coming to get you, Mr. Mandelson, it'll be sharpish."

"And you expect me to sit here and do nothing for a week?"

"Yes." Ellis withdrew his hand from Randall's head. "I expect you to cooperate with the Constabulary's investigation into the disappearances of five people and the attempted kidnapping of a sixth. I expect you to sit here for as long as it takes for us to resolve this situation to the best of our ability. And I expect you to be more gracious about it, because while we're here babysitting you, we might be missing out on an opportunity to protect someone else."

He heard Mandelson take two steps.

Randall growled a warning.

"Read a book or something," Barb drawled into the sudden silence. "Pretend like we ain't even here. In fact, if you've got some board games or something we could all entertain ourselves while we wait."

"No," Mandelson grated. "I don't have games."

"Then we're in for some great nights of literature, in't we? Sit your arse down."

Mandelson's steps receded.

Ellis leaned his head back against the seat and closed his eyes. It made no real difference, but he liked to think it allowed him to concentrate on his hearing better.

He could pick out a couple to one side of the house, discussing their daughter's horse-riding escapades. There was little strain in their voices, no slack in the vocal chords, so he estimated they were no older than mid-thirties and the daughter still a child.

To the other side, he heard nothing. Not only no people, but no house sounds either. No electrical devices humming, no plumbing or heating. His best guess was this was an end-of-terrace house, but he supposed it was also possible that the house on that side stood empty.

That was how he entertained himself as they waited. He tested the limits of his hearing. He listened to the traffic outside and the trains nearby. He learned more about the neighbours' daughter's dressage than anyone ever needed to know. He listened as a very drunk Hen party staggered its way past the house at around one o'clock in the morning. Randall's breathing slowed to the gentle, shallow inhalations of sleep.

Mandelson went from ungracious host to irate host. He stomped about fetching different books, flicking through them, and discarding them before fetching another. He surfed through fifty channels of television, over half of which sounded like teleshopping and advertorials. He texted with his phone volume up as high as it would go so that every poke of a stylus made loud *tik tik tik* noises.

If he had to put up with another night of this, let alone week, Ellis would damn well have to start bringing something to read. Randall could download some audiobooks for him, maybe, and then Mandelson would have to hear those while he was trying to be passive-aggressive with his own noises.

It hardly seemed fair on Aaron and Barb, though. Maybe Barb had the better idea. They could find some games. Something Ellis could memorise the rules to so that he could play without referring to them. Or Trivial Pursuit. He'd be bad at it, but at least it wasn't a complicated game.

"This is ridiculous," Mandelson said for what was probably the twentieth time now.

Ellis felt his watch. His touch ran across the raised markers and the ball bearings which indicated minutes and hours.

It was almost four in the morning.

"Couldn't agree more," Barb grumbled. Any humour she might have had at the start of the night had long since faded.

"I'll talk to Asquith about this. I'm not having any more—"

Mandelson stopped. Ellis opened his eyes.

Someone had opened the gate at the front of the house.

Ellis sat forward, then shook his head faintly. There were two people approaching, not one. Two sets of feet, two pulses, two pairs of lungs.

Someone used the doorbell, and Randall's breathing picked up. He yawned, then rumbled faintly.

"May as well," Hughes sighed.

Mandelson's feet stomped out of the room.

Randall growled.

Then everything went horribly wrong.

TWENTY-ONE

RANDALL SMELLED the other werewolf's scent seconds after he was woken by some knocking sound. He'd barely had the time to remember where he was and why he was a wolf before the soft scent of the shifter's human form tickled his nostrils.

He growled a warning to Ellis and scrambled to all fours. Mandelson was already most of the way to the front door.

Randall's heart thumped. The adrenaline sloughed off the rest of his slumber. His hackles bristled. He tongued his nose.

There was a second scent.

Not a shifter, not an animal. A human, then.

Get back, he rumbled to Ellis.

Ellis held the folded harness to his chest, and moved cautiously across the unfamiliar room. Hughes seemed to get the idea and stepped in to guide him to a corner, where Ellis all but jammed himself with all the composure of a man who fully expected to be eviscerated in a minute.

"Who the hell are you two?" Mandelson snapped.

There was a scuffle at the door, and Mandelson was

propelled backward into the living room. He remained on his feet, but his assailant stepped in after him.

There he was. The scent was *his*. The shifter was older, though Mrs. Uddin had said something once about shifters ageing more gracefully than humans, so it made it difficult for Randall to judge. His face was lined and dark, and he wore the expression of a man who had very little interest in life. His shoulders sagged and his eyes were dull. There were paler splashes of hair at his temples, but for the most part his afro-textured hair was short and dark. He wore cheap trousers and an even cheaper T-shirt. Without a coat, even a shifter would be cold in this sort of weather, but he hadn't bothered to wear one.

Randall supposed that if he expected to rip his way out of whatever he wore, he wouldn't bother putting a coat on either.

The shifter turned to stare at Randall, and something stirred in his gaze. His body language didn't change, though. Mere curiosity, then? Or threat assessment? Randall couldn't tell.

The vampires cautiously spread throughout the room. Mandelson had been talking a big game earlier on, but now he sure looked happy to step back and let Barb and Hughes handle things. Randall's lip curled at the hypocrisy of the man, but he kept his attention on the other shifter in the room and kept Ellis at his own back.

Another person stepped into the room, and the shifter immediately backed himself up to protect her in some strange reflection of Randall's own stance.

The woman was seventy if she was a day. Her face bore deep creases, but her eyes were bright. Pale hair was drawn back into a neat bun at the back of her head. She wore a simple dress, and its greyish tone suggested it was a warmer colour.

Randall looked between her and the man protecting her. It didn't make much sense, but here he was putting up the same stance to defend a vampire. Was this woman the shifter's lover, then?

"I'll ask again," Mandelson snapped from his position of cowardice. "Who are you? What're you doing here?"

The shifter ignored him, and the woman looked from one vampire to the next.

Then she looked directly at Randall and said, "Let me get a good look at you, youngster. Take your human shape."

Not bloody likely.

Randall's body shuddered, then began the transformation. He yelped with shock, but he couldn't stop it. It was almost like being under Devitt's control, except this felt more direct. It was as though she'd spoken and his body had obeyed without waiting for his mind to bend to her will.

"Randall?" Ellis whispered.

"I can't help it!" And by the time he said it, it was with a human mouth.

"Bloody hell!" Mandelson stared at him.

Randall snarled softly.

"Stand up."

His body jerked him to his feet, and his mouth dried in an instant.

She had complete control over his body.

Her eyes were blue. He could see that now. Her dress was a burnished orange thing made for elderly ladies. She looked like she knitted sweaters for teacups as a hobby, and he wouldn't have looked twice at her on the street. Now, if he survived this, he'd probably have a fear of old white women for years to come.

Ellis' hand touched the small of his back. Randall glanced back to him and found the vampire frowning with concern.

"You're a good-looking one, aren't you?" She smiled, but it didn't reach her eyes.

Randall wasn't wholly sure what came next. He suspected that Hughes had chosen to attack the old lady, and he couldn't blame the Constable for prioritising her over the shifter between them, but it didn't seem to work out that way.

One second Hughes was in front of Mandelson, and the next he was flying backwards through the air and into a flat-screen television. Both Hughes and the TV crashed to the floor in a heap, and Hughes swore as he plucked glass from his arm.

Ellis stepped up alongside Randall. His hand still rested against Randall's back, as though to reassure him.

"Who are you?" Ellis asked. His voice was level, but Randall saw the strain of concentration in his shoulders. "Tell us what you want."

She turned away and looked to Hughes, then to Mandelson.

Ellis' teeth clamped together in confusion. His eyebrows drew together.

Did he try it? Randall swallowed tightly. Had Ellis just tried to use Devitt's power on her?

Her gaze drifted over Barb, then fell on Ellis.

"That one," she finally said. One crooked hand gestured to Ellis. "Get me that one."

Hughes was on his feet again before anything happened, but then the shifter began to change.

And he wasn't dropping *down*. He was growing *up*. Mandelson's house was huge, the room easily tall enough for Randall to stand in if he took on his war shape, but Randall was on the shorter end of the scale, and this bloke had a couple of inches on him in human form.

Those two inches would be a couple of feet by the time the change was done.

Hughes became a blur, but again he was thrown back. This time he slammed into the wall where the television had hung moments before.

"What the hell?" he snarled.

The shifter's skin rippled and fur breached the surface. His muscles gained mass as his bones twisted and grew. His fingers splayed and spread. His nails darkened and lengthened, curving and sharpening. His face stretched as it grew, and for a brief moment he was in that awful state between human and beast where he was both and neither at the same time, and then his body was silent as his head scraped the ceiling.

"Shitting hell!" Mandelson scrambled back against the far wall.

The shifter's eyes were still cold and emotionless as he launched himself at Ellis.

HUGHES WAS A BLUR AGAIN, but the next time he reappeared it was in front of Ellis. He had something in his hand, and as Randall looked to it, Hughes blurred slightly and a sheath fell to the floor.

The cold glint of silver was unmistakable.

Randall pushed Ellis back as the towering shifter batted at Hughes with the back of his paw, but failed to connect. Hughes disappeared for a brief second, like he'd flickered out of existence, and the shifter howled in pain.

The blade was embedded in his chest. Hughes hadn't wasted any time. He'd gone straight for the heart, but in his war shape, the shifter's chest cavity was too deep and the blade wasn't in far enough.

Randall began to shift up.

"No," the old woman snapped.

His transformation aborted itself.

Randall snarled with frustration. "El, get out. Get out of here, come on!" He grabbed Ellis by the arm. He'd have to apologise for that later.

"Stop interfering, child."

Randall stood helpless as his body refused to go any further. He dropped Ellis' arm and whimpered.

Hughes withdrew the blade and struck again. Barb came in with a flurry of punches of her own, though Randall couldn't imagine that they achieved much.

"Fine. Come here."

This time it wasn't Randall who obeyed her command. The older shifter batted Barb aside and sent her flying as he returned to his mistress, and she reached into the air.

She plucked a two-foot wooden stake from nothingness. Absolutely nowhere. With a gesture of her fingers, her hand closed around the thick end of a stake identical to the one dropped at Baxter's house.

The werewolf took it from her and turned back toward Ellis.

"Jesus Christ, how hard is it to stop one of these bastards?" Hughes leaped in and sank his fangs into the beast's wrist.

It was a good location. The fur was thin there. It offered little armour, and a vampire's fangs could reach the skin through it. If Hughes could immobilise the werewolf, Barb would be able to take up the blade and finish the job.

It wasn't ideal. Randall had never wanted to kill the guy. He doubted even Hughes wanted that. Questioning a corpse was a lot harder than interrogating someone who was still alive. But though the monster was bleeding and wheezing in pain, it hadn't stopped under the knife's assault.

But he had once Hughes was attached to his wrist.

The room seemed to hold its breath.

"Stake him," she said.

Randall stared in impotent horror as the shifter's body obeyed her order. He drove the stake through Hughes' chest so fast that Hughes' split-second hesitation in disengaging cost him the opportunity to react.

The shifter tossed the Constable's inert body aside.

"Hughes!" Barb ran for the blade, but she had nowhere near Hughes' speed. The shifter raked her with his claws and slammed his elbow into her.

Something snapped, and she rolled aside.

The old woman idly checked her watch while she pulled another stake from the air.

"For God's sake," Randall whispered. "Stop."

He urged his body to move. To push Ellis toward the kitchen, to shift into any other shape, to do *anything* but stand rooted to the spot. And when his body refused, he stared at Mandelson as if he could make the Elder do something useful just by scowling.

But of course Mandelson was all talk. The slimy bastard had made it all the way to the stairs and looked about to run off up them.

The shifter took the second stake and ran it through Ellis' heart.

Randall screamed. He swore. He threw words he'd never expected to use in his life at the creature which was bleeding from stab wounds all over his torso. He used language his mother would clip him around the ear for.

But all the creature did was shrink back down into his human shape and toss Ellis over his shoulder like a sack of potatoes, mindful of the shard of wood which penetrated his chest. He cast Randall a muddy look. A look filled with loathing and sorrow, and maybe even apology.

The old woman moved aside for the wolf shifter and his burden, and then he was gone.

"I wish I had room in my arsenal for a second werewolf." She looked Randall over slowly. "Especially such a prime specimen." Then she shrugged and turned away. "Still. I can always come back for you later. You'd make a fine replacement for Carter some day."

Barb screamed and flung herself at the old woman's back, only to be tossed through the air like a rag doll herself.

The woman hadn't lifted a finger. She hadn't even *looked* at Barb.

And then she was gone. She walked out in no particular hurry, and no matter how hard Randall swore, she didn't come back.

Ellis didn't come back.

Randall stared in dawning horror at the empty doorway.

Carter?

TWENTY-TWO

Randall snarled. He thrashed-

No. He tried to thrash. He tried desperately to move. His body refused to obey him.

Barb picked herself off the floor. Her broken bones snapped and ground as they knitted back together, and she hurried to Randall and grabbed him by the arms. "Randall? Are you okay?"

"I can't move." His chest ached and his eyes itched. "Barb, I can't... they took Ellis..."

"I know. I know, just—" She stopped and scowled toward the doorway.

Mandelson had returned.

"You absolute *coward*," she snapped. "Don't you dare show your face 'round 'ere!"

"It's my house!" he roared. "And frankly if that's your idea of protection you can get the hell out of it!"

Barb swore and shook Randall some more, then stomped away and crouched by Hughes. One hand curled around the stake and the other pushed against his chest. With a jerk of her arm she wrenched the wood free.

Hughes' eyes snapped open and he grit his teeth.

"Easy, tiger," Barb muttered. She tossed the stake aside and stood, then offered Hughes her hand.

Randall stared. Hughes sprang to his feet like absolutely nothing had happened. There was a hole in his shirt, but the skin under it was pale and smooth, already whole.

Which meant Ellis would be okay. They just had to get that thing out of his heart.

Randall blinked quickly. His eyes still itched, and now the wetness spilled slowly down his cheeks.

"Looks like you were wrong," Mandelson snapped. "They're not after Elders at all."

"Or she assumed Ellis was the Elder here. Maybe she only has addresses, but he's the one with Randall bodyguarding him. It makes sense he might be the most important guy in the room." Barb's lip curled.

Hughes shook his head and grabbed his knife, then sheathed it. "What happened?"

"Bastard staked you, then did the same to Ellis and took him," Barb said.

Hughes eyed Randall. "She able to control shifters or something?"

"Looks that way." Barb frowned.

Randall fell forward, and barely managed to hold himself upright. "Oh God. Oh God, I think it's worn off. Oh *God!*"

He felt sick. Panic clenched in his gut, wrenching his insides into a tight ball.

She'd taken Ellis from him and he'd just fucking *stood there*.

"Randall—" Hughes began.

Randall's skin prickled and he threw himself forward, taking on his wolf shape. He hit the ground running.

She couldn't have Ellis. She *couldn't*. Ellis was *his*. His to love. His to hold. His to protect.

He bolted, chasing the shifter's scent. They couldn't have gotten far. They mustn't have.

Carter.

Randall howled as he ran out onto the street. His voice reverberated off walls and windows. He leaped the low gate and slid across the icy pavement.

Their footprints had crushed the thin dusting of snow and left footprints which went to the kerb and then disappeared.

No. No!

Rage welled up inside him. He ran. He chased the tyre prints and then he chased shadows. He ran blindly through the streets desperate to catch any trace of that scent, and at every failure he screamed his fury at the night. Anyone out early enough to run into him earned a threatening snarl for their trouble, and they hurried out of his way.

Cars slid across ice-coated streets to avoid him. Horns blared. Metal crashed into metal, and a whining car alarm began to sound.

None of it mattered. He had to find her. He *had* to.

She took the man he loved.

She had his *father!*

Randall slid to a halt and howled a promise to the sky.

I will find you, and I will ruin you.

TWENTY-THREE

ELLIS WOKE.

His chest itched briefly as his body frantically repaired itself, then it was done. Good as new, though for a second he couldn't work out why the hell he'd need to heal just for waking up.

Randall had told him to go. Then he'd whispered to stop. He'd heard a shifter change, but it wasn't Randall if Randall could still talk.

Then something had stabbed him, and he'd blacked out.

He rolled slowly onto his side and felt the floor. It was cold and hard, coated with some latex-like substance. Rubberised paint, possibly, or a thin mat. He dug his nails into it but it didn't budge, so he stuck with the paint theory for now.

Footsteps moved away from him. They didn't reverberate very clearly. The floor absorbed much of the noise, but the rest of it seemed to wander away, never to return. There was no wind here, though, nor ice or snow.

He was indoors, then, but in a space far larger than Mandelson's living room.

There were two heartbeats. The one which backed away from him was sluggish and calm. The other was from a shorter body, and it raced with excitement.

He took a breath. A slow one. He inhaled through his nose.

One werewolf, and the human woman.

Ellis lifted himself onto his knees and then stood with care. He ran his hands down himself to straighten his clothes, and his fingers faltered at the ripped material over his heart.

They'd staked him.

He drew breath again. He focused his thoughts and pushed his doubts aside for now. He needed Devitt's power. He was so sure it had come when he called on it earlier, but it hadn't worked. He couldn't risk another failure.

The strange sensation coiled around his breath, and he released it. "Tell me what you want," he said.

Neither of them answered.

Ellis tongued the tip of a canine as he considered his situation.

"What are you?" She sounded elderly. Her tone was crisp, but her voice had a weak crack to it that suggested less flexible vocal chords.

Ellis raised a hand to idly scratch at his ear. He couldn't feel the weight of glasses against his nose, so he used the gesture to run a forefinger up to his temple in search of the plastic arm. His finger only confirmed his suspicion that the glasses were gone, and he tucked a lock of hair behind his ear then lowered his hand to his trouser pocket. "You already know." She had to know. You didn't ram a wooden stake into someone if you didn't know exactly what they damn well were. "Where are we?"

She laughed. It was a dry sound, and one which bore little interest in answering his question. "Your magic is no use to you here." Her footsteps were light things, and they padded idly against the coated floor on her approach.

He frowned faintly and did what he could to resist the sudden urge to step back from her. "I don't use magic."

Her laugh was more genuine this time around. "It's funny. They all say that. And yet your very existence is magic. And you in particular..." She stopped perhaps four feet away from him at most. "You have so much more power than any I've ever seen. Heck, you've got more than the others combined." He heard material rustle, then the dry sound of skin rubbing over skin. "Dear, if I'd known you existed I could have saved myself a whole lot of messing about. But you're not Mandelson, are you? So who are you?"

Ellis eased his hands into his pockets. She *needed* something from him. Power, information, either or both, and it put him in a strong position to negotiate. Selling paintings was hard; nobody needed art. They wanted it, they coveted it, but they could go on without it if a negotiation failed. This woman, though, spoke with the sharpness of need. It was disguised, relaxed, because she believed she held all the cards — or that Ellis held none — but ultimately something between them had shifted, and he needed to appear relaxed if he was to capitalise on that.

"You went for Mandelson," he stated. It was best to begin with things they both knew to be true, things that could be agreed on without resistance.

Think, damn it! Think!

She went for Mandelson for his power. She bypassed Aaron and Barb to hone in on Ellis instead, which meant she considered Ellis to contain far more power than Mandelson. But until now all her targets had been Elders, which implied that she linked age with power.

Could she work out, if he released his age to her, what he'd done? Where his power had come from? Did she believe that age and power were incontrovertibly interlinked? If so she might not even believe him if he revealed his age to her, and that would weaken his position if she began to believe he would talk about anything.

God, he would've given anything to have Randall here right now.

The thought that she might have hurt him, that she might have done worse than hurt him, gripped his heart. Ellis had been staked. Anything could have happened after that. Days could have passed. Or months, maybe years…

Christ, no wonder she behaved like she had all the negotiating strength here. She *did*.

"Boy, I've cherry-picked what I could out of this useless town. Turns out just about everything of value got wiped out in the Blitz, or fled after. I feel like I'm chewing on scraps." Glee entered her voice. "And then there was you, you beautiful beacon you, shining like a lighthouse from a sea of dross."

He turned to his right and took a step. "Where are the others? Where's Cooper? Victor?"

"They didn't last."

Ellis stopped in his tracks and turned to face her. "They're dead?"

"Oh, they were far too flimsy. It isn't their fault." She chuckled like she was discussing the failure of her soufflé to rise in the oven. "Not made like they used to be. Not like you. And that magic you wield, the magic to control minds?" She gave a low whistle. "That's a rare thing indeed, boy. Is that how you stay hidden? Convince them all you're just a fledgling nobody?" But she continued before Ellis could find a lie that fit. "Well, it doesn't matter now. And rare as it is, I'm looking for something more slippery than that. If I'm fortunate, I'll find it before the search unweaves you."

Ellis drew his hands from his pockets and spread them warily. "Wait, what do you mean 'unweaves'?"

"The magic. It's everything you are. Once you're turned, you're nothing but magic, tightly wound. Like a ball of string. Like the werewolves, only they're magic from birth. Harder to spot until they've hit puberty, but still magic. Wrong kind of magic, though, for what I need."

Let's just go back to this unweaving! Ellis clamped his mouth shut. The ball of string analogy was more than enough for his imagination to run wild with, and it almost trampled roughshod over her admission.

"Say I help you," Ellis murmured, slow with caution. "Say I work with you to find what you need…"

"You can't help. You are magic, young man, but you can't ever use the magic that isn't already inside you. That's the problem with vampires. By the time they gain the gift of magic they also lose any ability to *learn* magic." She sighed. "You seem a pleasant enough sort. But needs must."

It didn't need a negotiator's skills to realise she'd just ended talks. Ellis stepped toward her, praying there weren't any obstacles on the floor, but his outstretched hands slid across something cold and wet.

He managed to stop before he bumped into it, and his palms spread further apart. The surface was flat as glass, but slick as ice, yet when he withdrew a hand and rubbed finger and thumb together his own skin remained dry.

If there was something solid between him and his captors, it should have muffled them, but he heard them as clearly as if they shared the same space.

Ellis backed away from the wall. He managed eight steps

before he hit another. His heel clipped it first, then his backside and shoulders.

He spread his hands across it, not daring to turn from her.

The same substance. Solid. Cold. Slippery.

"They all do this," she said. It didn't seem aimed at him. Was she addressing her werewolf? "The amusement value wears off after the first few times you see it, doesn't it?"

Ellis snarled and pushed away from the wall.

"Ridiculous creature." Her voice came at him now, bitter and derisive. All effort at polite talk had sloughed away.

She knew. She damn well knew all along.

She'd held all the cards. She'd toyed with him in case he would volunteer information, but she'd *known* she had him.

"Do you think I'm going to interact with your kind without wards?" she sneered. "Vampires. God, what am I reduced to when I have to deal with you filthy little corpses?"

"Then don't!" Ellis shook his head. "If we're so—"

"Shut up! I've had enough. I am too old to entertain your prattle. You're a vile little parasite, and there's no purpose wasting time here any longer. You might last longer than the rest, boy, but the search *will* unravel you in the end."

"But if I knew what you were looking for—"

"There's magic in you," she snapped. "Magic in every vampire. The *same* magic. But picking it out is like trying to play Jenga with arthritis. Every time I grab a hold of it, the whole lot comes down. They were all weak, though." She stepped in closer. "And you're not. And if I'm *really* lucky I can extract what I need without losing it when the tower falls."

Jenga. That's what his life was to her. A child's game. "There has to be some non-destructive—"

"Oh, I'm trying, boy. I am really trying. But I'm getting good at this now, and there's one thing I've noticed each time I do this."

He tilted his head, desperately trying to hear some clue as to where they might be. Or, even better, the sound of Randall bursting in to rescue him. That would be a damn good sound right about now. "What's that?"

"You're going to scream," she sneered. "A lot."

TWENTY-FOUR

RANDALL SLUMPED TO THE GROUND. His body shook. He was exhausted, but it wasn't from the running, or the howling. It wasn't from the night spent sleeping on some stranger's floor. It was bone-deep. He felt drained, like all his energy had been sucked from him and scattered to the wind.

He couldn't find Ellis, and he couldn't find his dad.

The man had looked so weary, so dead inside.

Was this where he'd been for nearly twenty years? Had he gone out one day and just stumbled into this woman's path and that was that? She'd spoken like she felt "Carter" was a disposable item, something in her toolkit. No. What was the word she'd used? Arsenal.

Randall's dad was a weapon.

Did she control him the way she'd made Randall stand there and do nothing? It seemed that way. Her commands had controlled the massive beast's body even though Hughes' fangs were in his flesh.

He retched at the thought of it. Taken away from loved ones, puppeted off to be a weapon without the chance to even say goodbye, and then piloted around like a goddamn drone for years on end. No freedom. No autonomy. No *life*. Years upon years of existence trapped in a body he had no control over.

No wonder he looked so hollow. And that pain in his eyes, that look as he took Ellis away…

Randall sobbed and clawed at the pavement.

The man knew how Randall felt. At that moment, he tried to offer what little comfort he could, because he knew what Randall had experienced.

It was his whole existence.

The horror of it tore through him, and his body convulsed. What little he'd eaten for dinner last night came right out and splattered the frozen pavement, and he lay trembling beside it, too weak to move.

"Hey."

Randall stirred. He turned his head slowly and swivelled his eyes until he caught Hughes by his side.

The vampire wore an expression of sorrow as he crouched by Randall. Then he reached out and placed a hand on Randall's back. "We'll find him," he said.

Randall bared his teeth, but his heart wasn't in it.

"Come on. Come with me. We'll ponce some clothes off Mandelson then get you home, yeah? Then we'll figure this shit out."

Randall growled weakly.

"Yeah, I have no idea what you're saying, mate. But you've got to get your arse in gear. We've got just about enough time to get Barb home before the sun comes up if you pull your thumb out of your arse and get moving now."

Randall blinked, then began to haul himself to his feet.

"Don't worry about me. I can get back in a minute if I gotta. I don't *have* to wait for the tube." Hughes slid an arm under Randall's chest to help him up. "Them tunnels are just sittin' there all by themselves otherwise. All I gotta do is vault a few maintenance guys on the way. They never know I'm there." He grinned and patted Randall's back. "There you go. Back on all fours. Come on, let's steal you some clothes, and you can show Mandelson them fine gnashers of yours. If you 'appen to sink 'em into the fucker while you're at it, I'll look the other way."

Randall shook himself down and rubbed his shoulder along Hughes' knee. The vampire could have walked away, but he'd come and found Randall. He wanted to find Ellis. And he was probably Randall's best chance of doing so himself.

He let Hughes lead the way. Randall hadn't a clue where they were or how far it was from Mandelson's, so they jogged through the streets with the Constable in front until it came up ahead. Randall's own scent came and went like Silly String from his reckless criss-cross of the entire Bayswater area. If he'd tried to follow that back it could've taken ages to find the house again.

Hughes got him into the house and shut the door. "May as well," he said. "The arsehole's already seen your face."

Randall grimaced, then shifted up anyway. Charging around at night was one thing. Dawn would come soon. He'd already frightened a few early movers. Trotting through the streets once service personnel began their journeys to work would be madness. The last thing he needed was baristas telling customers they'd seen a wolf on the streets.

"You know," Barb said in a conversational tone, "I never get tired of seeing your meat and two veg just hanging out like that. You should do it more often."

Randall blinked at her. She was joking, he knew she was, but the humour failed to reach him.

She offered an apologetic smile and gestured to the

bundled-up harness in the crook of her left arm. "Right, let's pinch you something to wear, yeah?"

"He's not having—"

Randall cut Mandelson off with a ragged snarl.

"I might have something spare." The Elder stumbled toward the stairs, then hurried up them.

Randall eyed Hughes. "Why didn't you go after them?"

Hughes crossed his arms. "I was staked, remember?"

"No, after that." Randall stalked toward him. His shoulders hunched forward. He was far shorter than the Constable, but Hughes still took a step back in alarm. "You could have followed them. They couldn't have gone far. You're too fast to be seen, you could have searched all of Bayswater and found them before they got away and we'd know where Ellis was now! We'd know where—" His throat choked his words off.

"Listen 'ere," Hughes said. He said it gently, but still firm with it. "I'd no way of knowing how long I'd been out when Barb took the stake out. Could've been seconds. Minutes. They could've been gone half an hour for all I knew. And what was important right then was *you*."

Randall stared at him. "No, what was important—"

"Was you," Hughes repeated. "Me, Barb, that wanker upstairs? We all could move. You were stuck like a pig in tar, and then you were *gone*, and I needed to make sure you were okay. They left me alive. They took Ellis alive. But you could've got yerself hit by a bloody car the way you were carrying on, and how'd you think Ellis'd react if he found out I'd let that happen to you on my watch, eh?"

Randall's skin prickled. His teeth ground together, and his lips pulled back in a threat.

"He's right." Barb placed her cool hand against his bare shoulder. "Don't go ripping his face off, eh? It's pretty. I like looking at it."

He wanted to punch something, tear pieces off anything. It wasn't the full moon, and even if it were he was still an Alpha, yet he still felt like his control was little more than a thin, fragile thing.

"We are going to find him," Hughes repeated.

Randall exhaled slowly and rubbed his hands over his face. "Yeah." He was numb. Weary. "Yeah, we will."

"Good man." Hughes squeezed his bicep. "Fuck me, you're built like a brick shithouse. I doubt Mandelson's got anything that'll wrap 'round them guns, mate."

"Probably not." Mandelson came down the stairs with a pile of clothes in his arms and a look of sheer disdain on his weaselly features. "Here. This is what I have." He thrust the pile at Hughes rather than Randall.

Hughes caught them and nodded. "Cheers." He passed them to Randall one by one.

Randall dressed perfunctorily. The trousers were too long, but Mandelson's waist was larger. He had to roll the ends up and tighten a belt around his midriff. The shirt was likewise too long, and clamped tightly around his arms whenever he tried to bend them. He pulled on socks and a sweater that was so dusty it made him sneeze several times, but shoes weren't going to happen. Mandelson's feet were two sizes smaller than Randall's.

"You gonna be okay in just socks?" Hughes frowned.

"Yeah. It's fine." It'd be horrible. The ice would permeate the socks until his feet were wet and freezing, but his body would prevent any real damage occurring, which just meant he'd go the entire way with slush between his toes. "Thanks," he added, looking to Mandelson.

Mandelson breezed past him and into the living room. "My house is a wreck," he sniffed. "An absolute wreck!"

"You're welcome." Hughes pulled a face at the Elder's

back. "Come on, Councillor. Let's get you 'ome in one piece before the sun comes up, eh?"

Mandelson glowered at them, but Hughes' well-placed reminder that Barb was the one in the room with all the authority kept his mouth shut.

IT WASN'T until they were well past Paddington Station that Hughes said, "Right. How're we gonna do this?"

Barb shook her head. "I have no idea what the hell happened back there."

"Magic," Randall rumbled.

They stared at him.

"She had me like it was nothing," he muttered. "And she had him, too..." He shook his head.

"Yeah." Barb shook her head, then bit her lip. "Randall... you know I gotta ask, right?"

Randall shook his head faintly. "I don't know."

"Ask what?" Hughes frowned.

Barb thumbed over her shoulder. "Bitchtits back there. She had that werewolf with her, and she called him *Carter*."

Hughes' gaze flickered between them. "Okay, what'd I miss? Tell me all of it."

Randall walked in sullen silence as he listened to Barb relay the moments during which Hughes had been staked. Her words picked at his hurt like a scab and left it fresh, raw.

"I think he's my dad," he whispered. "Christ, Aaron, I think that cow's got my *dad*. All these years we thought he'd just run off with another woman, or been hit by a bus, or walked out, or jumped in front of a train. The police never found him, they never found a body, and now he's..." He shuddered. "She took him. She *took my dad*."

Hughes stopped and faced him, then wrapped his arms around Randall and squeezed.

Randall's breath caught, then he returned the hug so tightly that Hughes grunted.

"Sorry. Sorry, I—"

"It's okay, mate." Aaron pulled back and stared at him. "We're gonna get them *both* back, okay?"

"How?" Randall shook his head. "How can we do that? She just has to say something and me and Dad, we can't... we don't get a choice. And you and Barb just bounced off her like she was rubber."

"Yeah." Aaron started moving again. "Yeah, the faster I went at her, the harder I got thrown off. I didn't even get a hand on her. She bounced me from like two feet away. Didn't even move. She couldn't have seen be coming."

"So she's got like a force field or something, right?" Barb nodded.

Randall bit his tongue. It had to be more than just a force field to have rebuffed Ellis' power from across the room. Or perhaps that's exactly what it was, and it had stripped the power from his words before they reached her. Either way, it suggested that it wasn't merely a physical barrier.

"Right." Aaron nodded like he'd reached a decision. "We need to pick up the pace. Come on."

They broke into a jog, which soon became a run, and Aaron steered them toward Hyde Park.

"Uh, Aaron." Barb eyed him as they ran. "Park's closed."

"Yeah, whatever."

The park was bordered by a low wall, which was topped by iron railings with spikes sticking up from them. Behind the railings was an even taller hedge. The entire assembly was around six feet high, but the railings capped out at about five.

Randall worked out Aaron's plan seconds before the Constable enacted it.

The vampire ran at the wall and leaped onto it, then launched himself up. One foot landed neatly between two spikes, and then he was gone, over the hedge. He landed with a crash of broken twigs. "All clear!"

Barb grunted. "Bloody hell. If I spear my foot on this shit…"

"Why don't I just give you a leg up?" Randall offered?

"Nah. Magic wall-running powers, remember? I just want him to feel guilty for a second." She sprinted over the fence and landed with far fewer complaints from the undergrowth.

Randall sighed. Public athletics weren't his favourite pastime, but if Hughes wanted to cut a corner, Hyde Park was the only way to do it.

He threw himself up and over, and landed in a low crouch to distribute the weight.

"Hang on." Barb blinked as she offered Randall a hand up. "What're we even doing in here? Soho's that way!" She pointed back out toward the street.

"Yeah." Hughes smirked. "But we're going to Pimlico."

"You said—"

"You reckon I'm gonna tell that bastard Mandelson all our business?" Hughes laughed. "Come on. Still gotta get there before sun-up. Then we can work out how we're gonna save the world."

They ran as fast as they could without Aaron outpacing them, and Randall wondered what harebrained scheme the Constable had cooked up.

TWENTY-FIVE

They had to vault their way out of the park too, and when they finally made it to the house in Pimlico, Randall was panting and his heart pounding.

"Nice." Aaron checked his phone. "Few minutes spare." Then he looked at Randall.

Randall had his hand on the door before he remembered he didn't have his keys. He shook his head. "Ellis has got them." He groaned.

Barb peered down at the harness in her arms. "No pockets in this, eh?"

Aaron grunted and drew out his roll of lockpicks. "Keep an eye out. Let's not get reported for breaking into yer own house, yeah?"

Randall and Barb shielded him with their bodies while he worked, then the door was open and Aaron pushed his way inside. "Where's the best place to stay out of the sun?"

"Master bedroom. Uh. Top floor." Randall followed them in.

He really had to talk to Ellis about getting some kind of

security system so that people couldn't just poke metal into the keyhole and let themselves in.

"Right. 'Ello, Tiberius!" Aaron sprinted off up the stairs and fussed the dog en route, and Barb trotted up after him.

Randall bolted the door and followed. "Right, let's hear it, then. What's the plan?"

"Wow." Barb stopped the moment she got in through the bedroom's door. "This is huge!"

"Yeah." Aaron moved to the windows and fussed with the curtains, but no light came in. "This is some serious effort Devitt put in here."

Randall turned the light on, which made both vampires flinch. "Sorry. I'm not all night-vision in this shape." He crossed the room to sit on the edge of the ridiculously ostentatious four-poster bed. At least Devitt hadn't had curtains around it, or whatever rich people did with these things. "The plan?" he prompted.

"First off, we need to talk about your dad." Hughes dropped into an armchair with gently curved wooden legs. "And maybe then we can move on to who exactly needs armchairs and a bloody table in their bedroom!"

Randall snorted at that. "He put chairs everywhere. There's one in every bathroom, too. Maybe it's a Victorian thing."

"Weirdo." Barb put the harness on the bed, then dropped into the other armchair.

Tiberius sat himself down between Randall's knees and yawned, then slid himself down to the ground to doze off again. It was far, far before his wake-up time, and he didn't seem all that impressed that his owner wasn't home, but not yet awake enough to worry.

"Randall."

Randall sighed and ran a hand over his hair. "Being a werewolf, it can run in the family. Does run in the family," he corrected. "But shifters can successfully bear children with humans, and after a while it becomes recessive, and you can end up with shifters born to human parents. That's how it was with everyone in my last pack. We didn't know what we were, didn't know how or why we'd come into being. None of us had a shifter parent, some of us had killed our families when we first changed..." He laced his fingers together and squeezed. "I didn't learn any of this until we bumped into this other pack last year. People died. But... this new pack, they've got shifter parents, some of 'em, so they go find people before the change and they help explain what they're going through."

"That's gotta be tough," Barb murmured.

"Yeah. Yeah, it is." Randall peeled Mandelson's soaking wet socks off his feet and tossed them to the floor. He wriggled his toes. "Some people change when they're twelve, I've heard of some not changing until they were eighteen. I changed when I was just a few days off fifteen. Dad had been missing since I was ten."

"Ah." Aaron nodded. "Right, so you had no way of knowing what he was, and he wasn't there when you changed."

"My brother, Kieran... he's not a shifter. Nor's my mum. But Kieran used to get so angry when kids picked on me at school. It's like he had all the anger and none of the biology. He'd thump anyone who even tried to say anything about our dad or our mum." He rubbed his forearm. "Mum thought Dad'd been hurt. That he might be in a hospital. But he never came home, and the police never found him. She grieved. She grieved for *years*. And she still won't believe he's dead, and I thought she had to be a bit bonkers, that he had to be dead, or why hadn't he ever come back, but this woman, she took him. She took my dad and she's been using him as some kind of fucking errand boy—"

"Whoa. Stop." Aaron raised his hands. "Take a breather. We'll get her. You hear me? We're gonna find them, and we will screw her to the wall for this."

"How?" Randall's voice cracked.

"First we have got to figure out where they are." Aaron pulled out his phone and swiped it with his stylus. He tapped away at it, features creased in thought. "She knows about werewolves, 'cause she's got one. She knows 'bout vampires, 'cause she's pinchin' 'em. She can control werewolves, but she can't control vampires—"

"Why'd you say that?" Barb crossed her legs.

"Because she'd just walk in, give us orders, and walk out again," Aaron reasoned. "Hell, she wouldn't even have to send Carter Senior to do her dirty work for her if she could walk in and tell us to follow her off home. So, she can't control us. But she can keep us at arm's length."

"Which she probably does *because* she can't control us," Barb offered.

"Yeah. My thinking exactly." Aaron stopped his typing for a moment. "Why didn't she take you?" He looked straight at Randall, pale eyes glinting in the light from the lone bulb overhead.

Randall shook his head slowly. "She said she could come back for me later."

"Which meant she couldn't take you at that time." Aaron pointed his stylus toward Randall. "Because surely two werewolves under your thumb is better than one?"

"And if she could get three people into a car, she could get four," Barb muttered.

"So it's a control problem, maybe," Randall said.

"If I had pinched a werewolf and used it as my personal whatever for nigh on twenty years, I'd bag myself another the moment I had the chance." Aaron sniffed. "Right. She knows about werewolves, but if she can't handle more than one of you with ease she might have avoided the shit out of shifters all that time. But she's hunting vampires down left, right, and centre, so she knows about us. She must've sussed by now we don't pick up on cameras, microphones, stuff like that."

"I don't follow."

Aaron smirked. "Phone Ellis."

Randall almost laughed. "What'd be the point of that?"

"Nobody phones a vampire. But you're in his phonebook, right?"

"Of course."

"Right. So you're not a telesales caller. You're someone he knows. And that means you know he can't answer, which tells her you're probably the werewolf she just dissed."

Randall's head felt sore just following Hughes' logic. It *seemed* to make sense, but he was so exhausted he wasn't entirely sure he got the point. "Uh-huh…"

Hughes put his own phone away after reading a message, then spoke slowly. "Just by phoning, you're telling her you want to talk to *her*. And if she's really interested in bagging you for her toolkit, she'll answer."

"We're assuming the old bag knows what a mobile phone is," Barb huffed.

"Yeah." Aaron nodded. "It does hinge on that, yeah. I'm not gonna deny it."

"I'm really tired. I've just found out my dad's been a prisoner almost all my life. The man I love's been kidnapped by the same woman that took my dad all them years ago. I've been sick. I've been running for a couple of hours." Randall rubbed his forehead. "Please just explain to me what talking to this woman on the phone is supposed to achieve? You reckon she's going to *tell* me where to find her?"

"Maybe not in so many words, no." Aaron sighed. "You put

her on speaker, Randall, and you do whatever it takes to keep her talking. Me and Barb will listen out and if there's a single damned thing that gives away her location in the background, we'll pick it up."

Randall stared at him. "That's your plan?"

"Yeah."

"This is like the worst plan I have ever heard."

"Maybe." Aaron looked cagey.

"You swore to me you had a plan!" Randall surged from the bed and made it halfway across the room before Aaron was in his face, hands against his chest.

"Randall, listen to me." The vampire's cold hands leeched warmth through the flimsy shirt Mandelson had handed over. "Every single part of this city sounds different. Every part! And I've been all over it. I've spent decades going all over it."

"You're asking me to pin everything on the hope that you can recognise one sound out of six hundred square miles of city?" Randall bared his teeth. "You're insane!"

"You give me something else, then!" Aaron shouted in his face. "God dammit, Randall, give me *something*! Tell me you can track your dad if you taste his blood! Tell me you've got some kind of soul bond thing you can follow all the way to Ellis! Give me an alternative! Tell me how we can find someone when they've been spirited away by a goddamn sorcerer and I will be all over that shit!"

Randall's pulse rushed in his ears. His breath came heavily. A weight settled into his gut, and dragged his shoulders down with it. "I can't," he breathed.

"Then this is the best shot we've got, innit?" Aaron sighed and gave Randall's shoulders a supportive squeeze. "You get some rest first though. You can't hold onto a train of thought right now, let alone a conversation with some evil witch."

"But—"

"No. Rest now, because we've got one shot at this, and if we fuck it up we've lost."

He wanted to fight, to argue, to scream at Aaron to get this thing done now, but he knew the vampire was right. Even if Randall did manage to pull himself together enough to keep the woman on the phone, what would happen next? She'd have an entire day with Ellis, and Aaron and Barb were both trapped indoors.

He took a deep breath, then let it go. "All right. Okay. You guys can have this room. I'll be downstairs."

"We'll get 'em, mate. By hook or by crook."

"We'd better." Randall patted his thigh and urged Tiberius to follow him, then he left his own bedroom and shut the door.

TWENTY-SIX

ELLIS HAD no way of knowing whether he was awake. Nothing was real, nothing made any sense. His heart was beating, juddering in his chest as though it could overcome if it put a bit more effort in, and it was such an alien sensation that he could only assume he'd finally cracked and gone insane.

One thing was true: he was screaming.

Maybe this was what it was like to get dissected if you were still alive at the time. His skin felt like it was splitting apart, and his veins were filled with silver. Each thud of his heart pushed fire through his body, and something, somewhere, something tiny and helpless felt like it was unravelling.

"Art?" Ellis hadn't ever seen his father's face so red in his entire life. "You want to go to university to study art?"

"Aye." He resisted the urge to run. Bad enough when Da' shouted, but that red?

"I worked all my life to get here. All my life! You boys have had the best of everything, no expense spared! And this is how you repay me?"

"I'm an artist!" Ellis' voice rose as his anger broke its banks. "I want to study art! I don't want to be a bloody lawyer, Dad!"

"You're a pansy! Is that it? Art is for poofters, boy!"

"Maybe I am! Not that it's any of your business!"

He expected more shouting. He even expected threats. But he hadn't expected the fist that exploded across his cheek.

No, the agony was still there. Time was meaningless. He was breathing only to scream because somehow that was better than silence. Or *was* he alive? He felt warm, warm enough that the air around him was cold against his skin. Was he breathing because he had no choice?

A ribbon of anguish twisted in him. A rib snapped.

It didn't heal.

"I've got your test results here."

"I should hope so, or I'm wasting your time." Ellis flashed his flirtiest smile, but only because this particular doctor was sexy as hell. It was a long shot, since doctors were ethically bound not to take patients up on such things, but statistically his odds were definitely increased by trying.

"I'm afraid you're not wasting my time at all, Mr. O'Neill." Dr. Bhattacharya's expression was neutral. No smile, only business. "The electroretinograph confirms our suspicions. There is a marked reduction in rod functionality around the edges of both retinas."

Ellis' smile faltered. "But it's okay, right?"

"It's retinitis pigmentosa, Mr. O'Neill."

"I don't…" He licked his lips. It wasn't the C word. He had no idea what it was, but it wasn't ocular cancer, right?

"It's a progressive genetic condition. Your retinas are dying."

Ellis' heart pounded. He had a degree in Fine Art. He knew damn well what retinas were for, and he was a hundred percent sure they needed to be alive to do it. "I'm going blind?"

This was ridiculous. He couldn't go blind. He sold art for a living, for crying out loud. How could he pick which artists to represent if he couldn't fucking see?

"Not all cases of RP lead to total sight loss. But it is degenerative, and there is no cure and no way to halt its progression. All we can do is monitor your eyes and put you in touch with specialist services. There are several charities which offer support, too. The clinic staff will give you all the information you need."

"No. No, there has to be a mistake. I've always been clumsy, that's all it is. My new optician decided to do some retinal photography when I mentioned it. Nobody else has thought it were a problem!"

Dr. Bhattacharya gave a small nod. He was calm. Of course he was; he delivered this news day in, day out.

"You said it was genetic?"

"Your grandfather's pathology is indicative of a form of RP, yes."

Ellis shrank in his chair. "No..."

"No!" The scream left his throat in tatters.

He heard faint muttering. It made no sense. None at all. The voice was female, dispassionate, but the words were like a nonsense poem. "Subject's response is consistent with that of previous attempts, though the amplification of the mana seems to stem from some commingling of blood and the blood of a lycanthrope, most likely the creature encountered during the subject's apprehension..."

Ellis tuned it out. It meant nothing and, more importantly, didn't make the pain stop.

"You're the most beautiful thing I've ever seen."

Ellis laughed hysterically. This bloke had been pawing at him for an hour already, but this was the cheesiest line yet. How could this berk think Ellis was beautiful? He was mashed off his face, he hadn't had a haircut in weeks, and he hadn't even damn well shaved in days. In a moment of lucidity he realised he had to look like a fucking mess, but he had no way of knowing how he looked, did he? None whatsoever. And he never would again.

*"Okay, it wasn't a joke, but maybe you've had a few too many…"
The man had a honey-like laugh. "Should I get you to a taxi?"*

*"Aye, why not?" Ellis laughed still. 'An' if I'm reet lucky we'll go
back to your place, eh?"*

*"Yeah. I'd like that." Cool lips brushed against Ellis' jaw, and
fingers slid over his stomach.*

*Ellis swallowed as his cock began to swell. Well, it tried its best
under the conditions, anyway.*

*"Come on." Hands helped him stand, and then an arm tightened
around his waist. "God, you're so beautiful. The world needs you."*

*"Uh-huh." Ellis lurched against his helper, arm around the man's
slim shoulders. "I don't bottom," he mumbled.*

"Whatever you want, sweet thing."

*The cold air rushed into his lungs as they stepped out of the club,
and it was like getting drunk all over again. They stumbled along and
even the music faded away.*

Weren't they looking for a taxi? Aye, that were right. A taxi.

*Those lips were on him again. Were they in the taxi already? Had he
blacked out?*

*When the other man's hand cupped his cock through his trousers,
the taxi issue became irrelevant. Ellis moaned and ran his hands
wherever he could. He felt a thin body, but not a weak one. Silk shirt.
People still wore silk shirts to nightclubs?*

*As the other man's mouth found the soft skin at the crease of his
neck, Ellis realised he didn't think he knew the bloke's name.*

Then his teeth broke Ellis' skin, and that didn't matter anymore.

His chest was vibrating. Buzzing. It was odd, but he
couldn't tell whether it was because of the torment or yet
another thing which caused him pain. Was he falling apart
now? Was this what it felt like?

But the pain turned dull, and his heart stopped. He felt his
rib heal. Other bones he didn't remember breaking also knit
themselves back together.

The buzz continued. It was almost like a flurry of text messages. Or maybe someone was daft enough to actually phone him.

He laughed with the absurdity of it.

"Get that thing off him, Carter."

Hands felt across his chest, then the buzzing flew away like a drunken bumblebee.

"What kind of fool tries to phone a vampire?" She paused. "Randall? Who is Randall? Answer me, vampire!"

Someone's heart rate picked up all of a sudden. For one insane moment Ellis thought it might be his own, but no. It came from near his persistently-buzzing phone.

The werewolf.

"It can't be another of you wretched creatures. And you wouldn't hand your number out to mortals, would you? Not without a lot of explaining as to why you never answer. Which leaves your handsome werewolf friend, doesn't it?" She sounded triumphant, and the buzzing stopped. "Yes?"

"We need to talk."

It was Randall's voice. Oh *God* it was Randall's voice!

"Randall!" Ellis rolled onto his front and tried to stand, but his limbs felt like jelly. "Randall!" He screamed the name hysterically as his nails clawed at the floor.

Randall couldn't hear him, not over a phone. It didn't matter how loudly he yelled.

"I'm busy," his torturer said. "What is it you want to talk about?"

"I want the vampire and the werewolf. Give them both to me and I'll let you live." Randall sounded angry. Furious. And *hot*.

Ellis giggled and pressed his cheek to the floor. This wasn't the best time to think of Randall in that way, was it? No. No, it wasn't.

"Since when has there been an allegiance between vampires and werewolves in this city?" She sounded only vaguely curious. "Honestly, you think you know a place, but you go away a while and everything changes."

"Shut up." Randall's speaker-borne voice carried a snarl to it.

"He's so beautiful." Ellis rolled onto his back and ran his hand across the slippery surface of the ward. "I've seen him."

"I want my vampire," Randall continued.

Ellis grinned. That had a nice ring to it. *My* vampire.

"I want my werewolf."

That didn't sound quite so sexy, but Ellis was willing to let it slide.

"And if you hand them both over, you get to walk away."

"I get to walk away regardless, sweetheart." Her voice shed all pretence of amusement. "You don't live to my age without breaking a few eggs. Your offer is weak, so here's mine. How about I take you to replace the godawful werewolf I've already got, since he's past his prime, and I kill this one right now to make room for you?"

Ellis heard Randall's growl. It did things to him. *Naughty* things.

A tiny voice suggested to him that he might have lost the majority of his sanity.

"Shhh." He shook his head. "I'm listening to Randall."

"But you'd let the vampire go?" Randall said. It sounded like he was talking through clenched teeth.

Ellis' angel of misery laughed like breaking glass. "If he survives, I'll let him go. If he doesn't, his ashes are welcome to go wherever the wind takes them."

"You dare—"

Randall's voice went away. It was there, then it was gone, and Ellis sighed at its absence.

"Might as well empty his pockets, just in case he's got other phones in there or something."

The werewolf came closer. It patted him down. Took some things. Ellis smiled as warm hands touched his body.

"Randall," he breathed.

But then the werewolf was gone, and it was just him and his jailer.

"Right," she said. "Where were we?"

Just as the little voice tried to say something about the word *Carter* to him, he began to unravel all over again.

TWENTY-SEVEN

It took all of Randall's willpower to remain still while the vampires worked. He didn't want to distract them, didn't dare risk either of them forgetting some vital clue.

The second the call ended, Aaron's pencil had sped across his notepad. He filled three pages with scrawl within two seconds while Barb was still jotting down her first note. Still, Aaron waited for her, too, and the silence made Randall's patience ever harder to maintain.

"Okay." Barb finally put her pen down. She scrutinised her notes, nodded to herself, and looked up at Aaron. "What'd you get?"

Aaron had his own phone on the little table in the master bedroom, and he poked at it with his stylus. "Call lasted two minutes thirteen seconds, starting at 15:47:11. She's in a large space, but it's enclosed, not outdoors. She had someone with her, whose pulse was elevated. For the sake of argument I am going to work on the assumption that it was Randall's dad."

Barb nodded and reached for her notes. "Okay. I got that. Apart from the insanely precise timestamp, obviously." She gave Aaron a look that clearly suggested she thought that was weird.

"Every single detail could be the one we need," was Aaron's simple answer. "What else'd you get?"

Randall watched the back and forth while he wrung his hands together. These two were his only hope.

His hope for *what*, he couldn't pin down to one single thing. For the safe return of Ellis, and for that of Randall's father, yes. But also for Randall to exact revenge, and the more he dwelled on the idea the more it took root. His dad deserved that, didn't he? Revenge for what had been done to him? For the years stolen off his life, and for the family who grew up without him?

What kind of revenge was there, though? The vampires had their own very neatly constructed system of justice, though it wasn't flawless. His pack didn't seem to have one, leaving everything to regular law, which had left them without any tools with which to decide how to proceed after Briar had killed Zev. But this lady was neither vampire nor werewolf. Whatever she was, did her own contemporaries have some set of laws which should deal with her, or was this sort of thing completely acceptable to them?

The thought that there could be more with her kind of power wasn't one he wanted to entertain, but Mrs. Uddin had warned him, hadn't she? She'd been so set on her view that magic was a dangerous thing that they were all best off staying well away from, and Randall's wide-eyed idealism had turned that into *let's go find some magic!* Well, now magic had found them instead, and it had taken away the most important thing in his life.

If he couldn't get Ellis back, what would happen to his pack? Sadia's period of mourning would end soon. If she still loved Zev, would she be able to become Alpha while Randall mourned his own loss?

He couldn't bear thinking about it. It made his skin itch.

"A lot of road noise in the background," Barb was saying when Randall forced himself to tune in again. "Lorries as well as cars, so it's outside the Congestion Charging zone."

"And a big road that sees consistent use this time of day." Aaron nodded. "But too much other noise for it to be the M25. Too much random stuff."

"Yeah. Pretty sure I heard a lorry reversing, too."

"You did, yeah. The whole *beep beep beep*. Really faint." Aaron delved into one of his many pockets and withdrew an A to Z, and began to flick back and forth through it so fast that all the pages blurred together. "So there's either something nearby that accepts deliveries by the lorryload, or some bloke was proper lost."

Barb snorted. "I'm pretty sure there was some overground, too."

"Trains?" Randall scratched his ear.

She nodded and re-read her notes, then stole Aaron's and let out a low whistle. "You got all this in two minutes?"

"And thirteen seconds," Aaron said absently. "I'm going to guess this is the North Circular we heard. It's three lanes each way, goes right through suburban areas and past supermarkets and stuff, runs right under or over some train lines."

Randall hissed and stood, prowling back and forth with his arms wrapped around himself. The North Circular was miles upon miles of road. It ran from Woolwich in the east all the way around to Gunnersbury in the west, then crossed the Thames to become the South Circular and complete the circuit around Central London.

"Keep yer 'air on," Aaron murmured. "If we run with the idea that she's only pickin' on targets somewhere near where she's based herself we eradicate everything east of Finchley. That cuts it down to, what, about a twelve-mile stretch? She probably ain't crossing the river if she wants to keep her vampires intact—"

Randall prowled toward the table and nodded. "And there's a pack in Richmond who would've sniffed out my dad by now if she was down that way."

Aaron's eyebrows lifted. "Good to know. So we're looking around here." He flattened the A to Z against the table and indicated an arc of the North Circular with his pencil. Other circles already dotted the page, lightly pencilled in with names scribbled next to them. *Cooper. Baxter.* Others Randall couldn't read in Aaron's light hand.

Barb leaned over and pointed. Her finger moved from one thin line to the next as she murmured, "Okay. Overground lines here... here, and... here! God, are there really this many?"

"Don't forget the underground comes up to surface level 'round 'ere an'all." Aaron poked at a mass of grey lines. "And up 'ere 'round Neasden's an entire maintenance depot."

Barb grunted. "Right. What about Stonebridge Park? Got loads of lines. Though you'd have to be mental to hang around there at night. Maybe she's a biker chick."

Aaron laughed briefly. "Probably would've heard motorbikes if she was anywhere near the Ace Cafe."

"Nah, they've gone all respectable these days. They've got a car park!" She sniffed like the idea of people *driving* to the Ace Cafe was deeply offensive to her. "Not that I'd know or have ever ventured outside my own territory, nudge nudge, wink wink," she added.

"You are a Councillor now," Randall reminded her.

"Fuck."

Randall looked down at the map. "Okay, if Stonebridge Park is out, what about Gunnersbury or Acton?"

"Maybe." Aaron flicked through his notes. "Didn't hear nothing like a golf course, though, or a driving range."

"We were only on the line two minutes."

"Yeah." Aaron tapped his pencil against the table. "But Neasden's got all them supermarkets and the IKEA."

"The lorry reversing," Randall said.

"Right. Then Staples Corner crosses over the Thameslink route, and it's got all them retail units around it."

"So we reckon Neasden or Staples Corner, and if those turn up nothing we go down to Gunnersbury, right?" Barb leaned back in her chair. "That's a lot of ground to cover."

Randall paced away from the table and toward the door, then all the way around the room in frustration. "Too much ground. This is hopeless! I can't even track him once he's got into a car. How are we ever going to find—"

"Oi. None of that." Aaron put his pencil down. "They got into a car, or maybe they just bloody teleported away, I dunno. But they have to reappear somewhere. They have to *be* somewhere. And if you can sniff 'em out before they go, you can sniff 'em out when they get back an'all, can't you?"

"And if I can't?" Randall felt like he was going to be sick. "God, what if I can't?"

"You *can*. And that's all there is to it."

Randall sat heavily on the bed and dug his fingers into his knees. It wasn't as easy as Aaron made it out to be. The Constable had to know that, didn't he? He wasn't crazy enough to think that wanting something to happen was enough to make it so. He couldn't be. He'd learned the hard way, if nothing else, that people didn't always get what they wanted out of life.

His chest heaved as the realisation blindsided him.

Aaron had been here. He'd been where Randall was now, worried sick that the man he loved had been taken, that Aaron could lose the love of his life. And he had. He'd lost Marcus. Hell, Devitt had forced him to kill Marcus. Yet here he was without any indication at all that he was allowing his own past to get in the way of his determination to find Ellis.

If Aaron could knuckle down and focus on the job at hand, Randall damn well could.

"I'm sorry," Randall whispered.

Aaron and Barb both looked at him, confusion writ on their features.

"I'm sorry," he repeated. "You're right, Aaron. You're right. I can. I'll find them. We'll find them." He stood slowly and dropped his hands to his sides. He was an Alpha, for God's sake. Maybe not a very good one, maybe not the one Zev's family deserved, but he had love on his side, and that gave him a stillness of thought which was supposed to help him keep not only his own temper in order, but that of every other shifter in his pack.

He was an Alpha, and it was time to behave like one.

"That's more like it," Aaron snorted.

"Yeah. Come on, let's get cracking."

He got one step toward the door, then Aaron was in front of him, hands outstretched. "Whoa, hold on there, tiger! Where do you think you're going?"

"Staples Corner. The sooner we start—"

"It's daylight out there."

Randall blinked. "Oh. Shit. Right, but—"

"No. You can't go running around as a wolf while everyone's awake and chargin' around the streets, can you? Let alone the fact that we can't back you up. If you find them, and you go in alone, you're gonna be just as screwed as we were last night. Or have you gone and learned some kickboxing or something while we were asleep?"

Randall's shoulders drooped. "No."

"Right. So take Tiberius for his walk and poo or whatever, and we can go out once the sun's down, and go sniff half the town."

Randall bit his lip, then adjusted his weight and crossed his arms. "I've got a better idea."

"Maybe run it by me, yeah?"

"Yeah." Randall grinned slowly. "I reckon twenty noses are better than one. And that might push the odds more in our favour when we find wherever she's hiding out."

"You can't be serious," Barb whispered.

"I can." He rolled his shoulders, then cracked his knuckles. They made gratifyingly loud popping sounds. "And I am bloody well going to. Tell Mandelson to expect visitors. I've got some friends who need to pick up a scent, and he better not get in our way."

TWENTY-EIGHT

HE WAS HEALING. Over and over, always healing.

There was a moment when he'd tipped into some weird kind of psychotic state, like he'd been on the brink of starvation, but he wasn't hungry. He still wasn't hungry. Other than the sweet tingle of his body stitching itself back together, everything was peaceful.

He'd seen a film once, when his eyes still worked. An older film, one of Gilliam's finest. A thing of utter despondent beauty in which the protagonist finally broke away from his misery into glorious freedom.

Only the audience knew that he'd failed, that his freedom was only in his mind.

Ellis reckoned that's where he was now. The soothing cocoon of darkness had him and held him close, but beyond it, beyond the protection of his mind shutting down, she was still there, still tormenting him, still picking him apart like a rat in a lab.

He couldn't hear her. Her non-stop gibberish had gone away.

That could be part of his disassociation. Yes, that made sense. He'd blotted her out. She wasn't a part of his freedom, his peace, so he'd made her go away.

Still, he listened while his flesh tingled. Maybe he *was* present. Could she have stopped?

Hope sparked in his chest.

Had she found what she wanted and let him go?

He laughed, and it sounded weak to his ears, so he stopped. But the laughter turned into something else.

Whump-thump. Whump-thump. Whump-thump.

What *was* that? It was like something he should recognise. A sound he heard every time he was awake, from everyone around him. It had a name. There was a thing inside people that did this noise. Except in Han. Han's had broken, but Ellis had saved him anyway. He'd taken away the thing and replaced it with blood.

Heart, said the little voice. *It's a heartbeat.*

Just the one?

Just one.

Ellis inhaled slowly for the scent. Dry blood. Interesting, but not edible.

There was another scent. He picked out a delicate odour like earth and woodlands in fresh rain.

A werewolf.

Ellis' exhale brought with it a slight groan as the air left him too quickly.

The shifter came closer. Air stirred.

Ellis smiled. The werewolf had come to end his life. That made sense, didn't it? The witch was done with him, and now he would be disposed of and his pain would end.

Warm skin clamped over Ellis' mouth. Fingers came to rest against his jaw.

"Vampire," the man whispered. "Are you awake?"

Ellis wasn't entirely sure, so he shrugged.

There was a grunt. "Close enough. I'm gonna take my hand away and you have got to be quiet, understand?"

Oh! Secrets!

Ellis was good at secrets, so he nodded.

The hand left his face. The werewolf stayed close. "Don't move," he breathed. "If you touch the wards, Bryce will be down here like a shot. You get me?"

"I don't know any Bryce," Ellis said, his voice quiet.

"The witch," the werewolf whispered. "She'll wake the moment you try to escape, yeah? So just stay put."

"Oh." Ellis smiled again. The movement made the skin of his face feel taut. Did he have something on him? "Areet."

"The man who rang you." The werewolf kept his voice low, but Ellis heard the tension which entered it. "What's his name?"

Oh! Ellis' smile grew. He'd heard of this sort of thing! They called it Good Cop, Bad Cop, didn't they? He'd had the Bad Cop, and now the Good Cop had come to sneak some information out of him. "I'm not falling for it," he said. "Ye must think I'm reet cabbage-lookin'."

"It's Randall, right?" The werewolf's voice cracked and his pulse began to race. "What's his full name?"

"Nooo. No, no no." Ellis shook his head idly, then reached a hand up to touch his face. It was caked in some dry, flaky substance, and the smell of dead blood spiked. "Is this mine? Was I bleeding?" What a strange concept. Vampires didn't *bleed*. Their blood very much liked to stay on the inside, where it belonged. He had to suck some of the stuff out of himself just to get it into Han's mouth.

"Yeah. Look, we don't have much time. Listen to me." The werewolf drew a breath, then let it out slowly before he continued. "Is it Carter?"

Ellis shut his mouth again and dropped his hand to his side.

"Randall Carter? Does he have an older brother called Kieran?"

How does he know?

Easy, said the little voice. *Magic.*

Ellis scowled. "Werewolves don't use magic," he reasoned.

"Shh!" The hand clamped over his mouth again. "Come on, vampire, snap out of it. For God's sake, pull yourself together. Is he Randall Carter?"

Ellis bit the inside of his own cheek, then shrugged a little.

The hand left him. "For Christ's sake, vampire. He's my *son.*"

Ellis shook his head slowly. "No. That doesn't make sense. His dad's gone. Gone, he went ages ago. Just *poof*, like that, into thin air." He waved a hand, but the werewolf pushed it down to the cold, rubbery floor.

"He's a werewolf," the shifter breathed. There was a thump by Ellis' side, soft, like meat landing on a worktop. "Oh god, he's… what about Kieran? Him too?"

Ellis shook his head again. No, he'd met Kieran. The man didn't smell the same.

Carter. She called him Carter.

Wake up. For fuck's sake wake up, this is important!

"Carter," Ellis whispered.

"George," said the werewolf.

"George," Ellis repeated. He felt like it was an anchor, something to cling to while the world carried on being terrible beyond this little spot. He struggled to figure out whether this was a nightmare, but it was impossible to tell. His body continued to tingle. "You… you can go. Go find Randall."

"I can't." George's voice was a sore thing, rusty, like a

disused part which wasn't well-oiled. "You can't get up. I can't leave. Not until she says otherwise."

"Why are we here?" Ellis turned toward the voice. "What does she want?"

"From you?" George sighed. "She's old, vampire. She's old, and she's frail, and she wants to live."

Ellis almost laughed, then managed to stop himself. "If she wants to be turned—"

"No. Vampires can't use magic. Not like she can. Everything she knows would be worthless. She's convinced she can take apart what makes a vampire and identify the single piece of you which makes you immortal. Once she works *that* bit out she wants to weave it into herself without all the vampire stuff that goes with it."

Ellis crinkled his nose. "Sounds bollocks."

"Yeah," George said. "I dunno. I think the world could do without this crazy bitch in it any longer." He sighed. "She keeps pulling vampires apart trying to work out what makes 'em tick, but in the end they just unravel and she's got nothing but ash on her hands. They all go crazy way before she's done with them. You're holding up pretty well."

Ellis had to laugh at that, and George covered his mouth while he did it.

"Sorry," he whispered once the hand left him.

"They don't last long." George sounded grim. "Couple of days maybe. They're crazy within a couple of hours. You're doing better, believe me."

Ellis shook his head at that. "She can't just want immortality. That's never the dream. People always want youth and beauty to go with their immortality."

George grunted. "Yeah, I'm pretty sure that's part of it. Maybe she thinks whatever she finds can turn the clock back. I don't know. I don't care. I just wanted to know whether that was my boy." He sighed, and his breathing caught softly. "I can't let her take him. God, vampire, she can't do this to him."

"Ellis."

George hesitated. "Ellis."

"We're getting out of here."

George snorted. "I've been stuck at this woman's side for years. Nobody gets away from her. You want to know what she took me for?"

Ellis gave a slow nod.

"She'd made so many enemies she was up shit creek. They were after her. When she found me, she didn't even think twice. I'd only gone to the shop to get the bloody paper—" George broke off as his voice wavered.

Ellis frowned and reached for the werewolf. He found warmth, and laid his hand against it.

"She made me kill them. One by one. We turned up, they'd be protected against her magic, and I would walk through all their wards and kill them. And I couldn't stop myself, I couldn't do anything but what she told me to. And then because she was paranoid that it was a tactic that could be used against her, she never let me go."

"We are getting out of here," Ellis said more slowly. "You're going home to your wife and your children, George."

The pulse juddered. "Naomie?" George's breath spoke the name as though it were a long-lost treasure.

"She hasn't moved on, George." Ellis blinked. "She's still there for you." He felt as though his mind were finally ticking over.

He was awake. Yes. He was absolutely awake. This was *real*. Happening, right now.

"You love her," Ellis whispered. "You still love her. You'd be a frothing mess by now if you didn't."

"Of course I still love her—"

Ellis raised his finger to his own lips.

George stopped himself.

"I need to know the limitations this Bryce woman has on you," Ellis whispered urgently. "How does it work? You can talk to me, touch me, so you're not completely static. What are the rules of this thing?"

"It's a talisman. She made it from wolfsbane and silver. She never takes it off. Anything she commands of me, my body does without any kind of pause. I don't get a say in it."

"Can anyone use it?"

"I don't know. I reckon maybe, if they could use magic, but I don't know."

"So we have to destroy it." Ellis nodded. His thoughts had begun to pick up speed now that they had a problem to chew on. "You can't get it off her or you would have already." That much was obvious. "You can't attack her, or you'd've done that too."

"Right."

"But you can move around here."

"I'm on guard. I can't leave the building, but I can look outside. I have to make sure I'm not seen. I can't use a phone, I can't shout, I'm not allowed to change shape without her permission unless it's to protect her from immediate harm."

Ellis bit his lip. "Where are we?"

"Near Brent Park. It's an industrial estate behind the supermarket. Not a big one."

He ran his hand across the rubberised floor. "This is a warehouse?"

"Yeah. There's like a mezzanine level with what's probably supposed to be an office up there. That's where she's living for now. We don't stay in one place too long, maybe a year at most. I don't remember ever staying in a place for more than one winter."

Ellis' brain ticked and whirred.

A plan, a plan, my kingdom for a plan.

"There have to be facilities here," he realised. "Kitchen, loo, yeah? Even if it's just the basics?"

"Yeah. There are."

Ellis cracked a grin. It pulled on one side of his face more than it did the other. "Then here's what you're going to do."

This isn't a plan. You're insane!

He ignored the voice. Only crazy people heard voices. Instead he focused on George's pulse as he quickly outlined what steps the shifter would have to take.

"You're mental," George whispered. "What do you think that even achieves?"

Ellis raised his eyebrows. It was so obvious. But maybe George couldn't see it.

"Randall's coming," he whispered. It sounded evangelical, but he didn't care. "He will come. So we're going to send up a flare for him."

You're crazy.

"Yes." He couldn't disagree.

TWENTY-NINE

MANDELSON COMPLAINED BITTERLY at the intrusion, despite both Aaron and Barb telling him to stick it up his jacksie. Randall led each wolf in turn to the correct scents, though the house was largely bereft of others and it was impossible to fail to pick out the shifter's scent from that of the woman who gave him the orders. He wanted to make absolutely sure they didn't mess it up.

Ameera and Hasan stood by him. They'd helped him gather everyone together quickly, and not a single person had refused the call.

Family was family.

He grumbled softly as Farah took her time with the scent. She was young, new to all this, and Randall wasn't convinced that she should have come.

"There has to be a first," Ameera had said.

"Surely her first was when Jim stabbed her," was Randall's answer.

"First hunt." Ameera squeezed his arm. "I'll watch out for her."

Randall watched the young shifter as she switched back and forth, her nose to the floor.

I have it, she rumbled. Her tail rose and her ears perked forward in readiness.

Good. Randall yipped a summons and leaped up onto an armchair.

"Which one of you is that?" Mandelson pointed at him. "Constable, get this damn dog off my—"

"You're gonna want to stop right there," Hughes snapped.

Randall bared his fangs to Mandelson, then regarded the pack. They were cramming themselves into the room. Some came from the kitchen. Some had waited upstairs for others to take their turn with the scent trail.

Wolves. The house was full of wolves.

Randall bristled as a shiver of anticipation ran through him. This pack was *his*, and they were going to hunt down the person who had brought misery to his family for almost two decades. They were going to rescue his father and his lover, and they would do it together.

He growled and yipped, his ears twitching, his nose lowering as necessary as he addressed them.

We have the scent.

The room burst out into a low thunder of agreement, and Mandelson slid himself behind Hughes for protection.

You know your tasks. Go.

The wolves filtered from the house and spread out across the streets and alleyways of west London as Randall cast his net as widely as it could possibly go.

———

RANDALL HAD the vampires with him. Aaron and Barb, but

not Mandelson — that coward was not interested in helping anyone but himself.

Aaron had parcelled up the search areas by postcode and explained to each and every shifter how to operate a thorough search pattern. He didn't seem convinced that they'd understood, but they'd pored over maps of their areas and how to reach them with intense focus.

Some, such as Farah, had been set aside as communicators rather than searchers. In the wild a wolf's howls might reach several miles, but that wouldn't fly here, so there was one dotted every mile to act as a message relay. They would keep the lines open between each little cluster of searching activity and, more importantly, they would repeat the cry should anyone locate the scent they all sought.

All knew the value of discretion, but it was a worry to know that there would be so many wolves charging around the suburbs. Randall prayed that their silhouettes would be mistaken for foxes by anyone who caught only a brief glimpse of a wolf, but they'd cross that bridge if they ever came to it. The task at hand took priority.

They filtered out of Mandelson's house in all directions. Some fled through the back door and disappeared into the warrens of back gardens, while others took the front door and sprinted down the street at top speed.

Randall himself took the street. With Barb and Aaron at his side he had the luxury of passing as a family pet out for a run with his owners, though maybe if Aaron could wear something other than Eighties goth-a-like shirts and Barb could possibly look less like a biker they might be more convincing. Randall was pretty sure as-is that onlookers were more likely to mistake them for drug dealers on the run.

They ran all the way to Stonebridge Park. Five miles, Randall reckoned. Barb was the slowest of them, but that was when compared to a wolf and a man who could probably outrun a bullet if he pushed himself. They still made it in well under half an hour.

"Thank God I don't do lactic acid any more," Barb said. "Right. I know this place like the back of my own hand. You do your thing, Randall. I'll make sure we don't overlook any little cubbyholes."

"Right," Aaron agreed. He had his A to Z in hand, and referred to it. "I'll keep us in the right area. Let's crack on."

Randall nodded and bayed into the night.

I have begun.

He loped toward the Ace Cafe with his nose to the ground, and his cry was relayed along the chain in a diminishing series of howls.

BACK AND FORTH, back and forth. Randall licked his nose to keep it fresh, but he found nothing.

Mournful howls punctuated the hours. Some were his own, others were those he heard and repeated to pass along the chain. He ducked in and out of shadows, he hid behind bins and walls, he scoured every possible inch of his allocated area, but there was nothing here.

Had he gone noseblind? He couldn't have, not yet, surely? He might not be used to acting as a sniffer, but wolves were better at this than dogs. He shouldn't have grown addled so soon, should he?

"Oi. Randall. Stop."

He skittered to a halt and blinked up at Barb.

"We're gonna do this, right?" She crouched and gazed into his eyes. "I see that tail drooping, kid. Don't—"

She paused as another distant howl sang mournfully through the air. It lingered, long and drawn-out.

Randall sprang to his feet, and passed the howl on with excitement.

"Is this good?" Aaron whispered.

"I think so," Barb said.

Randall looked up at them both, and parted his jaws in a satisfied smile.

Yes.

Oh, yes.

I hope you're ready to run!

RANDALL WASN'T the first to arrive. He wasn't the last.

A half-circle of wolves gathered around a little row of industrial buildings. The bright light-polluting glow of a supermarket sat less than half a mile behind it, which made the squat terrace seem darker still. It was unlit at night. People didn't live here, they didn't need street lights.

There was a car bodywork shop, and a small company which made signage. A couple of the units sat empty, presumably victims of the recession.

And then there was one in the middle which had a stream of wolf spoor trailing from a tiny upper window which stood out so brightly that it was virtually a flag.

"That's the only camera I can find that covers the front," Barb said. Her voice was low as she tossed a couple of wires to the floor.

Randall tore his gaze from the near-fluorescent scent trail to look up at the post which housed the problem camera. He hadn't paid attention as she ran off to destroy it. She must've run all the way up the post to reach it.

He snorted, impressed.

"You're welcome." Then she gestured to the door. "Aaron?"

"Yeah. Piece of piss." The Constable picked his way past the wolves and examined the door's lock.

The unit had two entry points that Randall could see. A small door that people could use, and a larger garage-style rolling door which would presumably enable vehicles or movement of pallets. Aaron had picked the smaller of the two, and unleashed his lockpicks on it.

More wolves arrived. Some chuckled at the spoor, and Randall glanced back up at it.

It was like a bloody Bat Signal. You didn't go pissing out of a window like that unless you *wanted* werewolves to find you.

His hackles rose at the thought, and he rumbled low in his chest.

It could be a trap.

Hasan nodded. *I agree.*

Something snapped in Aaron's hand, and the vampire swore while he fished a replacement bar from his tools. "Why not?" he whispered.

Randall's ears flicked.

Aaron swore, then glanced to Barb. "You and me, we can't go in."

Barb folded her arms across her chest and glowered at the door, then said, "That's bullshit."

Randall heard something quiet from inside. Quiet, but familiar.

Ellis!

He howled the moment Aaron stepped away, and shouldered the door.

"Randall—" Aaron breathed.

"Let them go," Barb muttered. "Go, Randall. We'll keep watch."

Not that he would have stopped.

THIRTY

THEY FLOWED into the building like water through floodgates.

It was odd underfoot. Rubbery without being rubber, like the floor was coated in a sheen of latex paint. His father's scent was dense in here, but there was blood, too.

The space was large. By his reckoning, the entire ground floor was one big open space. Above them was a mezzanine level which ran along three of the four walls, with only two sets of metal stairs which led up to it. There were walls up there with doors in them, so presumably that was where things like offices, toilets, maybe a little kitchen area and other facilities for workers lay.

The space here wasn't heated, and the bitter cold from outside had seeped inside. The only thing the roof and walls kept out was the wet.

The wolves fanned out with caution, nosing into corners and at the bottom steps. Their paws were muted against the almost sticky floor, which Randall guessed was there to help maintain footing for people who might work in the space.

He saw odd lumps. There were clothes, scattered across the floor, discarded and covered in grainy particles. Another pile of clothes, with a body in them, surrounded by patterns painted onto the ground.

Ellis!

He snarled as he ran toward the huddled form. Little puffs of dust had fallen around him, and the scent of blood came from him.

Randall took human form as he reached the body. "Ellis! Ellis, it's me!"

Ellis' head turned toward him, and Randall's heart stammered at the sight.

His skin was pale as paper. Dried blood ran in spidery lines from his eyes and lay in cracked trails down his cheeks. His lips were caked in it, as though he'd vomited blood at some point. His irises were bright red, still with their faint glow, which made them seem lit from within.

Ellis laughed briefly. "Shh." He raised a blood-stained finger to his lips. "I knew you'd come." His voice was slurred. He almost sounded drunk, but there was a tense gleam to his eyes that no intoxicated person could hold. It was the sort of look that Randall had seen in Briar's eyes not so long ago.

It was the look of a man who was not in full control of his faculties.

Bile surged to the back of Randall's throat and burned so much it made his eyes water. "What the hell did she do to you?"

"Your father's here." Ellis curled himself up again. "You don't have long now. She's awake."

"I need to get you out of here!" Randall slid his hands under Ellis' shoulders to try to lift him, but the vampire was like a dead weight.

"You can't." Ellis' words were filled with despair. "She has wards. I can't leave. Aaron and Barb can't come in. Randall, listen!" He turned to face Randall again, and his unsettling gaze passed straight through him. "She has a talisman—"

A ripple of snarls passed through the pack, and claws clattered against metal. Randall turned toward the commotion.

It was his father.

The shifter came midway down the stairs in his wolf shape before he took human form, and he gazed out across the assembled wolves before his dark eyes settled on Randall.

Christ, how could he not have seen it before? He looked like an older version of Kieran. The eyes, the nose, the jaw, it was all *right there* for anyone to see, and Randall hadn't damn well noticed it last time.

"Dad?" he whispered.

"Randall, I..." His dad shook his head quickly. "I can't help you!"

One of the doors up on the mezzanine level opened inwards. Some of the pack surged toward the stairs, but Randall's dad took his war form the moment one paw was laid on the lowest step. He shifted from human to monster in two seconds flat, and snarled a low warning.

"Wait!" Randall set Ellis down gently and stood. "Just wait."

The woman who emerged through the opened door seemed every bit as old and frail as she had when Randall last saw her. Anyone who passed her in the street would step around her and not think twice. She looked like she might have ten cats and a black-and-white television at home, wherever home might be.

She stepped forward and laid a wrinkled hand on the metal rail, the only barrier between the mezzanine level and empty space. Her gaze swept the ground floor with disdain, before she focused on Randall. Her voice rang out in the sudden quiet.

"You are a very persistent young man."

Ellis seemed to find that amusing, if the snort which came from behind Randall was any indication.

"I told you what I wanted," Randall said. He tried to keep the snarl from his voice. It didn't happen.

She tapped her fingers against the rail a moment. "Very well. You can have Carter."

Carter blinked and stared up at her. Randall couldn't blame him.

"It's not enough." Randall gestured to Ellis. "I'm taking him, too."

She laughed at that. "That stays with me."

"Oh go on, Bryce!" Ellis snorted. "You're not going to find what you want. You're just going to keep on failing." Randall glanced down at him in time to catch a disturbing, wild laugh as it came out of Ellis like a spasm. "That's what you do, isn't it? Fail. And everyone else suffers for it. Well, tough. Now it's your turn to suffer."

Bryce just tutted. "I think it's broken anyway," she said to Randall. "You may as well leave it here."

Randall's fingers curled into fists. His heart pounded, and his skin itched. His war form wanted to come out, and he had half a mind to let it. "What did you do to him?"

"Nothing that matters to you."

"Torture," said Ellis, his voice suddenly flat.

Randall's anger turned into a cold thing. He breathed in, and when he breathed out again he let go of his restraint. It wasn't fury, it wasn't some out-of-control tantrum which twisted his body and pushed him to his fullest mass. It was ice-like and bitter, and it enveloped him in a sense of calm.

Subdue my father, he snarled. *Do not kill.*

The wolves closest to Carter surged up the stairs, taking their own war forms. That staircase became a seething mass of claws and fur as bodies piled in on bodies.

It left the other staircase free, and Randall strode toward it. *With me!*

Ameera took on her largest shape and followed, and moments later Randall had half his pack behind him, all towering, all climbing the stairs, all ready to help him do what he had chosen to do.

Bryce looked so small once he reached the mezzanine. So frail. How had this tiny human done so much harm?

"Stop!" She reeked of fear, even though her face betrayed only a glimmer of it.

Randall's body obeyed, and he snarled. But others bumped into him from behind.

"Stop!" Bryce's voice grew louder. Panic crept into her gaze.

Ellis' laughter echoed around the hollow space. It was wild, and when Randall looked over the rail toward him he found Ellis standing still, a frightening mask of hatred on his face. From up where he was, he could see that the markings in the floor surrounded Ellis in a tight circle. "Don't stop, Randall," he sang. "Don't you dare stop!"

Ameera pushed past, and Bryce stepped back from the railing. "Stop!" She almost screeched the order.

Ameera snarled as she ground to a halt.

Randall's fingers flexed, and he took a step forward.

Bryce's eyes flicked between the two, and Randall smelled her terror.

Kill her, he bayed. *She can't stop us all.*

Farah bounded up the stairs. She leaped the pile of bodies which pinned Randall's dad against the metal steps and rocketed toward Bryce. She was a lithe thing, no taller than

Randall and with far less muscle, but she was still more than enough for a frail human body, and Bryce turned to face the oncoming beast.

"Stop!" Bryce screamed now. "Everybody stop!"

Randall's body was filled with ice-hard rage, and he pushed forward. The witch was trying to do too much, control too many of them. She couldn't do it, and that knowledge was written in her posture and in her pheromones.

He howled in satisfaction. His prey would lose. It didn't matter to who. Her time was limited and there wasn't a creature in this building who didn't know it.

"He's going to kill you, Bryce," Ellis' sing-song continued. His musical joy contrasted sickeningly with the dried blood that ran like tears down his cheeks. The glow of his eyes was dark in Randall's current sight, seething with fluorescence. Ellis threw himself forward and rebounded off thin air, just as Barb and Aaron had the night before, but he laughed and did it again. "He'd better kill you before I do!"

Bryce's attention slipped toward Ellis for a second, and in that instant, her grip on Randall weakened just a hair more.

He dug the balls of his feet against the walkway and pushed himself into her. Her mouth opened, and he watched as her fear coalesced into horror.

Randall was out of time. He couldn't let her speak another word.

Without a sound, he drove the claws from his right hand into her stomach. The left he closed around her neck. He would hold her in place while he disembowelled her.

Eighteen years he'd been without a father. Eighteen years his father had been without any agency, without his wife, without his children, trapped in his own body and without any hope of escape.

Then she'd taken Ellis, too. Taken him, tortured him,

driven him insane in one single day. *One day*. Not content with destroying one generation of his family, she'd come back to get the next.

Randall spilled her intestines across the floor as he snapped her neck.

THIRTY-ONE

RANDALL'S CLAWS dripped blood onto the fallen body.

Howls of triumph lifted into the air, and he felt nothing. No satisfaction, no pride. He stared down at the broken old body and couldn't shake the feeling that it was nothing more than a Pyhrric victory.

He shoved the monster back into the box, easing down into a shape which convinced even himself some days that it was human, and all the red which splashed across the body and the floor became visible to him. Some was bright. Some was almost as dark as it had been with his wolf sight. It oozed from the body like the last few drips of a tap whose supply had been turned off. By contrast, her skin had turned a stomach-churning yellow-grey.

Randall tore his gaze away and looked down to the ground. Aaron and Barb were inside, now, and picking Ellis up off the floor. Randall couldn't hear what they said; his pack were making too much noise.

He stepped over the corpse and made his way past Farah, past Hasan. A flutter of hope stirred, but he didn't want to succumb to it just yet. "Dad?" His voice was drowned out by the howls, so he tried again. "Dad!"

"Randall!"

Werewolves disengaged from their wrestling pile, and a battered, bloodied form emerged from beneath them all. He'd been clawed here and there as the pack had pinned him down, but Randall saw no serious injuries.

"Oh, God. Dad?" Randall rushed in to hug him tightly, but it was too weird. He let go again. "I... I have to—"

The older Carter nodded. "I know."

He swallowed and ran past, then across the floor, his bare feet slapping against the latex paint. "Ellis?"

Barb looked grim, and Aaron's expression was blank.

Ellis stood between them, looking calm. "Randall!" He cracked a lop-sided grin. "I see you've met George. He says he's your da'." Then Ellis leaned in, and Aaron caught him. "I'm inclined to believe him," Ellis whispered.

"There's a bathroom upstairs." George said it quietly, a step behind Randall. "It's not much, but we can clean him up, get him presentable."

Randall nodded. "Why?"

"We can't take him out like this," Aaron muttered.

"No. Why." Randall turned to raise his gaze to his father. "Why'd she do this? What reason is there for any of this? How could she take the man I *love* and do this to him?"

George blinked, but answered, "Greed, nothing more. She always wanted more. Prestige, power, control. And once she had it all, she wanted it for longer." He shrugged. "She thought she could find the secret of immortality in one of these vampires. None of the others survived."

"She tortured them all?" His bile rose again, and swallowing it down made him cough. Christ, he hadn't exactly been Victor's best friend, but the guy hadn't deserved that. None of them had.

"It was a side-effect. Not one she cared about." George shrugged. "She picked them apart like a watchmaker and she didn't care about the cogs she wasn't looking for."

Randall ground his teeth together, but the witch was dead now. There wasn't anything he could do about it.

He scooped Ellis into his arms and carried him toward the stairs. The pack parted for him and closed in after, and he stood by the corpse of the woman who had broken his lover.

"We wouldn't be here," he said, "if it weren't for all of you." He cleared his throat as the baying, the celebration, began to die down. "But we can't stay here. We can't linger." He glanced down to Ellis, whose head lolled against his chest. "Go home. Be careful. Don't be seen, don't be caught. Keep the noise down, eh?" He smiled, but it was empty. "Thank you. Thank you. I had no right to ask this of you, but if you hadn't come, we'd have lost everything."

His eyes stung, and he blinked rapidly. He couldn't cry in front of them. Not now, not...

Hasan sank down to human form and whistled sharply. "All right, you heard 'im. Let's get a wiggle on! Shift down, get out of here. Don't nobody go alone. Pairs, all the way home, whichever way you go, okay? You pick a buddy and you get back in one piece! Go, go, go!"

"That went well, I reckon," Ellis breathed.

"Yeah?" Randall clutched him tight and sniffled as tears fell onto the vampire's forehead.

"Aye. When I told *my* father I were gay, he lamped me one right in the face."

Randall blinked rapidly. It was all becoming too much. He didn't know what to say, and he felt like he was being torn apart. "Oh god."

"Go. We can tidy up 'round here," Ellis whispered. "Look after your da'. Get him home to your mum. He loves her. He loves all of you."

"I can't leave you, El." Randall's grip on him tightened. "I only just got you back!"

Ellis laughed faintly. "I need a wash. And we need to clean this mess up before people start comin' to work in the morning. You get him home and you look after him a while, petal. He deserves that. He needs it."

Randall stared down at Ellis' blood-red eyes and swallowed tightly. "And if anything happens to you while I'm gone?"

"It won't." Ellis placed a hand against Randall's chest. His touch was cold, even though he'd only fed a couple of nights ago. "I can stand."

Randall set him down with care, and guided him to the bathroom. "You're sure?"

"Petal, I love you. But I think we're gonna do things here you don't want to see." Ellis flashed his teeth in a cold, humourless smile. "You should go."

"I love you," Randall whispered. "You better be home when I get there."

Ellis drew a finger over his own heart. "Scout's honour."

Randall wasn't sure Ellis had ever been a scout. But he had two utterly different problems tugging on him, and one of them had just given him permission to go and deal with the other one first. He kissed Ellis' jaw, a patch free of encrusted blood, and tried not to think of the look in Bryce's eyes as the light had gone out.

RANDALL RAN. His father was at his side, but he felt alone; stuck in his head with his thoughts.

He'd killed. Deliberately. He'd thought it through, reached a decision, and he had carried it through to the ultimate conclusion.

That was murder. It was brutal, premeditated vengeance, and now he had blood on his hands.

Did Ellis feel this way? About his own actions, about Randall's attack on Bryce, about any of the blood they'd been forced to spill...

He stumbled, and the wolf at his side nudged him with a shoulder to bump him back on track. Randall yipped in gratitude and looked up to work out where they were.

Islington.

God, they'd covered most of the distance already? Ten miles from Brent Park to Spitalfields and he still hadn't figured out how the hell to tell Mum that he'd found Dad at last. How did anyone do that? He'd seen shows on TV which reunited long-lost families and he wished he'd paid more attention to the fine details.

It will be all right, his father said.

Randall blinked and looked over at him as they ran. *What if it isn't?*

This is more than I ever thought I'd have. George snorted and his ears flicked back in the breeze. A snowflake landed on his nose and melted, and he huffed a laugh. *I am proud of you.*

Randall's lungs burned and his chest ached. Everything he wanted to say to that cascaded through his thoughts, but his current body couldn't express such a complicated mess of words. For now, all he could settle for was, *Thank you.*

George's tongue flapped as he panted, and they bounded along until they passed by the lingering scents of closed shops and still-open restaurants.

They reached the tower block Randall had grown up in, and George stared up at it.

Still here? He shook his head.

Yes. Randall nudged the door with his nose. *Still smells of pee.*

George grunted in amusement as he followed. *What is your plan?*

Randall sprang for the stairs and led him up them. *The truth,* he chuffed.

Are you crazy?

Maybe. Randall snorted. *You've got three floors to think up something better.*

Three floors passed, and neither of them had anything, so when they reached his mother's flat, Randall leaped up and hit the doorbell with his nose.

It was the middle of the night. Maybe they should go. Maybe they should head to Pimlico and get some bloody clothes then come back here in daylight. Maybe-

Randall's ears perked forward. Someone was coming to the door.

"You better have a damn good reason for ringing a woman's doorbell at five in the bloody morning!" His mum's voice reverberated past the thin door and out into the hallway. Metal scraped as bolts drew back, and then she opened the door.

She'd been looking out at eye-level, so it took her a second to notice the two wolves on her doorstep. And by the time she did, they'd run in past her legs.

"What? No! Get out! Is this a joke? Go, I don't want dogs!"

Randall made it to the living room before he began to change. He grabbed a cushion the moment he had hands so that his mum didn't have to see things that were much, *much* smaller the last time she'd seen them. "Mum, just wait. I can explain! Shut the door!"

She uttered words he'd never heard pass her lips in his

entire life, and she pushed the door shut, then followed warily into the living room. "Randall?" She looked him over, her expression one of total confusion. Her eyes went to the wolf in the room, then back to her son. "Ah, pinch me, this is nonsense!" She took a wedge of flesh between thumb and finger and squeezed so hard that she yelped.

"Mum, no. It's not... it's not a dream." He took a deep breath and rubbed at his eyes. "I reckon maybe you should sit down."

"Don't be so ridiculous. What're you playing at?" She gestured to the wolf. "Weren't there two? How did you get in here?"

"Mum..." Randall trailed off and waved to the wolf. "I found Dad." His voice gave out on him, and the last word came out as a whisper.

"Randall, that's not funny!"

George's fur rustled, and his body grew. He lifted his paws onto the sofa, then once he had enough of the right shape for balance he pushed up to his feet. As the last of his fur receded into his skin, he gazed to the woman in the room.

"Naomie," he croaked. "It's me."

She stared, then lowered herself slowly into an armchair. "George?"

George nodded numbly.

"Oh," said Mrs. Carter. "This better be *damn* good!"

THIRTY-TWO

Water flowed over Ellis' hands. It was soothing and clean, though he couldn't quite tell whether it was hot or cold. It wasn't until he turned the other tap and the temperature rose that he figured out he'd had his fingers under the cold tap all this time.

It didn't matter. The goal was to get the blood off.

There was a bar of soap in the sink. Aaron had placed it in his hands and stood waiting nearby, but once Ellis had washed his face he let the soap sit in the sink while he leaned his elbows on the hard ceramic and felt the water.

"Councillor O'Neill?"

Ellis turned both taps off and flicked water from his hands. "You can just call me Ellis, Aaron."

"Are you okay?"

He didn't feel qualified to answer. "Is there a towel?"

"Yeah." He heard the rasp of cloth through plastic, then Aaron nudged his elbow. "Here."

"Thanks." Ellis patted his hands dry with it, then his face.

"She had a talisman. It's made of silver and wolfsbane. Could you find it and make sure it gets destroyed?"

"Would it be something she wore, do you reckon?"

"No idea. Sorry."

"I'll find it." Air sucked away from him as Aaron vanished.

Barb's boots thudded on the floor. She came toward him. "Let me look at you," she said quietly.

Ellis chuckled and turned to face her. He spread his arms as though he'd just gone through an airport metal detector. "Here I am."

She hissed between her teeth, and her fingers took hold of his jaw. They were warm against his skin. She was well-fed, then.

He let her turn his head one way and then the other. "It's not going away," she muttered.

"What, my face?" He smiled his best smile. "No, not yet. Is it supposed to?"

"Your eyes," she answered. "They're red."

"Oh." Ellis lowered his arms. "I can carry it off, right?"

"No." Barb released him and sighed. "No, it stands out like a vegan at a barbecue."

"Hm." Ellis shrugged and slid his hands into his pockets. It didn't seem terribly important.

Nothing did.

"I think I've got it," Aaron called. "You reckon just melting it down will do the job?"

"I don't know." Ellis shrugged. "I'm not a sorcerer. None of us are. Or can be." He laughed. "Which is funny, because we're all made of magic."

Neither of them answered him, so he felt his way out of the bathroom. The stink of cooling blood was strong out here, but like all dead blood it wasn't remotely tempting. His foot squished in something gelatinous.

"Oh, Bryce," he mused. "What did you do?" He crouched by the corpse and cupped a hand to his ear. "What was that? No? Nothing to say?"

"Ellis…" Barb didn't say anything else.

"Holy shit. You should check this lot out." Aaron called from somewhere to Ellis' right.

Barb led him along and he didn't object to it. There was little point. No dog, no Randall, no sight. All he would do without them was fumble around in the entrails. When Barb gave a low, appreciative whistle, he assumed it wasn't at him, but couldn't see the point in asking for an explanation.

"Books," Aaron said. "It's all makeshift in here. A camping bed, and then there's just suitcases, boxes, that kind of thing. Looks like they both lived out of a case and only one of them got to have a bed."

Ellis shrugged. "Tiberius sleeps on the floor."

"Tiberius is a dog."

"And that's all George was to her." Ellis shook his head. "We should take it all. Sort through it later."

"Or we can just torch it with the rest of the place," Barb muttered.

The idea made Ellis' head hurt. Even if only half of Bryce's possessions were magical in some way, who knew what else she might have? "No," he concluded. "It needs to be curated."

"How do you reckon we get all this stuff away from here, then? I ain't got a car, and we'll look suspect as shit trying to cram all this into an Uber."

"What time is it?" Ellis felt for his watch even though he knew it wasn't there.

"Coming up on five."

"We can get a car if you find my phone and keyboard."

Aaron paused. "You've got someone with a car?"

Ellis gave a lazy smile. "It's not someone I would usually

consider at my beck and call, Aaron. But he won't mind that we won't show up in the rear-view mirror."

"What makes you so sure?"

"Because he doesn't either."

"SO THIS IS THE GUY?" Aaron's voice was terse.

Ellis could understand that. He was putting the Constable in an even more dangerous position than he was already in. It was one thing to know about Han's existence, and another to meet with him face-to-face. "Aye."

"What kind of car's he got?"

"I don't know." Ellis waved his hands. "A car."

Aaron tutted as he paced, boots muted by the flooring. "Sunrise is at half seven."

"It'll be areet."

"Are you okay? I mean, you seem..." Hughes' pacing stopped.

"Out of it," Barb supplied.

"Aye." He didn't bother to specify whose statement he was answering. It seemed pointless.

Tyres crunched against asphalt outside, and doors slammed.

"Why can I hear a breather?" Aaron hissed.

"Oh, that'll be Jay, I expect." Ellis beamed. "It's fine. He knows everything."

"*What?*"

The door squeaked open. Footsteps entered. The door clattered shut. Jay's pulse, his breathing, brought some sense of life to the dead space.

"Oh my God!" Jay squealed. "Is that- is that a dead body?"

"I've had better five a.m. callouts," Han muttered.

Ellis shook his head. "Han, Jay, Aaron, Barb." He gestured in the direction of each — or at least where he'd last heard them speak from. "Han, Aaron's a Constable. No, I'm not turning you in. Yes, you're still a secret. No, he's not going to arrest either of us." *Yet.* "I'll explain later, but for now we need to clear some things out of this place."

"You've killed someone and now you're looting the body?" Han still seemed unimpressed.

"Yeah, pretty much," Barb said.

"She deserved worse." Ellis surprised himself with his flash of vehemence. For the first time in hours, he *felt* something.

Hatred. Bone-deep loathing.

Then it was gone again, and he smiled. "We haven't got long. Aaron, could you show them?"

Most of the voices walked away. "Where are we going after this?" Han was asking. "I had to come here from Southwark, which meant the Rotherhithe tunnel, and that thing gets crammed in rush hour. If we have to cross the Thames again—"

"There are safe-houses this side of the river," Aaron answered. "If it comes to it, you'll be okay for a day."

"But I have a business to run!"

A hand took Ellis by the elbow, and warm breath touched his cheek. "Ellis?" Jay spoke softly. "What happened?"

Ellis turned toward the voice, and heard a soft gasp. "It's okay."

"You're sure? I mean, your eyes…"

"She staked me, brought me out here, and tortured me for hours on end. Randall killed her."

Jay swallowed with a little wet sound. "Where is he?"

"It's complicated."

"He should be here with you."

"No. Believe me, he's got something he needs to do."

Jay sighed. "You need to stop sending him away when you need him the most, Ellis."

"I don't do that." Ellis laughed.

"Yeah. Yeah, you really bloody do."

Jay wrapped long, warm arms around him, and Ellis leaned against the other man.

Then, quietly at first, he began to sob.

THIRTY-THREE

RANDALL CLUTCHED the cushion to his lap as his parents talked.

George talked about the day he was taken and about the early years when he tried everything he could think of to escape. He talked about the sorcerers he'd been forced to kill and the nights he'd dreamed he was home with his family. He talked until his voice gave out, and Randall fetched him a glass of water so that he could continue.

His mum listened. And at first, Randall wasn't sure she'd believe any of it, not even after she'd seen her husband change. But the longer he talked, the softer her eyes became.

"It's you," she whispered. "George, it's... it's really you." Her eyes glistened with moisture.

"It's me, Naomie. I've missed you so much. So much. I thought I'd never see you again—" His words choked off, and he pushed to his feet, his arms reaching toward her.

"My sweetheart." She stood and tumbled into his arms, and her tears fell. "Oh, George, I knew you were out there. I *knew* it in my heart. They told me you had to be dead, but I couldn't... I couldn't let go of you. You were always the one. Always!"

"I love you. Oh God, I love you so much." He clutched her to his chest, and his own tears fell as freely.

Randall glanced away and rubbed at his eyes. He'd need to talk to the neighbours about cutting onions this time of the day. Totally careless of them. He sniffed, and wiped tears across the back of his hand.

"How come you never told me you're a werewolf!" His mum teased. "And you're standin' here naked in front of God and everyone! Oh, you're *both* naked, my goodness! I'll have to get clothes, and you must be hungry, and we'll need to—"

"It can wait." George nuzzled against her neck. "Let me hold you the way I used to. That's all I need."

Randall hugged his cushion as a pang of loneliness swept through him. "Is it okay if I go?"

"So soon? But your father—"

"Wants to spend time with you," Randall cut in. "And I... there's somewhere I gotta be."

George looked to him and gave him the slightest of nods. "Ellis?"

"Yeah. Yeah, he's... he's in a bad way. I think I need to be there."

"You can't go out like that!"

"Yeah. I can." Randall leaned forward so that he would fall to the carpet as he shifted, and the cushion dropped from his lap as he did so.

She gawped at him, then came to her senses to go open the front door.

"You'll always be my son," she whispered. "Go, be with him."

Randall cast a look past her to his father, then nodded, and slipped out of the flat.

He ran along the Thames Path and wove in and out of hedgerows. He hadn't slept in at least twelve hours, and it felt as though he'd spent most of that time on his paws, but if he'd done himself any harm by it he didn't notice. His body healed such minor things as a matter of course, so he was without any aching joints or sore foot pads despite the miles he'd covered.

Damn it, Ellis.

The vampire had done it again, hadn't he? He'd been hurting, so he'd sent Randall away. He'd done it after Preeti had died, he'd done it after each and every nightmare, and now he'd bloody well done it again after Bryce had tortured him.

Randall snarled at himself. How could he have been so dumb? Ellis was the one who had fallen in love so easily, so quickly, and so unreservedly. It had taken longer for Randall's feelings to make themselves known. And yet now it was Ellis who kept pushing Randall back to give himself space when what he really needed was the love they'd built together.

No more. Randall was an Alpha. He, unlike the vast majority of people in the world, knew with absolute surety whether or not his feelings were genuine, whether they were deep enough to stand the test of time. He'd seen how strong the bond was, now.

George had been a prisoner for eighteen years, yet that bond had kept him sane. It kept him in control when the full moon came. It was there to comfort him every single day, and to give him hope on the loneliest of nights. And Randall's mum had *waited*. She'd never given up hope, never remarried. She *knew* it was love. She knew George was the one. Without even knowing about the bond or what it meant for a shifter, she had waited.

Randall delved between trees then shot across roads like greased lightning. The was no way he could avoid all the commuters, but he could at least streak past them so fast they mistook him — he hoped — for a dog on the loose.

There was a car in the permit-holders bay outside the house, a dark Range Rover with tinted rear windows which was too high for him to see whether it had a permit on the dashboard. He scooted past and leaped up at the house's front door to growl at the letterbox.

It's me.

The door unlocked soon after, and Ellis smiled down at him. "Petal."

Love.

He pushed his way into the house and shifted up the moment Ellis closed the door. His hands found the vampire's hips, and he pressed Ellis against the wall as he kissed him as deeply as he could.

Ellis' fingers trembled as they gripped Randall's biceps. The red of his eyes was more pronounced in the light of day. His lips were weak, and his mouth unresisting.

"I'm sorry," Randall whispered. "El, I'm so sorry. I was gone for so long."

"It's areet," Ellis said.

"No, it's not."

"I was about to make Jay a cuppa. Did you want one?"

Randall blinked quickly, and pulled back to glance toward the office.

Ellis nodded. "Han, Jay, Aaron, Barb. They're here."

"Right." Randall swallowed. "Right, yeah. Tea. Tea's good. But later, we talk, okay?"

"Later." Ellis nodded and patted Randall's arse, then he

slipped free and wandered toward the kitchen, one hand trailing idly along the wall for guidance.

"Right," Randall echoed.

He shook his head and frowned, but stepped through into the office while his brain chewed on the problem. He couldn't toss everyone out onto the street. Only Jay would survive it, or maybe Aaron too if he ran fast enough to get underground before he burned.

There was always something in the way, wasn't there?

He blinked at the sight which greeted him. Suitcases were lined up against one wall, piled two high. Aaron sat in a chair flicking through books at high speed, placing some in one pile and the rest in another. Barb was picking through piles of clothing and folding them neatly while Tiberius sniffed at each item. Han sat at Ellis' desk and tapped furiously away at a laptop, presumably doing actual work rather than this bizarre car boot sale that Aaron and Barb were engaged in.

Jay was by Aaron, picking out arbitrary books from each of the Constable's two piles and making two more piles with those.

"Hey, Randall. Oh, Christ, put it away, you'll frighten the kids!" Aaron looked up, then his eyes widened and he tore his gaze away.

"Anyone'd think you'd never seen a naked werewolf before," Barb muttered. She was far more willing to let her gaze linger on Randall, and she flashed him a grin.

"Oh!" Jay's cheeks flushed, and he clutched a book to his chest as though it could protect his eyes. "Randall! Glad you're here. You can settle, um." He shook his head, then waggled the book. "You can settle something for us."

Randall moved over to a chair and scooped up his second cushion of the day, if only to stop Barb staring at his cock. "What's up?"

Jay gestured to the books. "Which of these piles is glowing?"

Randall stepped across the room and frowned uncertainly. There were leather-bound books, painted books, embossed books. Books with gilt edges, books with coloured edges, books with crinkled edges. Some of the books bore titles, others didn't. A few were hinged and had locks.

But none of them glowed.

"None of them?" he offered.

Jay's features went from hope to chagrin. "Oh my God, they totally are!"

"They aren't, Jay," Han said without looking up. "Stop taking the pee."

"I'm not!" Warmth flushed through Jay's cheeks again and he gestured to the book in his arms. "This one's glowing. *All* of these are glowing!" He placed the book onto one of his two piles and waved at both. "I thought maybe it was just vampires who couldn't see it."

"Maybe shifters can't either?" Randall shrugged. "Or maybe only sorcerers can. Try it on Christy later?"

Jay laughed weakly. "I'm not a sorcerer."

"Says the man who works magic with my schedule," Han said absently.

"Tea." Ellis came in with a cup at each hand. "We can worry about whether books are glowing later."

Jay scurried over to take the cups and bring one to Randall, and Randall took it with thanks.

"We're gonna be okay in here all day, right?" Barb asked.

"Worked for Devitt for over a century," Ellis said cheerfully. "And we're all younger than he was. But if things get uncomfortable the master bedroom is completely safe."

Any other time, Randall would have believed Ellis' smiles. But not today.

He had to stop falling for them so easily.

THIRTY-FOUR

IT FELT like forever until they had the house to themselves again. Randall slept. Jay had curled up in an armchair to doze the afternoon away after his early start. By the time night fell, Ellis had settled into a mechanical daze.

He wasn't going to let himself sleep. Not while others were here. No. That wouldn't do.

He took Tiberius for a walk before Randall woke. That would keep him on the move, keep him from giving in.

Wasn't it ridiculous that vampires needed to sleep? They weren't even dead. Ellis had believed they were, but Bryce showed him that he was anything but. He wasn't alive in the traditional sense, but he certainly wasn't dead.

He was Magic.

He waited for Randall. Beautiful, sweet Randall. He knew, didn't he? He knew Ellis had pushed him away.

What else was he to do? Drag the man down into this nothingness with him? Drown him in it?

No. No, Randall needed to be free of him. And if he wouldn't listen to reason, well, Ellis had other means. He could make Randall go away, make him forget Ellis, make him live a better life. A life with someone *sane*.

Randall deserved that. He deserved more than Ellis could give him.

It was clear as day, and so Ellis waited. It wasn't right to wake Randall just to punt him out onto the street. The man needed his rest.

The shifter's breathing changed. Not in the way it did for a dream, but in the slow stretch of a chest which was waking.

Ellis let himself into the bedroom and closed the door to keep Tiberius out. He walked to the bed and reached for one of the turned wooden posts, then slid his arm around it. It was something to hold onto while he broke the news.

"We need to talk." His voice echoed oddly, and it took him a second to realise that Randall had said the same thing at the same time.

"El, I know what you're doing."

Ellis laughed. How could Randall know that? Ellis barely had a clue himself.

"I'm serious. Please, come and sit?"

He slid free of the post and perched on the bed. The mattress shifted as Randall moved, and then the man was at his side, all warm and firm, his arm around Ellis' waist.

"If you want to talk," Randall said, "I'll listen. If you don't want to talk, I'll wait for you. But don't ever think the way to deal with any of this is to make me leave."

Ellis turned toward him, but there wasn't enough light in here. It made no difference.

"Don't give me that look. You do it all the time, El. I'm not going to let you do it again. I'm here for you, and you're going to learn to live with that, because you're always here for *me*. And you've got to start letting me look after you."

His lips parted. But what could he say to that? What could

he possibly use to fill the chasm which yawned between them all of a sudden?

You could make him go.

Randall's pulse quickened, and his palm covered Ellis' mouth. "Don't," he growled. "Don't you even think about it."

Ellis' brows furrowed in confusion.

"Because you get this look in your eyes," Randall rumbled. "Every time you use it, every time you so much as think about using it when you know it's the wrong thing to do."

You need to work on that.

"You're so cold." Randall gently lowered his hand. "Do you need to feed?"

Ellis shook his head slowly. "No."

"Talk to me, El."

Ellis shook his head again. "How many ways can I find to say that she tortured me, petal? How many ways are there to say that I felt as though my blood was on fire, that my eyes had been torn out, that my entire body was unravelling? I had a *pulse*, Randall. For hours on end, I had a heartbeat. I bled. I don't know. I don't know if I imagined that, if I dreamed it. I dreamed so many things." He gasped for breath. "I wanted to die because it would mean it was *over* at last. I dreamed, I saw things I haven't seen in years." He rubbed his cheek as though his father's fist had hit him all over again. "I screamed. God, I screamed and I screamed and she didn't stop, she wouldn't stop. I couldn't stop her. All because she wanted to live forever, all because she had the power and thought it gave her the right to do what she wanted, and I'm such a hypocrite. I haven't got the right, petal. I haven't the right to tell you what to do, with or without the power. I'm sorry." His body shook, and he leaned against Randall's chest, weak as a newborn. "It was only a day. Only one day."

Randall groaned and slid his other arm around Ellis'

shoulders, pulling him tight against himself. "I'm here, El. I'm right here. You're safe now. She's dead." He rubbed Ellis' back and rocked him in his powerful arms. "You're safe, and I love you. I'll always love you."

"I need you," Ellis whispered. "I can't explain it."

"You don't have to."

Ellis shook his head slightly.

"No, El. You really don't." Randall's hand slid down to unbutton his shirt. Ellis felt the warmth brush his skin as Randall worked one button free at a time. "You've had to stand alone for years, baby. But it's okay to need someone. It's okay to be weak once in a while. We can't all be these towering beacons of independence every day, every week, every year. We all need to let go. To trust someone else. To let them catch us when we fall." His lips fell to Ellis' shoulder as he tugged the shirt from his waistband. "Let me catch you, baby."

"What if we both fall?" Ellis tipped his head aside.

"Then we fall together. It doesn't matter. What matters is I'm with you, and you're with me."

Randall guided Ellis back onto the bed and undressed him. He eased free trousers and shoes, socks and underwear, all with firm and methodical hands which didn't waver, didn't hesitate.

Ellis felt bare. More than merely naked. He couldn't see a thing, and everything about him was exposed to Randall. His thoughts, his emotions, his fears, his pain, it was all there like a butterfly pinned in a display case. He drew his hands across his chest, but Randall gently brushed them aside, so he laid them on the mattress by his hips.

"I don't know what to do," he said.

"Me either. But I know what makes me feel better. And I don't mean it like that, you dirty git." His palm smoothed across Ellis' stomach. "But I kind of do, too. Because when you're inside me, everything else goes away. All the chatter, the worry, the fear, the anger, it all melts, because you've got me. You've got me, and you make me whole, and you complete me in a way I can't even begin to explain."

Ellis felt for Randall and traced the outline of one thick, strong bicep. "I don't know. I haven't ever... I don't..."

"We don't have to if you don't want to."

Ellis gripped the hard muscle beneath his hand. It was one thing entirely to have this commanding creature surrender beneath him, but to give himself over? To have Randall inside him, claiming him, taking him over?

He didn't bottom. He hadn't *ever* bottomed. Back when he was sighted it was something he wasn't able to bring himself to do. Not without his father's sneer at the back of his mind. But once he'd been diagnosed, he'd lost the ability to trust anyone with that kind of intimacy — if he'd ever had it in the first place.

Could he do it? Could he give himself to Randall? Could he afford not to?

Randall eased over him and nudged his knees apart, and Ellis was pinned beneath his weight, his heat, with those strong arms sliding under his shoulders and those soft lips pressing against his own.

His heart thudded.

He gasped, then groaned into Randall's mouth and coiled his legs around the shifter's. "Please," he whimpered. "God, Randall, do it. Do it."

"I'll get there, I promise." Randall's lips pressed against his jaw. His hips rolled slowly against Ellis', and their cocks stiffened together, growing harder with each thrust. His fingers kneaded Ellis' shoulders, and his mouth closed around his throat gently.

Ellis writhed with need. He could *feel*, and he needed more. "Please!"

Randall leaned away from him for a moment, and Ellis rocked against him, desperate for his attention. He heard the drawer, the plastic cap, the *shlick* of liquid.

One hand ran along Ellis' leg, then lifted it, steered it to rest against a broad shoulder. The position raised Ellis' hips from the bed, and Randall drew him into his lap, thighs spreading to support him there. Ellis bent his other knee, and Randall raised that leg to his free shoulder until Ellis was helpless, his calves on either side of Randall's head, his head barely able to lift from the mattress. His arms spread for balance, and his cock butted against his own stomach, heavy and hard.

Randall brushed his balls softly as his hand eased past them, and then wet fingers circled Ellis' entrance, a curious mingling of coolness and warmth.

Ellis' stomach knotted. He gripped the sheets.

"Take your time," Randall whispered. He turned his head to kiss Ellis' calf. "I won't hurt you."

Ellis wanted to believe him.

A soft palm wrapped around his shaft and stroked slowly, and Ellis' hips lifted from Randall's thighs. He groaned, and a finger slowly eased into him before he understood what Randall was doing.

Then it touched something inside him, and he cried out.

"Randall!"

"Are you okay?"

Randall's touch surrounded him. It was inside him, it was wrapped around him, it was a tyrant and it demanded his complete submission.

Ellis nodded weakly. "Oh, God. Oh God..."

Heat spread from Randall's hands. Every motion of them,

every brush against that hardness inside himself brought him closer and closer to life, to feeling, to *sensation*, and he groaned but whether in protest or acceptance he couldn't tell. And when a second finger eased into him, his head fell back and he made wordless pleas and tried to move against it, to thrust into Randall's palm, but his body was weak and his leverage lousy.

Then there was emptiness. The warmth left him, and he whimpered. "I need you."

Click. Sssst. Snap.

Something hot, something slick, pressed against him, and he thought it might be a finger. The fingers had been good. They'd been *wonderful*.

It pushed slowly into him, and he groaned. It was thicker. Bigger. At once softer and harder at the same time. It eased into him, and it filled him, it penetrated him to the core, it took him over and still it kept on coming.

When it stopped at last, when Randall's thighs were flush against his arse, when he was stuffed full and helpless and oh so *God oh so full* he was almost overwhelmed with the sheer intensity of the connection he felt. Was this what it was, to take someone into you? To trust them not to hurt you? To be putty in their hands, to have them render you so feeble in so intimate a fashion?

He blinked as his eyes grew wet, and tears slid down the sides of his face. God, he hoped they were just tears.

"El?"

He smiled a weak, twitching smile. "Don't stop, petal. Don't stop."

Randall leaned over him, and it trapped Ellis' thighs between them, but it also pressed the hot, thick cock inside him up against his prostate so hard that it made him squirm.

Randall's hands gripped his shoulders, and only then did his hips begin to move, slowly at first.

"Oh," Ellis whimpered. "Oh, oh God."

"I love you." Randall peppered kisses over his jaw, stubble and all. "Christ, El, I love you."

Randall's hips pushed deep against him, hard and firm, and something inside Ellis gave way.

"Fuck me," he whispered. "Please, Randall, fuck me!"

Randall didn't answer. Not with words. His cock slid out, then thrust in hard. Fast. And again. His grip on Ellis' shoulders grew tight, and he snarled softly as he thrust, and every single thrust hammered through Ellis' body, rubbed over his prostate, sent sparks of pleasure to the tip of his cock as though it jolted right through his entire length.

Ellis lost the power of speech. He had no power, no control, no ability to draw breath or to move his own body. He was helpless in Randall's arms, and as Randall shoved him closer to the edge, his back arched, lips parted in a silent cry.

"Fuck, you're so beautiful," Randall grunted. "Oh... oh God."

"Do it," Ellis whispered.

Randall took a hand from Ellis' shoulder and curled it around his cock, and Ellis' world turned to light.

His orgasm ripped through him. It wasn't merciful, it took no prisoners. It made him buck and twitch in Randall's hands, and he felt white heat fill him as Randall's cock pulsed and jerked.

Randall growled with his release, then curled over Ellis, panting hard against the vampire's chest.

They lay together and, after a while, Ellis found the strength to wrap his arms around Randall's body. The werewolf was slick with sweat, and running his hands over the stocky, muscled body was a delight.

His legs slid free some time later. Randall moved one arm and then the other to let them go, and the motion made Randall's softening cock finally slide free with a gentle pop which made Ellis laugh faintly.

"Stay with me, petal," Ellis breathed. "Stay with me forever."

"On one condition." Randall's lips nibbled at Ellis' collarbone.

"Anything."

"You don't get to push me away, El."

Ellis nodded and held Randall tight. "Deal."

TOOTH & CLAW

Blind Man's Wolf

Blood Moon Rising

Balance of Power

Monsters Within

Mirror Flower, Water Moon

Visit https://ravenswordpress.com to discover more about the characters and world of Tooth & Claw, and to sign up to the newsletter.

Join the Discord server at https://ravenswordpress.com/discord.

INHERITANCE

Laurence Riley has too many problems, and his uncontrolled psychic powers are just the tip of the iceberg. But when he accidentally summons a god, his only hope for survival might be another wild talent: the enigmatic and aloof British earl, Quentin d'Arcy.

Lose yourself in a world like no other in this award-winning series.

RAVENSWORDPRESS.COM

ACKNOWLEDGMENTS

Thank you for reading this far!

Monsters Within was the book Tooth & Claw had always been heading towards. My interest in urban fantasy and the supernatural has always been where exactly the line lies between "human" and "monster", a theme I explore again and again in my writing, and I remain immensely satisfied with it all these years later. I hope you enjoyed reading it as much as I did writing it!

If you'd like to get sneak peeks of upcoming releases, why not join my Discord server? You can find it here:

https://ravenswordpress.com/discord

Love,

Amelia Faulkner, London UK, July 2024.

ABOUT THE AUTHOR

Raised on a steady diet of Star Trek and Doctor Who, Amelia Faulkner stood no chance in not becoming a grade-A geek. They have sat on the board of the British Fantasy Society, contributed fiction and fluff to various published roleplaying games, and written non-fiction for SciFiNow and SFX Magazines. For every positive there is an equal and opposite negative, and Amelia is forced to admit that they love Wild Wild West.

In their spare time they enjoy travel, photography, walking their Corgi, and trying to convince their friends to replay the Pathfinder Adventure Card Game with all the Goblins decks.

9 781912 349036